Epitaph of a Small Winner

Epitaph of a Small Winner

Machado de Assis
Introduction by Louis de Bernières

Translated from the Portuguese by
William L. Grossman

Drawings by
Shari Frisch

BLOOMSBURY

This edition first published in Great Britain 1997

Originally published in Brazil in 1880 under the title
Memórias póstumas de Brás Cubas

Introduction copyright © 1997 by Louis de Bernières

Translation copyright © 1952 by William L. Grossman
renewed 1980 by Mignon S. Grossman

Bloomsbury Publishing Plc, 38 Soho Square, London W1V 5DF

A CIP catalogue record for this book
is available from the British Library

ISBN 0 7475 3355 5

10 9 8 7 6 5 4 3 2 1

Printed in Great Britain by Clays Ltd, St Ives plc.

Contents

INTRODUCTION

The rise of Machado de Assis to world eminence was even more of a miracle than it normally is for those few writers who attain it. He was of mixed race, epileptic, an orphan, half-educated, unhealthy, and myopic, and he never once left his native Rio de Janeiro, yet he taught himself English and French, inveigled himself into Brazil's literary milieu, wrote a vast amount in almost every literary vein, and became (by unanimous vote) the President of The Brazilian Academy Of Letters from 1897 until 1908 . . . and all this whilst holding down a regular job as a civil servant. He was one of the very few writers who not only received a state funeral, but actually deserved it.

Modern readers receive a surprise upon delving into Machado's work for the first time; 'Oh, it's Brazilian,' they think whilst hefting the volume in their hand, 'it's bound to be exotic, full of strange animals and customs, and beautiful prostitutes, and magic, and gods with African names, and revolutions, and violence . . .' They think wrongly, however, for Brazil's literature has always been wider and more varied than we foreigners have realised, and, furthermore, Machado was writing at a time when Brazil's literary consciousness was still almost completely European. He inhabits the same territory as Manzoni, of Italy, (1785–1873) and Eça de Queirós, of Portugal(1843–1900). His influences were at first French, and then English, but naturally and inevitably he also kept abreast of Portuguese letters, once famously accusing Eça de Queirós of having plagiarised Madame Bovary in *Cousin Basilio*.

Despite this, Machado's voice is more similar to Eça than to any other of his great contemporaries. There is the same irony, the same mockery, the same limpid style, the same urbanity and lightness of tone, and the same preoccupation with protagonists who have plenty of time and money, but who make nothing of their lives. Eça de Queirós has been neglected in the English-speaking world, but he is at least comparable to Flaubert, Dickens, Zola, and Balzac, whilst Machado, on the other hand, is not only comparable to Eça, but also seems to have been born one hundred years before his time, which is perhaps why he appeals to modern writers as diverse as Salman Rushdie, Paul Bailey, and William Cooper. The latter also, incidentally, writes like Machado, in snack-size chapters that tempt you to read just one more before you feed the cat, or get out of the bath, or turn off the light. Cooper also compares for wit and deftness of touch.

Machado would have laughed at me for what I am about to say (and please, dear reader, do not be put off) . . . but he is really a post-modernist writer. Of course we all know that there is nothing remotely new about post-modernism – Homer begins the *Odyssey* half way through, after all, and *Les Liaison Dangereuses* is composed of letters – but there *is* more of it about these days. Alongside Machado's very nineteenth century habit of confiding directly in his readers, we find a text that has been deliberately and playfully fragmented. We are offered delightfully whimsical and irrelevant passages of light philosophising, we find chapters that are only one sentence long, chapters which are quite strangely inconsequential, chapters about why Machado has not written a chapter, chapters consisting of dots and punctuation marks. We are referred to other chapters, as if Machado is spoofing a legal document or an academic tract, and he reflects often upon the text itself, so that, as he says, 'I have already compared my style to the progress of a drunk.'

But what an entertaining drunk! This is the kind of drunk who has had three glasses of excellent red wine, has loosened his belt by one notch, and has just hit his stride. 'I like jolly chapters,' says one of his characters, 'they are my weakness.' Fortunately for us, each and every chapter of Machado, however dismal, is a jolly one. Every sentence, in fact, is a jolly one, and a fair proportion of them ought to be collected in a small volume entitled 'The Wit And Wisdom Of Machado de Assis'. Here is a selection:

'The best way to appreciate a whip is to be holding it in one's hand.'

'Philosophy is one thing, and actual dying is another.'

'A ridiculous old age is the last and perhaps the saddest surprise of human nature.'

'God alone knows the power of an adjective, especially in new, tropical countries.'

'I know you have a certain philosophy – but let's talk about dinner.'

And, of course, 'To the victor the potatoes.'

Quite apart from the sheer pleasure that we derive from several passages, of great poetic force, this 'jolliness' is the reason that we do not go out and hang ourselves after reading Machado. That Machado is a pessimist is something that has been so frequently reiterated, that one hardly dares to controvert it; the case, after all, seems to have been settled. It is true that he presents us with the arbitrariness of fate and the inevitability of death. It is true that he appears to think that man is a futile passion. It is true that he tells us that our romantic loves are venial and ephemeral, and that our inveterate apathy always triumphs over our deepest passions and noblest aspirations. He tells us that a freed slave goes out and buys a slave of his own. He demonstrates the irresistible tug of our basest desires, and the emptiness of our high philosophies.

Dom Casmurro is perhaps an exception, but for the most part his books do not leave us downcast or depressed, or with a bitter aftertaste on the tongue. We have, it turns out, hugely enjoyed the experience of reading him, because Machado is quite unlike the greater majority of pessimists and satirists, in that he is not for one second a misanthropist. On the contrary, he likes us quite a lot, and there is no sourness, hostility, or contempt in his manner as, with a kind of detached amusement and with one eyebrow raised, he sketches out our foibles, follies, and delusions. This is not pessimism; it is a profound and affectionate celebration of the triviality, inanity, and fatuousness of the human race.

Machado is still laughing at us from six feet down, and cordially invites us to join him, both in his laughter and in his grave. Enjoy his books, and if you go to Rio, place a potato on his tomb.

The Epitaph of a Small Winner is the first in a quasi-trilogy which continues with *Quincas Borba, Philosopher or Dog?* and ends with *Dom Casmurro*. The 'Epitaph' is narrated by its dead protagonist, Braz Cubas, and is written with 'The pen of mirth and the ink of melancholy'. Braz relates the story of an adulterous love affair that finally fizzles out, and indeed, the entire story of his life, which also fizzles out. In the meantime Braz has suffered some reverses, betrayed lovers and friends, lost a fiancée in a plague, become a disciple of the mad philosopher, Quincas Borba, whose 'humanitism' is clearly a spoof of the optimistic philosophies then fashionable, and has become a deputy in parliament for only one term of office. He has wasted his life entirely, but, after all, what else can one do with it, and what else might it be for? In death he is consoled by the one small thing that there was on the plus side.

Louis de Bernières, 1997

Translator's Introduction: For all his restraint and good humor, Machado de Assis hurls at his readers a fierce challenge, unrecognized by many, offensive to some, a joy to those who are strong enough to accept it. The challenge lies in Machado's vast iconoclasm, which is likely to involve destruction of the reader's own icons. In his best work, Machado is perhaps the most completely disenchanted writer in occidental literature. Skeptics generally destroy certain illusions in order to cling to others. Machado rejects everything mundane.

The present novel sets forth Machado's pessimism with a fastidious minuteness that leaves the reader only two alternatives: to reject Machado or, with Machado, to reject the world. The latter alternative still permits affirmation of certain supramundane values which Machado does not touch. Many religious persons regard agnostic Machado as a great writer—perhaps because, by destroying so many false gods, he leaves room for none but the true.

Braz Cubas, the protagonist of this novel, is spiritually and psychologically a very ordinary man. Machado endows him with wealth, good looks, and health, doubtless to avoid dwelling upon the frustration occasioned by the lack of these characteristics. For Machado has more esoteric game in mind than the sources of unhappiness that everyone recognizes as such. Braz's pursuits embrace sex, politics, philosophy, even "doing good." Yet in the final chapter, when he comes to calculate the net profit in his life, he finds it to be zero—until he remembers that, having had no children, he has handed on to no one the misery of human existence. And so, he concludes, he is a little ahead of the game, a small winner.

The abject and ironic pessimism of the book is based on nature's indifference and man's egoism. Indeed, virtually all of Braz's interests can be reduced to one: the affirmation of Braz. In the other two of Machado's three great novels—*Quincas Borba* (1892) and *Dom Casmurro* (1900), Machado emphasizes a third factor, which is perhaps implicit in egoism: the indifference of the human environment to the individual's welfare. Braz Cubas betrays himself; the chief character in *Dom Casmurro* is betrayed by the indifference (to him) of his wife and of his friend. A commonplace triangle becomes, in Machado's hands, a tragedy of the frustration of a sensitive man's love by the ruthless but natural lust of two stronger persons. In a sense, the human environment takes on much of the aspect of the physical environment, leaving the individual without recourse.

More than twenty books and innumerable shorter essays have been written about Machado. Much of this literature is directed to the solution of two problems: how Machado came to acquire his pessimism and how he managed to develop a lively, classic taste in the midst of the prevailing romanticism. The known events in his life leave much to be explained.

Joaquim Maria Machado de Assis was born in 1839 in Rio de Janeiro, the son of a mulatto house painter and a white woman from Portugal. His mother died in his early childhood, and he was raised by the kindly mulatto woman whom his father then married. Some of his time was spent in the aristocratic old house of his wealthy godmother. Machado went to elementary public school, which in Brazil offers at most a five-year course. His widowed stepmother took a job as cook in a girls' school, and Machado probably listened in on classes. He learned French from a neighboring French baker.

In adolescence, if not even earlier, Machado determined to become a man of letters. He kept himself in a literary milieu, working as typesetter and proofreader, making literary friends, and always writing. His collected (although not quite complete) works total 31 volumes. Machado tried his hand at almost every literary form: epic poetry, lyric poetry, drama, criticism, short stories, novels, journalistic commentary. But his fame now rests upon the three novels here mentioned, about thirty of his more than one hundred short stories, and two or three short poems, one of them an amazingly skillful translation of Poe's *Raven*.

Most of Machado's fiction prior to 1879 was in the popular romantic tradition. In that year his health, never robust, broke down so severely that he was forced to spend some months in a health resort. There he appears to have determined to free himself from literary conventions alien to his personality. The first fruit of this determination was the present novel, published in 1880. Dictated to his wife—some critics maintain that the process of dictation is manifest in the style—it represents a turn not only from romanticism to a sort of psychological realism but also from French influences to English. Machado had learned to read English and had become something of a literary Anglophile.

The book greatly enhanced Machado's already secure reputation. Before long, critical opinion established him as Brazil's leading man of letters. The Brazilian Academy of Letters unanimously elected Machado its president, a title that he held from the founding of the Academy in 1897 till his death in 1908.

In 1869 Machado married a white woman five years his senior, a cultured Portuguese who lived with him in what appears to have been complete harmony and devotion; she died in 1904. They had no children.

Through most of his life he worked as a public official—a bureaucrat, we should say—for it was almost impossible to earn a living as a writer. Epileptic, myopic, rickety, Machado had both the shyness and the intense need for companionship so often found in sickly persons. Among his friends one notes in particular the brilliant diplomat Joaquim Nabuco. Another friend—Ruy Barbosa, Brazil's great liberal statesman—delivered Machado's funeral oration. Symptomatic of the general unwillingness to grasp Machado's central thought is the resemblance of the tone of Barbosa's florid speech to that of the burlesque funeral oration in Chapter 1 of the present book.

In all this, there is little to guide one to a solution of the basic problems about Machado. His poor health may have been in part responsible for the Machadian irony, but it cannot account for—rather it makes all the more unaccountable—his rejection of the superman; there are surely Nietzschean elements in Quincas Borba's philosophy, which Machado ridicules in the latter part of this book. As for the source of Machado's classic taste, implicit in his rejection of false models and explicit in some of his critical writings, we are even more at sea and can hardly avoid reliance upon undiscovered, possibly undiscoverable, subjective factors.

Some of Machado's works have been translated into German, French, Italian, and Spanish. In English there are only three short stories, in an anthology, long out of print, by Isaac Goldberg; however, future publication of a translation of *Dom Casmurro* has been announced. Without denying the tragic power of *Dom Casmurro*, the present translator chose *Epitaph of a Small Winner* because the creative release of Machado's inhibited (by compliance with romantic conventions) sentiments makes it the liveliest and most inventive of his novels and because, as a cogent and nearly complete statement of Machado's attitude, it provides a suitable introduction to his work.

A few words at this point about the text will avoid a superfluity of editorial intrusions. Those that cannot be avoided are in every case the translator's.

With respect to monetary units, if the reader will think of a conto (one thousand milreis, *i.e.*, one million reis), in the period covered by the narrative, as the equivalent of about five hundred dollars, he will be near enough to the truth for literary purposes. A crusado was four hundred reis. The value of the dobra, a Portuguese coin, varied considerably, but the context generally suggests its value closely enough to give the sense of the passage.

"Nhonhô" (applied to Virgilia's son and to Braz) and "Yayá" (applied to Virgilia) were common nicknames for male and female children, respectively, of well-to-do families.

Except where the context indicates otherwise, places named are districts and suburbs of Rio de Janeiro.

Non-Portuguese words used by Machado have been retained, untranslated, except that the English word "luncheon" has been changed to "afternoon snack" (Chapter 73), which is what it meant to Machado and his public.

WILLIAM L. GROSSMAN

1952

EPITAPH OF
A SMALL WINNER

To the first worm that gnawed my flesh

To the Reader: When we learn from Stendhal that he wrote one of his books for only a hundred readers, we are both astonished and disturbed. The world will be neither astonished nor, probably, disturbed if the present book has not one hundred readers like Stendhal's, nor fifty, nor twenty, nor even ten. Ten? Maybe five. It is, in truth, a diffuse work, in which I, Braz Cubas, if indeed I have adopted the free form of a Sterne or of a Xavier de Maistre, have possibly added a certain peevish pessimism of my own. Quite possibly. The work of a man already dead. I wrote it with the pen of Mirth and the ink of Melancholy, and one can readily foresee what may come of such a union. Moreover, solemn people will find in the book an aspect of pure romance, while frivolous folk will not find in it the sort of romance to which they have become accustomed; thus it is and will remain, disrespected by the solemn and unloved by the frivolous, the two great pillars of public opinion.

But I still entertain at least the hope of winning public favor, and the first step in that direction is to avoid a long and detailed prologue. The best prologue is the one that has the least matter or that presents it most briefly, even to the point of obscurity. Hence I shall not relate the extraordinary method that I used in the composition of these memoirs, written here in the world beyond. It is a most curious method, but its relation would require an excessive amount of space and, moreover, is unnecessary to an understanding of the work. The book must suffice in itself: if it please you, excellent reader, I shall be rewarded for my labor; if it please you not, I shall reward you with a snap of my fingers, and good riddance to you.

Braz Cubas

1. The Death of the Author: I hesitated some
time, not knowing whether to open these memoirs at the beginning or at the end, *i. e.*, whether to start with my birth or with my death. Granted, the usual practice is to begin with one's birth, but two considerations led me to adopt a different method: the first is that, properly speaking, I am a deceased writer not in the sense of one who has written and is now deceased, but in the sense of one who has died and is now writing, a writer for whom the grave was really a new cradle; the second is that the book would thus gain in merriment and novelty. Moses, who also related his own death, placed it not at the beginning but at the end: a radical difference between this book and the Pentateuch.

Accordingly: I expired at two o'clock of a Friday afternoon in the month of August, 1869, at my lovely suburban home in Catumby. I was sixty-four, sturdy, prosperous, and single, was worth about three hundred contos, and was accompanied to the cemetery by eleven friends. Only eleven! True, there had been no invitations and no notices in the newspapers. Moreover, there was a fine drizzle, steady and sad, so steady and so sad, in fact, that it led one of those faithful friends of my last hour to work this ingenious thought into the discourse that he offered at the edge of my grave: "You who knew him may well affirm with me that Nature herself appears to be weeping her lamentation over her irreparable loss, one of the most beautiful characters that ever honored humanity by his presence in our poor world. This sombre air, these drops from heaven, those dark clouds covering the blue like a crepe of mourning, all manifest the harsh and cruel grief that gnaws at her deepest entrails and the praise that heaven itself bestows upon our great and dear departed." Good and faithful friend! I shall never regret the legacy of twenty government bonds that I left him.

And thus I arrived at the end of my days; thus I started on the road to Hamlet's "undiscovered country," with neither the anxiety nor the doubts of the young prince, but slow and halting, like a person who has lingered in the theatre long after the end of the performance. Tardy and jaded. Some nine or ten people saw me go, among them three ladies: my sister Sabina, who was married to Cotrim; her daughter, a real lily of the valley; and . . . Have patience! In a little while I shall reveal the identity of the third lady. Be content for the moment to know that this anonymous lady, although not a relative of mine, suffered more than the relatives. You must believe me: she really suffered more. I do not say that she tore her hair, nor that she rolled on the floor in convulsions. For there was nothing dramatic about my passing. The death of a bachelor at the age of sixty-four does not take on the proportions of high tragedy. And even if it did, nothing could have been more improper than that this anonymous lady display the intensity of her sorrow. Standing at the head of the bed, eyes glazed and mouth half open, she could hardly believe I had gone.

"Dead! Dead!" she repeated to herself.

And her imagination—like the storks that a famous traveler saw setting out in flight from the Ilissus to the African shores, heedless of the times and of the ruins—her imagination flew above the desolation of the moment to the shores of an ever youthful Africa.

Let her go; we shall go there later. We shall go there when I return to my early years. At present, I wish to die calmly, methodically, hearing the sobs of the ladies, the soft words of the men, the rain drumming on the taro leaves, and the piercing noise of a razor being sharpened by a knife-grinder outside in front of the door of a leather craftsman. I assure you that the music of this orchestra of death was much less sad than may appear. After a certain time, it was actually pleasurable. Life was shaking my body with the force of a great wave, my consciousness was fading away, I was descending to a physical and mental state of utter immobility, and my body was becoming a plant, a stone, clay, nothing at all.

I died of pneumonia; but, if I were to tell the reader that the cause of my death was less the pneumonia than a great and useful idea, possibly he would not believe me, yet it would be true. I am going to explain the matter to him briefly. Let him judge for himself.

2. The Plaster:

One morning, as I was strolling through the grounds of my suburban home, an idea took hold of the trapeze that I used to carry about in my head. Once it had taken hold, it flexed its arms and legs and began to do the most daring acrobatic feats one can possibly imagine. I just stood and watched it. Suddenly it made a great leap, extended its arms and legs until it formed an X, and said, "Decipher me or I devour thee."

This idea was nothing less than the invention of a great cure, an anti-melancholy plaster, designed to relieve the despondency of mankind. In the application for registration that I then prepared, I called the attention of the government to this truly Christian purpose of the plaster. Nevertheless, I did not deny to my friends that pecuniary advantages could be expected from the distribution of a product of such great and profound effects. Now, however, that I am here on the other side, I can confess everything: what influenced me most was the desire to see, printed in newspapers, on store signs, in pamphlets, on street corners, and on the little boxes containing the plaster, these four words: *The Braz Cubas Plaster*. Why deny it? I had a passion for showiness, for billboards, for pyrotechnics. Perhaps the modest will reproach me for this defect; I trust, however, that people of discernment will acknowledge my talent. Thus my idea, like a medal, had two sides, one turned towards the public, the other towards me. On one side, altruism and profit; on the other, thirst for fame. Or rather, let us say, love of glory.

An uncle of mine, a canon receiving a full prebend, used to say that the love of temporal glory was the perdition of the soul, which should covet only eternal glory. To which my other uncle, an officer in one of the old infantry regiments, would reply that the love of glory was the most truly human thing about a man and, consequently, his most genuine characteristic.

Let the reader decide between the soldier and the canon; I shall return to the plaster.

3. Genealogy:

But, as I have already spoken of my two uncles, let me first make a short sketch of my genealogy.

The founder of my family was a certain Damião Cubas, who flourished in the first half of the eighteenth century. He was a cooper by trade, a native of Rio de Janeiro, where he would have died in penury and obscurity if he had been *merely* a cooper. But no; he made himself into a farmer, planted, harvested, and exchanged his products for fine and honorable silver coins, until he died leaving a large fortune to a son, Luiz Cubas, Master of Law. In this fellow the line of my ancestors really begins—that is, of the ancestors that my family regularly acknowledged—because Damião Cubas was, after all, a cooper, and perhaps a bad cooper, but Luiz Cubas studied at Coimbra, became a prominent figure in the government, and was one of the personal friends of the viceroy, Count da Cunha.

As this name Cubas reeked excessively of the cooper's shop, my father, Damião's great-grandson, alleged that said name had been given to a nobleman, a hero of the African expeditions, in token of his achievement in capturing three hundred *cubas* [vats] from the Moors. My father was a man of imagination; he escaped from the cooper's shop on the wings of a *calembour*. He was a good sort, my father, worthy and true as are few on this earth. There was, to be sure, a certain amount of foolishness in his character; but who in this world is wholly free from folly? In justice to my father, one should note that he resorted to elaborate invention only after first experimenting with simple falsehood. He had related himself to the family of that famous namesake of mine, Governor Braz Cubas, founder of the town of São Vicente, where he died in 1592; this is why I had been given the name of Braz. However, the Governor's family had protested, and it was then that father invented the three hundred Moorish *cubas*.

Some of my relatives are still alive; for example, my niece Venancia, the lily of the valley; also her father, Cotrim, a fellow who . . . But let us not anticipate; let us finish once and for all with the plaster.

4. The Fixed Idea:

My idea, having performed its acrobatic capers, became a fixed idea. God deliver you, dear reader, from a fixed idea; better a mote in your eye, better even a beam. Remember Cavour: it was the fixed idea of Italian unity that killed him. True, Bismarck has not died; but this merely substantiates the observation that nature is immensely whimsical and that history is eternally irresponsible. For example, Suetonius told us about Claudius the simpleton—or "pumpkinhead," as Seneca called him—and about Tito, who was deservedly the delight of Rome. Now along comes a professor and finds a way of proving that, of the two caesars, the truly delightful one was Seneca's "pumpkinhead." And you, Madame Lucrezia, flower of the Borgias, if a poet painted you as the Catholic Messalina, a skeptical Gregorovius turned up and almost completely absolved you of that quality; so that, if you have not become exactly a lily, at least you have emerged from the mire. As for me, I take no sides between the poet and the scholar.

Then long live history, voluble old history, which is all things to all men. Returning to fixed ideas, let me say that it is they that make both supermen and madmen; supple, flexible ideas make only men like Claudius, *i. e.*, like Suetonius' Claudius.

My idea was really fixed, as fixed as . . . I cannot think of anything so fixed in this world: perhaps the moon, perhaps the Egyptian pyramids, perhaps the late Germanic Diet. Let the reader make whatever analogy pleases him most, let him make it and be content; there is no need for him to curl his lip at me merely because we have not yet come to the narrative part of these memoirs. We shall get to it. The reader, like his fellows, doubtless prefers action to reflection, and doubtless he is wholly in the right. So we shall get to it. However, I must advise him that this book is written leisurely, with the leisureliness of a man no longer troubled by the flight of time; that it is a work supinely philosophical, but of a philosophy wanting in uniformity, now austere, now playful, a thing that neither edifies nor destroys, neither inflames nor chills, and that is at once more than pastime and less than preachment.

Come now, uncurl your lip and let us get back to the plaster. Let us leave history and its elegant-lady capriciousness. None of us fought in the battle of Salamis, none of us wrote the Augsburg Confession; for my part, if I ever think of Cromwell, it is only to fancy that His Highness, with the same hand with which he closed Parliament, might have forced the English to use the Braz Cubas Plaster. Do not mock at the idea of a pharmaceutic victory alongside the Puritanic. Who does not know that, together with the great, imposing, public banner, there are often various other flags, modest and private, that are hoisted and wave in its shadow and that not infrequently survive it? By way of a questionable analogy, it is like the common people who used to seek protection in the shadow of the feudal castle; the castle fell, but the common people are still with us. In fact, they have become great and noble in its stead . . . I think I shall withdraw the analogy.

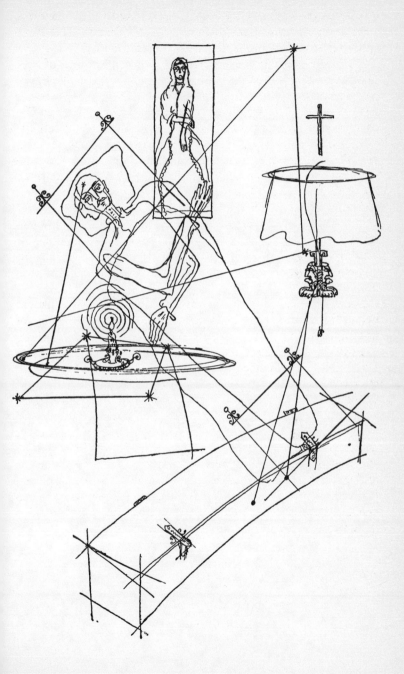

5. In Which a Lady Appears at the Door:

While I was developing and perfecting my invention, a draught of air caught me full on; I fell ill and took no steps to cure myself. I had the plaster on my mind, the fixed idea of supermen and of madmen. I would see myself, at a distance, rising above the common herd and ascending to the sky like an immortal eagle, and it is not before so grand a spectacle that a man can feel pain. The next day I was worse; I began then to take care of myself, but imperfectly, unmethodically, carelessly, sporadically. Such was the origin of the illness that carried me off to eternity. You already know that I died on a Friday, which is a bad-luck day, and I believe I have proved that it was my invention that killed me. Logical demonstrations less perspicuous than mine have been accepted as conclusive.

Until then, it appeared to be quite within my power to leap to the pinnacle of the age and to figure in the newspapers along with other big men. I was healthy and strong. Let us suppose that, instead of laying the foundations for a pharmaceutic innovation, I had tried to set up a new political institution or a religious reform. The current of air would have come along just the same and, with its efficacy greater than that of human plans, would have carried everything off with it. On such factors depend the destinies of men.

With this thought, I said farewell to the most, I shall not say discreet, but certainly the most beautiful woman of her time, the anonymous one of the first chapter, she whose imagination, like the storks of the Ilissus . . . She was then fifty-four years old, a ruin, an imposing ruin. You see, reader, we had loved each other, she and I, many years before, and one day, after I had fallen ill, I saw her appear at the door of my bedroom . . .

6. Chimène, qui l'eût dit? Rodrigue, qui l'eût cru?

I saw her appear at the door of the bedroom, pale, obviously moved, dressed in black, and remain there a minute without the courage to enter, or perhaps held back by the presence of the man who was with me. From the bed where I lay, I gazed at her this while, forgetting to speak to her, forgetting even to make a gesture. I had not seen her for two years, and I saw her now, not as she was, but as she had been; I saw us both as we had been, because a mysterious Ezekiel had made the sun turn back to the days of our youth. The sun turned back, I shook off all my miseries, and this handful of dust, soon to be scattered in the eternity of nothingness, became stronger than time, stronger than the minister of death. No fountain of youth could have performed this feat accomplished by mere nostalgia.

Believe me, remembrance is the lesser evil. Let no one trust the happiness of the moment; there is in it a drop of gall. When time has gone by and the spasm has ended, then, if ever, one can truly enjoy the event; for, of these two illusions, the better is the one that can be experienced without pain.

My evocation lasted only a short time; reality soon dominated, and the present expelled the past. Perhaps I shall expound to the reader, in some corner of this book, my Theory of Human Editions. The important thing now is to know that Virgilia—her name was Virgilia—entered the bedroom resolutely, with the gravity supplied by her clothes and her years, and came up to my bed. The man rose and left. He was a fellow who used to visit me every day to talk about the exchange, about colonization, and about the need to develop the railroad system; nothing, of course, could be more interesting to a dying man. He went out. Virgilia remained standing; for some time we merely looked at each other. Which of us would speak the truth? Of two great lovers, of two boundless passions, nothing was left after twenty years; there were only two withered hearts, devastated by life and sated by it, perhaps not in equal degree but definitely sated. Virgilia then had the beauty of age, an austere and maternal air. She was less thin than when I had last seen her, at a St. John's Day party in Tijuca; and, because she was one of those women to whom senescence comes tardily, only now was a little silver beginning to interweave her dark hair.

"Visiting the dead these days?" I asked.

"What do you mean, dead!" replied Virgilia, with a deprecative cluck of the tongue. And, after pressing both my hands, "I'm visiting lazy good-for-nothings so that I can throw them out of bed and into the street."

She did not have the caressing, almost lachrymose manner of earlier years, but her voice was affectionate and sweet. I was alone in the house with a manservant; we could speak to each other without danger. Virgilia gave me a long report of the news, telling it delightfully and salting it with a pinch of malice. I, soon to leave the world, felt a satanic pleasure in deriding it, in persuading myself that what I was losing was not worth keeping.

"What an idea!" interrupted Virgilia, a little annoyed. "You'll see, I won't come back. Talking about dying! We all have to die; that's what we get for being alive."

And, looking at the clock, "Heavens, it's three o'clock! I've got to go."

"Already?"

"I'll come back tomorrow, or soon after."

"I don't know if you ought," I replied; "the sick man here is an old bachelor, and there are no ladies in the house . . ."

"Where is your sister?"

"She's going to spend a few days with me, but she can't come before Saturday."

Virgilia reflected a moment, shrugged her shoulders, and said seriously, "I'm old. No one notices me. But, to avoid the possibility of gossip, I'll come with Nhonhô."

Nhonhô was a law graduate, the only child of her marriage, who, at the age of five, had been an unconscious accomplice in our love affair. They came two days later, and I confess that, seeing them together there in my bedroom, I was overcome by a shyness which prevented my replying immediately to the young man's polite words. Virgilia understood, and said, "Nhonhô, pay no attention to that crafty customer there. He doesn't like to speak because he wants people to think he's dying."

Her son smiled, I think I smiled too, and it all ended in pure fun. Virgilia was cheerful and serene; she had the aspect of one who had led an immaculate life. No suspicionable glance, no gesture that could reveal anything; an evenness of speech and of spirit, a self-possession, that I thought unusual in her. As we touched casually on an illicit love affair that was half secret and half overt, I heard her speak with scorn and with a little indignation about the woman in question, who happened to be a friend of hers. Her son felt pleased, hearing these stout and worthy opinions, and I asked myself what the sparrow hawks would say of us if Buffon had been born a sparrow hawk . . .

It was the beginning of my delirium.

7. The Delirium: So far as I know, no one has yet related his own delirium. I shall do it, and science will be grateful to me. If the reader has no taste for the contemplation of psychological phenomena, he may skip the chapter; let him go straight to the story part of the book. But, however lacking he may be in curiosity, I should like him to know that what occurred in my head during this period of twenty or thirty minutes is extremely interesting.

First, I took the form of a Chinese barber, rotund and skilful, shaving a mandarin, who paid me for my work with candy and pinches—mandarin whimsicality.

Soon after, I felt myself being transformed into St. Thomas' *Summa Theologica*, printed in one volume and bound in morocco with engravings and a silver lock—an idea that gave my body the most rigid immobility; and I still remember that, as my hands were the two overlapping parts that locked, I crossed them on my chest, and someone (Virgilia, doubtless) uncrossed them because they gave me the appearance of a corpse.

Finally, back in human form, I saw a hippopotamus approach. He carried me off. I remained silent and did not resist, whether through fear or because of confidence in him I do not know; but, within a short time, we were proceeding at such a dizzy speed that I ventured to speak to him, and tactfully remarked that the trip seemed to me to have no preconceived destination.

"You are mistaken," replied the animal; "we are going to the beginning of the ages."

I insinuated that it must be very far off; but the hippopotamus did not hear me or did not understand me, unless he was merely feigning one or the other. As he apparently could talk, I asked him whether he was a descendant of Achilles' horse or of Balaam's ass, and he replied with a gesture common to quadrupeds of both species: he wiggled his ears. For my part, I closed my eyes, relaxed, and abandoned myself to fate. I am not ashamed to confess that I felt a certain itch of curiosity to know just where the beginning of the ages was, whether it was as mysterious as the origin of the Nile, and above all whether it was more important or less important than the end of the ages: reflections of a sick brain. As I kept my eyes closed, I did not see the road. I remember only that the feeling of cold continually increased in intensity, and that after a time it seemed to me that we were entering the region of eternal glaciers. I opened my eyes and saw that my animal was galloping across a plain white with snow, with snow mountains here and there, snow vegetation, and various big snow animals. Everything of snow; we were even frozen by a sun of snow. I tried to speak, but could only grunt anxiously, "Where are we?"

"We have gone beyond the Garden of Eden."

"I see. Let's stop at the tent of Abraham."

"How can we if we are traveling towards the past!" derisively replied my mount.

I became annoyed and a little dizzy. The journey began to seem tiresome and absurd, the cold uncomfortable, the method of transportation violent, and the result uncertain. And afterwards— a sick man's thoughts—even if we arrived at the stated destination, maybe the ages, irritated by the trespass upon their origin, would crush me between their nails, which must be as frightfully old as the ages themselves. While I was thinking about these things, we were eating up the road, and the plain was flying beneath our feet, until the animal suddenly stopped and I was able to look more calmly about me. To *look* only; I *saw* nothing but the immense whiteness of the snow, which by now had even invaded the sky. Perhaps I saw an occasional plant, enormous, brutish, its broad leaves swaying in the wind. The silence of this region was like that of the tomb: one might have said that the life in things had become stupefied in the presence of man.

Did it fall from the air? Did it rise from the earth? I do not know. I know only that an immense shape, the figure of a woman, then appeared before me, with its eyes, shining like the sun, fixed upon me. Everything about this figure had the vastness of the primeval; it was indeed all too much for human perception, for its contours were lost in the surroundings, and what appeared at first to be dense turned out, in many cases, to be diaphanous. Stupefied, I said nothing, I did not even cry out; but, after a short time, I asked who she was and what she was called—curiosity born of delirium.

"They call me Nature or Pandora. I am your mother and your enemy."

On hearing this last word, I drew back in fear. The figure loosed a fierce laugh, which produced about us the effects of a whirlwind; the plants were contorted, and a long wail broke the silence of the surroundings.

"Do not be afraid," she said, "my enmity does not kill; it is through life that it affirms itself. You are alive: I wish you no other calamity."

"Am I alive?" I asked, digging my nails into my hands as if to make certain.

"Yes, worm, you are alive. You have not yet lost that tattered cloak of which you are so proud; you will taste for a few hours more the bread of pain and the wine of misery. You are alive; even though you have gone mad, you are alive; and, if your consciousness regains a moment of lucidity, you will say that you want to live."

As she said this, the vision extended one of her arms and lifted me into the air as if I had been a feather. Then for the first time I could see her enormous face close up. Nothing more pacific in the world; no violent contortion; no suggestion of hate or ferocity. Its sole, all-pervasive expression was that of eternal isolation, of changeless will, of the impassivity of complete egoism. Wrath, if she experienced it, remained suppressed in her heart. At the same time, in this face with its glacial expression there was an air of youth, a combination of energy and freshness before which I felt like the weakest and most decrepit of beings.

"Do you understand me?" she said, after a period of mutual contemplation.

"No," I replied, "nor do I wish to understand you. You are an absurdity, a fable. I am surely dreaming, or, if in truth I have gone mad, you are nothing but a psychopath's figment, a vain and empty thing, which reason, being absent, cannot govern. You, Nature? The Nature that I know is mother only and not enemy. She does not make of life a scourge nor does she wear such a face, indifferent as the tomb. And why Pandora?"

"Because I carry in my bag all good things and all evils, and the most remarkable of all, hope, man's consolation. Are you trembling?"

"Yes. The way you look at me . . ."

"I know; for I am not only life, I am also death, and you are soon to give me back what I loaned you. Come, my great lecher, the voluptuousness of extinction awaits you."

When these words had reechoed like thunder in that vast emptiness, I thought that it would be the last sound ever to come to my ears; of a sudden I felt as if I were being decomposed. Then I looked at her with suppliant eyes and begged a few more years.

"A few years would seem like a minute!" she exclaimed. "Why do you want to live longer? To continue to devour and be devoured? Are you not sated with the show and the struggle? You have experienced again and again the least vile and least painful of my gifts: the brightness of morning, the gentle melancholy of dusk, the quietness of night, the face of the earth, and, last of all, sleep, my greatest gift to man. Poor idiot, what more do you wish?"

"Just to live, I ask nothing more. Was it not you who gave me life and placed in my heart the love of life? Then why should you do yourself injury by killing me?"

"Because I have no more need of you. Time finds interest not in the minute that is already passing, but only in the minute that is about to come. The new-born minute is strong, merry, thinks that it carries eternity in its bosom; it brings only death, and perishes like its predecessors. But I do not perish. Egoism, you say? Yes, egoism; I have no other law. Egoism, self-preservation. The tiger kills the lamb because the tiger's philosophy is that, above all, it must live, and if the lamb is tender so much the better; this is the universal law. Come, see for yourself."

As she said this, she snatched me up and lifted me to the summit of a mountain. I looked down and, far off through a mist, contemplated for considerable time a curious thing. Just imagine, reader, a procession of all the ages, with all the human races, all the passions, the tumult of empires, the war of appetite against appetite and of hate against hate, the reciprocal destruction of human beings and their surroundings. This was the monstrous spectacle that I saw. The history of man and of the earth had thus an intensity that neither science nor the imagination could give it, for science is too slow and imagination too vague, whereas what I saw was the living condensation of history. To describe it one would have to make the lightning stand still. The ages moved along in a whirlwind, but nevertheless, because the eyes of delirium have a virtue of their own, I was able to distinguish everything that passed before me, afflictions and joys, glory and misery, and I saw love augmenting misery, and misery aggravating human debility. Along came voracious greed, fiery anger, drooling envy, and the hoe and the pen, both wet with sweat, and ambition, hunger, vanity, melancholy, affluence, love, and all of them were shaking man like a baby's rattle until they transformed him into something not unlike an old rag. They were the several forms of a single malady, which would attack now the viscera, now the psyche, and would dance eternally, in its harlequin trappings, around the human species. Pain would give way to indifference, which was a dreamless sleep, or to pleasure, which was a bastard pain. Then man, whipped and rebellious, ran beyond the fatality of things in pursuit of a nebulous and elusive figure made of patches—a patch of the intangible, another of the improbable, another of the invisible—all loosely sewn together with the needle of imagination; and this figure, nothing less than the chimera of happiness, either eluded them or let them hang on to its skirt, and man would hug the skirt to his breast, and then the figure would laugh in mockery and would disappear.

Upon seeing such misfortune, I could not repress a cry of anguish, which Nature, or Pandora, heard with neither protest nor ridicule; and—I do not know by what psychological law of inversion—it was I who began to laugh, with a laughter immoderate and idiotic.

"You are right," I said, "the thing is amusing and worth seeing; a bit monotonous, perhaps, but worth seeing. When Job cursed the day he had been born, it was for want of seeing the show from up here. All right, Pandora, open your belly and devour me; the thing is amusing, but devour me."

Her reply was to force me to look down and to see the ages continuing to go by, fast and turbulent; generation upon generation, some sad like the Hebrews of the captivity, some merry like the libertines of Commodus's reign, and all arriving punctually at the grave. I wanted to flee, but a mysterious force paralyzed my legs. Then I said to myself, "If the centuries are going by, mine will come too, and will pass, and after a time the last century of all will come, and then I shall understand." And I fixed my eyes on the ages that were coming and passing on; now I was calm and resolute, maybe even happy. Each age brought its share of light and shade, of apathy and struggle, of truth and error, and its parade of systems, of new ideas, of new illusions; in each of them the verdure of spring burst forth, grew yellow with age, and then, young once more, burst forth again. While life thus moved with the regularity of a calendar, history and civilization developed; and man, at first naked and unarmed, clothed and armed himself, built hut and palace, villages and hundred-gated Thebes, created science that scrutinizes and art that elevates, made himself an orator, a mechanic, a philosopher, ran all over the face of the globe, went down into the earth and up to the clouds, performing the mysterious work through which he satisfied the necessities of life and tried to forget his loneliness. My tired eyes finally saw the present age go by and, after it, future ages. The present age, as it approached, was agile, skilful, vibrant, proud, a little verbose, audacious, learned, but in the end it was as miserable as the earlier ones. And so it passed, and so passed the others, with the same speed and monotony. I redoubled my attention; I stared with all my might; I was going at last to see the end—the end!—but then the speed of the parade increased beyond the speed of lightning, beyond all comprehension. Perhaps for this reason, objects began to change; some grew, some shrank, others were lost in the surroundings; a mist covered everything—except the hippopotamus who had brought me there, and he began to grow smaller, smaller, smaller, until he became the size of a cat. Indeed, it was a cat. I looked at it carefully; it was my cat Sultan, playing at the door of the bedroom with a paper ball . . .

8. Reason versus Folly: The reader will no doubt understand that Reason was returning and was inviting Folly to leave, declaiming, and with justice, the words of Tartuffe: *"La maison est à moi, c'est à vous d'en sortir."*

But it is an old habit of Folly's to fall in love with houses that belong to others, and, once she has obtained possession of a house, she cannot readily be persuaded to leave. It is an old habit; she will never give it up; her sense of shame has long since been calloused over. If we just think of the vast number of houses that she occupies, some all year round, others only during the summer, we shall conclude that this amiable pilgrim must be the terror of property-owners. In the case under consideration, there was a minor disturbance at the door of my brain, for the trespasser did not wish to deliver possession of the house and the owner insisted upon recovery. Finally, Folly said that she would be content with a little corner in the attic.

"No, madam," replied Reason, "I am tired of letting you remain in attics; tired and experienced. Your plan of action is to pass almost unnoticed from the attic to the dining room, and from the dining room to the living room and the rest of the house."

"All right, but let me stay just a little longer. I am on the trail of a mystery . . ."

"What mystery?"

"Two, really," replied Folly; "of life and of death. Just give me about ten minutes more."

Reason began to laugh. "You'll never change . . . never . . . never . . ."

And, as she said this, she took Folly by the wrists and dragged her out; then she entered and locked the door. Folly whined a few more entreaties, muttered a few imprecations; but she soon accepted the hopelessness of her suit, stuck out her tongue, and went her way . . .

9. Transition:

Observe now with what skill, with what art, I make the biggest transition in this book. Observe: my delirium began in the presence of Virgilia; Virgilia was the great sin of my youth; there is no youth without childhood; childhood presupposes birth; and so we arrive, effortlessly, at October 20, 1805, the date of my birth. Did you note carefully? No apparent seams or joints, nothing to upset the reader's habitual attentive calm, absolutely nothing. Thus the book has all the advantages of system and method without the rigidity that they generally entail. In truth, it is high time that we began to follow some sort of systematic procedure. However, although system is indispensable, one should use it in a spirit of looseness and informality, in one's shirt-sleeves and suspenders, like a person who does not care what the lady who lives across the street, or even the policeman on the block, may think of him. It is like eloquence; for there is a genuine and vibrant eloquence, with a natural, engaging art, and a rigid eloquence, starched and empty. Let us go back to October 20.

10. On That Day:

On that day, the Cubas tree brought forth a lovely flower: I was born. I was received in the arms of Paschoela, famous midwife from Minho, Portugal, who boasted that she had opened the doors to the world for a whole generation of noblemen. Quite possibly my father had heard her say this; I believe, however, that it was paternal sentiment that induced him to gratify her with two half-dobras. Washed and diapered, I immediately became the hero of the house. Everyone predicted for me what best suited his taste. Uncle João, the old infantry officer, found that I had a certain facial expression like Bonaparte's, a thing that my father could not hear without nausea. Uncle Ildefonso, then a plain priest, scented a future canon in me.

"He will most surely be a canon, and I shall say no more for fear of appearing prideful; but I should not be surprised in the least if God has destined him for a bishopric . . . Yes, a bishopric; it is by no means impossible. What is your opinion, brother Bento?"

My father replied to everyone that I would be what God desired. Then he would lift me high in the air, as if he wanted to show me to the whole city and, indeed, to the whole world. He asked everyone whether I looked like him, whether I was intelligent, pretty . . .

I relate these things briefly, just as I heard them related years later; I am uninformed about most of the details of that great day. I know that the neighbors came or sent their compliments to the new-born, and that during the first few weeks we had many visitors. There was no chair or stool that escaped service. Many

Sunday coats and fine breeches put in an appearance. If I do not relate the caresses, the kisses, the admiration, the blessings, it is because, if I did so, I should never finish the chapter, and finish it I must.

Item: I can tell nothing about my baptism, for they told me nothing about it, except that it was the occasion for one of the jolliest parties of the following year, 1806. I was baptized in the church of Saint Dominic on a Tuesday in March, a fine, pure, clear day, with Colonel Rodrigues de Mattos and his wife as godparents. They were both descended from old families of the North, and did real honor to the blood that ran in their veins, blood that had once been spilled in the war against Holland. I believe that their names were among the first things that I learned; and surely I could repeat them with great charm, or I revealed a precocious talent in doing so, for I was obliged to recite them before every visitor.

"Nhonhô, tell these gentlemen the name of your godfather."

"My godfather? He is the Most Excellent Senhor Colonel Paulo Vaz Lobo Cesar de Andrade e Souza Rodrigues de Mattos. My godmother is the Most Excellent Senhora Dona Maria Luiza de Macedo Rezende e Souza Rodrigues de Mattos."

"Your little boy is so clever!" exclaimed the listeners.

"Very clever," my father agreed. His eyes spilled over with gratification, and, placing the palm of his hand on my head, he gazed at me a long time, lovingly, proudly.

Item: I began to walk—I do not know exactly when, but ahead of time. Perhaps to hurry nature, they had me hold on to chairs while they supported me by the diaper and promised me little wooden wagons as a reward. "There we go, Nhonhô, all alone now!" my Negro nurse would say to me. And I, attracted by the tin rattle that my mother shook in front of me, started forward, fell, arose, fell again; and walked, doubtless badly, but walked, and I have been walking ever since.

11. The Child Is Father to the Man:

I grew; and in this the family did not help; I grew naturally, as the magnolias and cats grow. Perhaps cats are less mischievous, and surely magnolias are less restless, than I was as a boy. A poet has said that the child is father to the man. If he is right, it is important that we examine some of the characteristics of this child.

From the age of five, I deserved my nickname of "little devil," for truly I was nothing less. I was one of the most malevolent spirits of the time, shrewd, bold, frolicsome, and impulsive. One day, for example, I hit a slave on the head so hard that blood ran from the wound, because she had refused me a spoonful of the egg-and-cocoanut paste that she had been making; and, not content with hitting her, I dropped a handful of ashes in the pot; and, not satisfied with this mischief, I told my mother that the slave had spoiled the paste out of spite; and I was only six years old. Every day, Prudencio, a little colored house-slave, had to play that he was my horse; he would place his hands on the floor and would take a rope (as a rein) between his teeth; and I would climb onto his back with a little stick in my hand, would beat him, and would turn him this way and that, and he would obey—sometimes groaning, but he would obey without a word or, at the most, with a "Gee, Nhonhô!" to which I would reply, "Shut your mouth, beast!" That I hid visitors' hats, tied paper tails to dignified people, pulled gentlemen's hair by the pigtail, pinched matrons on the arm, and performed many other exploits of the same order, was evidence of an unkind disposition, but I trust that it was also an expression of a robust spirit, for my father held me in great admiration; and if at times he scolded me before others, he did so merely as a formality: in private, he would kiss me.

One must not conclude from this that I spent the rest of my life breaking heads and hiding hats; but I did remain stubborn, egotistical, and somewhat contemptuous of men. If I did not pass the time hiding their hats, perhaps, metaphorically, I did occasionally tweak their pigtails.

In addition, I developed a taste for the contemplation of human injustice. I was inclined to minimize and to justify it, but I also tried to classify its parts and to understand it—in accordance not with a rigid pattern but with my reaction to the particular place and circumstances. My mother indoctrinated me after her fashion: she made me learn by heart certain precepts and prayers; but I felt that I was governed less by these than by my nerves and my blood. Good rules in my case lost their spiritual significance, which alone gives them life, and became empty formulas. Before my hot cereal in the morning and before going to bed at night, I would ask God to forgive me my debts as I forgave my debtors; but between morning and night I would work great mischief, and my father, when the excitement was ended, would pat me on the cheek and exclaim laughingly, "Oh, you little rascal! You little rascal!"

Yes, my father adored me. My mother was a weak woman, of little intellect and great heart, rather credulous, sincerely pious—a homebody despite her prettiness, with simple tastes despite her wealth; afraid of thunder and of her husband. He was her god on earth. These two were responsible for my upbringing, which, although it had its good points, was in general incorrect and incomplete. My uncle, the canon, would sometimes make remarks about it to his brother; he would tell him that he was giving me more license than instruction and more affection than correction. But my father would reply that he was applying to my upbringing a system wholly superior to the system in general use; and in this way, although he did not confute his brother, he managed to hide the truth from himself.

In addition to my inherited characteristics and parental upbringing there was the example set by other persons in the general domestic environment. We have seen my parents; let us look at my uncles. One of them, João, was a gay dog and a spicy conversationalist. From my eleventh year on, he let me hear stories, some true, some fictitious, but all of them full of smut and obscenity. He had no respect for my adolescence and none for his brother's clerical robe. The canon, of course, would flee as soon as Uncle João started on a doubtful subject. Not I; I stayed and listened, at first without understanding any of it, but later understanding, and finally finding it enjoyable. After a certain age, I used to call on him; and he was always glad to see me, would give me candy, would take me out. At home, when he came to spend a few days with us, I would find him, not infrequently, talking with the slave women behind the vegetable garden, where they did the laundry; as they beat the clothes, there would be a series of funny stories, sayings, questions, and bursts of laughter, which no one else could hear because the washing-tank was very far from the house. With apron-belts tied in such a way as to raise their dresses a few inches, the colored women—some of them in the washing-tank and some outside, bent over the pieces of clothing, beating them, soaping them, wringing them—would listen to Uncle João's jokes, would reply in kind, and from time to time would comment:

"Holy cross! . . . This Mist' João is the devil himself!"

Very different was my other uncle, the canon. He was full of austerity and purity. These gifts, however, did not set off a lofty idealism but merely compensated for a mediocre spirit. He was not a man who saw the substance of the church; he saw the external side, the hierarchy, the sacred objects, the genuflections. An omission in the ritual disturbed him more than an infraction of the commandments. Now, looking back through the years, I am not certain that he could have easily understood a passage from Tertullian nor that he could have expounded without error the history of the Nicene Creed; but no one at the holy commemorations knew better than he the number and kinds of reverences that were due the officiant. To be a canon was the only ambition of his life; and he used to say, in all sincerity, that it was the highest dignity to which he could aspire. Pious, severe in his habits, minute in the observance of rules, compliant, shy, respectful, he possessed certain virtues in the greatest degree, but wholly lacked the power to inculcate them in other persons.

I say nothing about my maternal aunt, Dona Emerenciana, although she was the person who exercised the greatest disciplinary authority over me; this differentiated her sharply from the others; but she lived in our company only a short time, about two years.

My other relatives and intimate family friends are not worth mentioning; they had no life in common with us but only inter- mittent contact, with long intervals of separation. The important thing is the general complexion of the domestic environment, and this the reader has doubtless already derived: vulgarity of charac- ter, love of loudness and ostentation, weakness of will, domination by whim and caprice, and the like. Of such land, fertilized by such manure, this flower drew its substance.

12. An Episode of 1814: But I do not wish to go on without relating, at least summarily, a gallant episode that took place in 1814, when I was nine years old.

At the time of my birth, Napoleon was enjoying all the splen- dor of glory and power; he was emperor and one of the wonders of the world. My father, in his effort to persuade others of our nobility, ended up persuading himself, and therefore felt obliged to nourish a hatred against Napoleon. This was the cause of many a lively argument in our house, for my Uncle João, whether be- cause of class loyalty or because of professional sympathy, par- doned in the despot what he admired in the general; my clerical uncle was unalterably opposed to the Corsican; my other rela- tives were divided: hence the conflicts and the controversies.

When the news of Napoleon's fall (the first one) arrived in Rio de Janeiro, there was, naturally, great excitement in our house, but with no mockery or humiliation of the losing faction. The erstwhile supporters of Napoleon witnessed the public re- joicing and decided that decorum demanded not opposition but a dignified silence; some even went so far as to join in the hand- clapping. The population, gay and hearty, did not spare itself in its demonstration of affection for the royal family; there were lights, fireworks, shouts, a *Te Deum*, and a parade. During those days, I cut an interesting figure wearing a little sword that my uncle had given me on St. Anthony's Day, and, frankly, the sword interested me more than Napoleon's downfall. This superior interest has never left me. I have never given up the thought that our little swords are always greater than Napoleon's big one. And please note that I heard many a speech when I was alive, I read many a page noisy with big ideas and bigger words, but (I do not know why), beneath all the cheers that they drew from my lips, there would sometimes echo this conceit drawn from experience:

"Do not deceive yourself, the only thing you really care about is your little sword."

My family did not content itself with an anonymous part in the public rejoicing; it found it opportune and necessary to celebrate the emperor's misfortune with a dinner, and such a dinner that the noise of the acclamations would come to the ears of His Highness or at least to those of his ministers. No sooner said than done. Down came all the old silverware inherited from my grandfather Luiz Cubas; out came the French tablecloths and the big pitchers from India; a gelding hog was killed; compotes and marmalades were ordered from the sisters of the Ajuda convent; the salons, the stairways, the candelabra, the chandeliers, all the apparatus of classic luxury, were washed, scrubbed, and polished.

When the time came, a select group sat itself at our table: the circuit judge, three or four military officers, several business men, lawyers, public officials, some with their wives and daughters, others without them, but all participating in the desire to bury the memory of Bonaparte in a breast of turkey. It was not so much a dinner as a *Te Deum;* this was the substance of a remark by one of the men of letters present, the famous extemporizer, Dr. Villaça, who added some delicacies from the Muses to the regular courses of the dinner. I remember as if it were yesterday, I remember seeing him rise, with his long hair tied in a queue, his full dress suit, and an emerald ring on one of his fingers, and ask my clerical uncle to supply a text. When the text had been given, he fixed his eyes for a moment on a lady's forehead, then coughed, raised his right hand, with all its fingers closed except the index finger, which was pointing to the ceiling, and, so posed and composed, extemporized a poem on the text. Indeed, he extemporized not one poem but three. Then, I think, he swore to his gods that he would never stop. He requested another text, they gave him one, he extemporized on it immediately and promptly requested another text and another. Finally, one of the ladies present could no longer suppress her great admiration.

"You are pleased to say this, madam," modestly replied Villaça, "because you have never heard Bocage as I heard him at the turn of the century in Lisbon. Of him your praises would be justified. What facility! What verses! We competed with each other in extemporization for one or two hours in Nicolas' cafe, to the tune of bravos and applause. An immense talent, Bocage's! The same opinion was expressed to me a few days ago in the course of a conversation with the Duchess of Cadaval . . ."

And these last three words, spoken with emphasis, made the gathering tremble with wonder and admiration. This man, so gifted yet so modest, not only fraternized with poets but also chatted with duchesses! A Bocage and a Cadaval! Association with such a man made the ladies feel socially distinguished. The gentlemen eyed him with respect, some with envy, not a few with incredulity. He, however, went right ahead, piling adjective on adjective, adverb on adverb, exhausting the possible rhymes for "tyrant" and "usurper." Dessert was ready, but no one thought any longer about eating. In the short interval between extemporizations, a happy buzz prevailed, the talk of persons with satisfied stomachs; the guests' eyes, soft and moist or lively and warm, looked off into the distance or leaped from one end of the table to the other—our table, laden with sweets and fruits, here slices of pineapple, there cuts of melon, elsewhere cheese, candied yams, yellow egg-and-cocoanut paste, and crystal bowls of compote in dark, rich sugar-cane syrup. From time to time a jovial laugh, full, unrestrained, an at-home laugh, would break the political seriousness of the banquet. In the midst of the great common interest, little private interests also were discussed. The young ladies talked about the popular songs that they were going to sing at their harpsichords and about the minuet and the new English dance. Nor was there absent the inevitable matron who promises to dance a few measures just to show how she used to do it in the good old days of her girlhood. One fellow, near me, was giving another man news of the shipment of Negroes that was soon to come, according to letters he had received from Loanda—one letter in which his nephew wrote that he had negotiated about forty head and another in which . . . He had them right in his pocket. This was not a good time for reading them, but he assured the other man that we could rely on receiving at least some hundred and twenty Negroes on this voyage alone.

"Sh . . . sh . . . sh . . . ," said Villaça, clapping his hands. The noise immediately stopped, like a sudden rest in a symphonic piece, and all eyes were turned to the extemporizer. Those who were far from him cupped an ear in order not to lose a word. Even before he started, a slight but eager suggestion of applause could be heard.

As for me, there I was, alone and forgotten, deeply in love with a certain dish of sweets that had aroused my passion. At the end of each extemporization my spirits rose, with the hope that it would be the last; but it was not, and the dessert remained intact. Nobody thought of making the first move. My father, at the head of the table, seemed to be drinking deeply of his guests' enjoyment; he beamed at their big, happy faces, at the food, at the flowers, relished the familiarity established between mutually remote spirits under the influence of an excellent dinner. I noticed his pleasure, for I shifted my eyes from the compote to him and from him to the compote, mutely asking him to let me have some; but in vain. He saw nothing but himself, reflected in his guests. And the extemporizations followed one another like the endless waves of the sea, obliging me to bridle my desire and to withhold my request. I remained patient as long as I could, which was not very long. I asked for dessert, first in a low voice, but soon I shouted, screamed, stamped my feet. My father, who would gladly have given me the sun if I had asked for it, ordered a slave to serve dessert to me; but it was too late. Aunt Emerenciana had snatched me from my chair and had delivered me to a slave woman despite my struggles and screams.

The extemporizer's guilt may be briefly summarized: he had delayed dessert and had caused my removal. This sufficed to lead me to plan vengeance, something impressive that would teach him a lesson, something, preferably, that would make him appear ridiculous. For he was a dignified man, Dr. Villaça, poised and deliberate, forty-seven years old, married, and a father. I would not be content with a paper tail nor with the pulling of his pigtail; it had to be something worse. I decided to watch him closely for the rest of the evening, to follow him in the garden, to which everyone had repaired. I saw him talking with Dona Eusebia, Sergeant-Major Domingues's sister, a robust, middle-aged lady, who, if not exactly pretty, was certainly not ugly.

"I am very angry with you," she was saying.

"Why?"

"Because . . . I don't know why . . . because it is my fate . . . Sometimes I think it would be better to die . . ."

They had entered a little thicket; it was dusk; I followed them. Villaça's eyes were sparkling with wine and voluptuousness.

"Let me alone!" she said.

"No one can see us. Die, my angel? What an idea! You know that I should die, too . . . What am I saying? I die every day, I die of passion, of longing . . ."

Dona Eusebia raised her handkerchief to her eyes. The extemporizer was racking his memory for an appropriate quotation and finally found the following one, which, as I learned at a later date, is from one of Judeu's libretti:

"Do not weep, my love, lest the redness of the dawn be reflected in your eyes."

He said this, and drew her toward him. She resisted a little, but only for a moment. Their faces met, and I heard the smack, ever so soft, of a kiss, a most timorous kiss.

"Dr. Villaça just kissed Dona Eusebia!" I shouted, running through the garden.

My words burst upon the gathering like a thunderbolt. Everyone stood still, stupefied and fascinated; then they turned their eyes to either side, and exchanged smiles and whispers behind their hands. The mothers led their daughters off, on the pretext that the night was becoming too damp. My father was genuinely annoyed with my indiscretion, and pulled my ears, although not

[33]

so violently as he pretended. The next day, at luncheon, remembering what had happened, he laughed and tweaked my nose, saying, "Oh, you little rascal! You little rascal!"

13. A Jump: Let's all get set and jump over the school, the tiresome school, where I learned to read, to write, to count, to hit my schoolmates, to be hit by them, and to raise the devil on the hills, on the beaches, wherever a young wastrel could find opportunity for mischief.

My cup of bitterness in those days was not empty: there were scoldings, punishments, and long, hard lessons; but, apart from these, my burdens were few and light. Heavy, however, was the switch, and yet . . . O switch, terror of the days of my boyhood, thou who wert the *compelle intrare* with which an old teacher, bald and skinny, drilled into my brain the alphabet, grammar, composition, and whatever else he knew, blessed switch, so deprecated by the moderns, would that I had remained under thy yoke, with my beardless soul, my ignorance, and my toy sword, that little sword of 1814, so superior to Napoleon's big one! After all, old schoolmaster of my first letters, what did you require of me? A lesson learned by heart and good behavior in the schoolroom; nothing more nor less than what is required by life, the graduate-school professor, with the difference that you, although you made me afraid, never made me angry. Even now, I see you enter the room, with your white leather slippers, your white work jacket, your snuff-box and handkerchief in your hand, and your clean-shaven face; I see you sit down, exhale through your mouth, murmur threateningly, take a pinch of snuff, and call us to attention for the first lesson. And you did this for twenty-three years, unnoted, obscure, methodical, shut off from the world in a little house on the Rua do Piolho, never boring the world with your mediocrity, until one day you took the great dive into darkness, and no one mourned except an old colored servant—no one, not even I who owe you the rudiments of writing.

You were known as Ludgero the Schoolmaster, but I want to

write your full name on this page: Ludgero Barata [cockroach] —an unfortunate name, that served as an eternal subject for our jokes. One of us, Quincas Borba, used to be cruel to the poor man. Two or three times a week, he placed a dead cockroach in the schoolmaster's trouser pocket, in his desk drawer, or next to the inkwell. If the schoolmaster found it during class, he would jump, run his flaming eyes around the room, and call us the worst and most ignominiously definitive names that he could muster: vermin, guttersnipes, dirty ragamuffins. Some trembled, others muttered; Quincas Borba, however, remained calm, gazing innocently into space.

A real flower, this Quincas Borba. Never in my childhood, never in all my life, have I known a boy more charming, more inventive, or more mischievous. He was the flower not only of the school but of the whole city. His mother, a widow with considerable property, adored her son, gave him everything he wanted. He was generally neat, if overdressed, and was followed by a handsomely outfitted manservant who, however, let us cut school and hunt birds' nests, or chase lizards in the hills, or simply wander the streets aimlessly like two unemployed dandies. And in the Espirito Santo festivities, what an emperor he made! It was sheer delight to see Quincas Borba on the throne. In our plays, he would always choose the role of a king, a minister, a general, some high office, whatever it might be. The rascal had poise, aplomb, and a certain magnificence in his attitudes and gestures. Who would have guessed that . . . Let us lift our pen and not anticipate Quincas Borba's fate. Instead, let us jump to 1822, the date of Brazil's political independence and of my own first captivity.

14. The First Kiss: I was seventeen; I was trying to convince the world and myself that the down on my upper lip was a mustache. My eyes, lively and resolute, were my most genuinely masculine feature. As I

conducted myself with a certain arrogance, it was hard to know whether I was a child with manly ways or a man with childish ways. At all events, I was a handsome lad, handsome and bold, and I galloped into life in my boots and spurs, a whip in my hand and blood in my veins, riding a nervous, strong, high-spirited courser like the horse in the old ballads, which Romanticism found in the medieval castle and left in the streets of our own century. The Romanticists rode the poor beast until he was so nearly dead that he finally lay down in the gutter, where the realists found him, his flesh eaten away by sores and worms, and, out of pity, carried him away to their books.

Yes, I was good-looking, elegant, rich; and you may well believe that more ladies than one lowered before me a pensive brow or raised to me a pair of covetous eyes. Of all of them, however, the one who captivated me was a . . . a . . . I do not know whether to say it; this book is chaste, at least in intention; in intention, it is super-chaste. But come, I must tell either all or nothing. She who captivated me was a Spanish woman, Marcella, "the gorgeous Marcella," as the young blades used to call her. And the young blades were in the right. She was the daughter of an Asturian vegetable farmer; she told me this herself in a moment of sincerity, for the accepted belief was that she had been born to a Madrid lawyer, a victim of the French invasion, who had been wounded, imprisoned, and shot by a firing squad when she was only twelve years old. *Cosas de España.*

But whether her father was a vegetable farmer or a lawyer, the fact is that Marcella was wholly wanting in rustic innocence, and indeed it is doubtful whether she accepted even the modest ethics of the legal code. She was a beautifully built young lady, gay, without moral scruple, but inhibited a little by the austerity of the times, which did not permit her to parade her extravagances through the streets; luxurious, impatient, a lover of money and of young men. In that year, she was dying of love for a certain Xavier, a fellow who was both rich and consumptive—a gem.

I saw her for the first time in the Rocio Grande on the night of the fireworks after the announcement of the declaration of independence, a celebration of spring, of the awakening of the public soul. We were two young men, the people and I; we were fresh from childhood, with all the eagerness and fervor of youth. I saw her get out of a sedan chair; graceful and bewitching, she had a slim, undulating body, with a sauciness that I have never observed in chaste women. "Follow me," she said to her manservant. And I followed her, as much her servant as the other; I followed her lovingly, vibrantly, full of the first dawns. I heard someone say "the gorgeous Marcella," I remembered what I had heard about her from Uncle João, and I became, I confess it, actually dizzy.

Three days later, my uncle asked me in private whether I wished to go to a supper party in Cajueiros, with women. We went; it was in Marcella's house. Xavier, for all his tuberculosis, was presiding at the supper, of which I ate little or nothing, for I could take neither my eyes nor my thoughts away from the lady of the house. How lovely was this Spanish girl! There were seven or eight other women—all more or less loose—and they were pretty and charming, but the Spanish beauty . . . My ecstasy, several draughts of wine, my imperious, impulsive nature, all led me to do an unheard-of thing: as we were leaving, at the street door, I asked my uncle to wait a moment and went back up the stairs.

"Did you forget something?" asked Marcella, standing at the head of the stairway.

"My handkerchief."

She got out of my way so that I could return to the salon; I seized her hands, drew her to me, and kissed her. I do not know whether she said something, whether she shouted, whether she called anyone; I know only that I rushed down the stairs, fast as a whirlwind and stumbling like a drunk.

15. Marcella:
It took me thirty days to go from the Rocio Grande to Marcella's heart, riding not the war-horse of blind desire, but the wily, stubborn ass of patience. For, in truth, there are two ways to overcome a woman's resistance: the violent way, as in the case of Europa and the

bull, and the insinuating way, as in the case of Leda and the swan or Danaë and the rain of gold, three of Father Zeus' inventions, which, because they are no longer in style, are here replaced by the horse and the ass. I shall not relate the tricks that I used, nor the bribes, nor my alternate feelings of confidence and fear, nor the frustrated hopes, nor any others of these preliminary matters. I assure you, however, that the ass is fully as excellent an animal as the charger. Moreover, it is, like Sancho's ass, a genuine philosopher. It delivered me to her house at the end of the period mentioned; I alighted, slapped it on the rump, and sent it off to pasture.

First ecstasy of my youth, how sweet you seemed! Much like you must have been the effect of the first sunlight in the biblical creation. Imagine the sun beating full upon the face of a world just formed. Well, my ecstasy was like that, friend reader, and if you were ever eighteen you must remember that yours was, too.

Our passion, or affair, or whatever you wish to call it (for names do not interest me), had two phases: the consular phase and the imperial phase. In the former, which was short, Xavier and I ruled jointly, although he never knew that I was sharing the government of Rome with him. However, when his credulity could no longer resist the evidence, Xavier abdicated, and all the power became concentrated in me—this was the Caesarean phase. The universe was mine; but, alas, not gratuitously. I had to raise money, multiply it, invent it. First, I exploited my father's generosity; he gave me everything I asked, promptly, without reproof, even agreeably; he would tell everyone that, after all, I was a young buck and he had been one, too. But my abuse of his good nature reached so great an extremity that he restricted his generosity a little, then more, and still more. I ran to my mother and persuaded her to give me, on the sly, a part of her household money. It was very little, however, and I therefore availed myself of my final resource: I began to borrow on my inheritance, to sign obligations that would have to be redeemed some day with usurious interest.

"Really," Marcella would say, when I had just brought her some fine silk or some jewelry; "really, I think you want to make me angry . . . Is this the sort of thing to do . . . so expensive . . ."

And, if it was jewelry, she would say this while examining it between her fingers, turning it one way and the other to see it in the best light, and then kissing me impetuously again and again; but, although she protested, her eyes almost spilled over with happiness, and, seeing her so, I, too, felt happy. She had a great fondness for old Brazilian gold dobras, and I would bring her as many as I could obtain; Marcella put them all in a little iron box, and no one knew where she kept the key, for she did not trust her slaves. She owned the house in Cajueiros in which she lived. Everything in it was substantial and in good taste: the furniture of carved rosewood, the mirrors, the vases, the silverware—beautiful silverware from India, given to her by a justice of the Supreme Court. Devilish silverware, it gave me terrible attacks of nerves. I said so to the owner herself; I never concealed from her the annoyance caused me by these and the other spoils of her former loves. She would listen to me and would laugh, a most ingenuous laugh—ingenuous and something else, which at that time I did not quite understand; but now, remembering, I think that her laugh was a hybrid such as might be expected of a creature born of one of Shakespeare's witches and one of Klopstock's seraphim. I do not know whether I have made this clear.

Perceiving my foolish jealousy, she seemed to like to provoke it. Thus, one day when I had been unable to buy her a certain necklace that she had admired in a jewelry shop, she assured me that she had been only joking, that our love needed no such vulgar stimulus.

"If I thought you had such a low opinion of me, I'd never forgive you," she said, threatening me with her forefinger.

And, as quick as a little bird, she opened her hands, took my face in them, drew me close to her, and made an adorable grimace, like a child. Then, lying on the couch, she continued to speak about the subject, with frankness and simplicity. She would never let anyone buy her affection. She had often sold the appearance of affection, but she had given the real thing to very few. Lieutenant Duarte, for example, whom she had really loved two years before, had been unable to buy her anything very valuable except at great personal sacrifice, as in my case; she had accepted from him without reluctance only inexpensive gifts, like the gold cross that he had given her on a special occasion.

"This one . . ."

As she said this, she put her hand in her bosom and drew out a delicate gold cross, tied to a blue ribbon hung about her neck.

"But this cross," I observed, "didn't you tell me it was your father that . . ."

Marcella shook her head deprecatingly.

"Didn't you know I was fibbing, that I said it in order not to make you unhappy? Come here, *chiquito*, don't be so distrustful . . . I loved Duarte, but it's all over, so what does it matter? Some day, after we have parted . . ."

"Don't talk like that!" I shouted.

"Everything must come to an end. Some day . . ."

She was unable to finish; a sob choked her voice. She reached out, took my hands, drew me close to her bosom, and whispered softly in my ear, "Never, never, my love!" I thanked her with my tear-filled eyes. The next day I brought her the necklace.

"To remember me by, after we have parted," I said.

At first, Marcella maintained a dignified silence. Then she made a magnificent gesture: she tried to throw the necklace out the window. I seized her arm; I begged her not to use me so ill, begged her to keep the necklace. She smiled and kept it.

However, she paid me in full for my sacrifices. I had no desire which she did not seek to satisfy with all her heart, apparently impelled by conscience and emotional necessity. Generally my desire was unreasonable, a childish whim: to see her clothed in a certain way, in this dress and not that one, with such-and-such accessories, to go for a walk, or some other little thing. Chatting and smiling, she was agreeable to everything.

"You are irresistible," she said; "I think you must have Arabian blood."

And she put on the dress, or lace, or earrings, with a prompt obedience that I found enchanting.

16. An Immoral Thought: There occurs to me an immoral thought, which at the same time may serve to correct an error in my choice of words. I believe I said, in Chapter 14, that Marcella was dying of love for Xavier. She was not dying, she was living. To live is not the same thing as to die—a statement that will be supported by all the jewelers in the world, and they are men of utmost refinement in the choice of words. Dear jewelers, what would happen to love if it were not for your baubles and your credit plans? You are responsible for at least a fifth and perhaps a third of the world's trade in hearts. This is my immoral thought. Perhaps it is even more obscure than immoral. What I mean is that the most beautiful brow on earth does not become less beautiful if encircled by a diadem of fine stones; neither less beautiful nor less affectionate. Marcella, for example, was no less beautiful and loved me . . .

17. Concerning the Trapeze and Other Matters: . . . Marcella loved me for fifteen months and eleven contos; nothing less. When my father learned about the eleven contos, he became really alarmed; he found that the matter had gone beyond the bounds of a youthful escapade.

"This time," he said, "you go to Europe; you shall go through a university, probably Coimbra. I want you to be a serious man, not a gadabout and a thief." And, as I made a gesture of surprise, "Yes, a thief. There is no other word for a son who does such a thing to me . . ."

He drew from his pocket the promissory notes I had issued, which he had already paid, and shook them under my nose. "Look at these, my fine-feathered good-for-nothing! Is that how a young man should protect the honor of his name and of his family? Do you think my ancestors and I earned our money in gambling houses and loafing in the streets? From now on, you will either behave yourself or get nothing."

He was furious, but his fury was tempered and brief. I listened in silence and expressed no opposition, although I had objected on other occasions, to his requirement that I go to Europe; I was thinking that I would take Marcella with me.

I went to her, explained the crisis that had arisen, and made my proposition. Marcella stared at the ceiling and said nothing. As I persisted, she finally said that she would remain in Rio, that she could not go to Europe.

"Why not?"

"I cannot," she said with a sorrowful air; "I cannot go and breathe the very air in which my poor father was murdered by Napoleon . . ."

"Which father? The vegetable farmer or the lawyer?"

Marcella wrinkled her brow and hummed a seguidilla through her teeth. After a few moments, she complained of the heat and ordered a glass of cider. A slave woman brought it on a silver tray that represented part of my eleven contos. Marcella politely offered me the refreshment; my reply was to upset the tray and the glass with a sweep of my hand. The liquid spilled all over the bodice of Marcella's dress; the colored woman shrieked, and I shouted at her to get out. Alone with Marcella, I loosed all the desperation that had been locked in my heart: I told her that she was a monster, that she had never loved me, that without even the excuse of sincerity she had let me descend to the depths of humiliation. I called her many ugly names, accompanied by the most unrestrained gestures. Marcella remained seated, snapping her nails on her teeth, as cold as a piece of marble. I had an impulse to strangle her or at least to humiliate her by making her grovel at my feet. I started to do the latter; but somehow the act reversed itself in the doing, and I threw myself at her feet, contrite and supplicant. I kissed her feet, I reminded her of our months of happiness apart from the world, I repeated the affectionate names we used to call one another. I was sitting on the floor with my head between her knees, holding her hands as tightly as I could; panting, distracted, I begged her, between sobs, not to leave me . . . Marcella looked at me a little while, both of us remaining silent, and then, as if bored, she pushed me away and said, "You get on my nerves."

She arose, adjusted her dress, which was still wet, and started toward the adjoining bedroom. "No!" I shouted. "Don't go . . . I don't want . . ." I was going to lay hold of her, but it was too late; she had entered the bedroom and had locked the door.

I went out into the street, stunned. I spent two deadly hours roaming the most out-of-the-way, deserted quarters, where I was unlikely to meet anyone I knew. I was feasting on my despair, with a sort of morbid gluttony. I was evoking the days, the hours, the moments of ecstasy. At times it pleased me to believe that they were eternal, that all of the coldness and conflict was a great nightmare; again, fooling myself in a different way, I would try to reject them entirely and put them out of my mind as an unnecessary encumbrance. Then I resolved to sail immediately in order to end, once and for all, that phase of my life and to begin a new one, and I relished the idea that Marcella, upon learning of my departure, would be overcome with longing and remorse. Because at one time she had loved me to distraction, she would at least have some feelings about me, some thoughts of me, as she had of Lieutenant Duarte . . . At this point, jealousy buried its fangs in my heart; my whole nature shouted that I had to take Marcella with me.

"I must . . . I must . . . ," I said, punching the air.

And then a salutary idea came to me . . . My trapeze, available for the service of carnal desires as well as the development of abstract concepts, came into play again. The salutary idea exercised on it, just as that of the plaster had done (Chapter 2). The idea was simply this: to charm her, to charm her completely, to dazzle her, and thus to take her; and I decided to use a means more concrete than supplication. Without fear of the consequences, I resorted to one last loan. I went to the Rua dos Ourives, bought the finest piece of jewelry in the city, three large diamonds mounted on an ivory comb. I hurried to Marcella's house.

Marcella was lying in a hammock, her physical attitude relaxed and lazy, one leg hanging over the edge and exposing her ankle in a silk stocking, her hair loose and down over her shoulders, her expression calm, almost somnolent.

"Come with me," I said, "we have plenty of money, you'll have everything you want . . . Here, look!"

And I showed her the diamond comb . . . Marcella started slightly, sat up, and, leaning on one elbow, stared at the comb for a few moments; withdrawing her eyes, she regained full possession of herself. Then I took her hair in my hands, entwined it, improvised a rough hair-do, and topped it off with the diamond comb. I stood back a little, came close again, and tried to impose some symmetry on the general disorder, adjusting the braids, lowering the hair a little on one side, and so on, all with the fussiness and loving care of a mother.

"Ready," I said.

"Silly!" was her first reply.

Her second was to draw me to her and to pay me for my sacrifice with a kiss, the most ardent she had ever given me. Then she pulled out the comb and admired greatly the material and the handwork, looking at me from time to time and shaking her head as if to scold me.

"What a thing to do!" she said.

"Will you go with me?"

Marcella reflected a moment. I did not like the expression on her face as she turned her eyes from me to the wall and from the wall to the comb; but my annoyance vanished as soon as she replied, resolutely:

"I'll go. When do we sail?"

"In two or three days."

"I'll go."

On my knees, I thanked her. I had found again my Marcella of the early days, and I told her so. She smiled and went to put away the comb, while I descended the stairs.

18. Vision in the Hallway: In the dark hallway at the bottom of the stairs, I stopped a minute to catch my breath, to compose myself, to collect my scattered thoughts—in short, to regain my self-possession after such deep and contrary emotional experiences. I decided that I was happy. Certainly the diamonds tainted my happiness a little; but it is certain also that a pretty woman can very well love both the Greeks and their gifts. Moreover, I had confidence in my Marcella; she may have had faults, but she loved me . . .

"An angel!" I murmured, looking at the ceiling of the hallway.

And there, mocking me, I saw Marcella's eyes, with the expression that had given me, a few minutes earlier, a shudder of distrust, and they were sparkling above a nose that was at once Bakbarah's nose and my own. Poor infatuated fool of *The Thousand and One Nights!* I saw you running the length of the gallery after the vizier's wife, she beckoning you to possess her and you running, running, running, until you came to the garden path and out into the street, where the leather venders laughed at you and beat you. Then it seemed to me that Marcella's hallway was the garden path and that the street outside was the one in Bagdad. Indeed, as I looked toward the street door, I saw three of the leather venders, one in a cassock, another in livery, and the third in ordinary clothes, come into the hallway; they seized me by the arms, put me in a chaise—my father on my right, my uncle, the canon, on my left, and the man in livery on the driver's box—and took me to the house of the local police captain, from which I was transported to a galleon that was to sail for Lisbon. You can imagine how I resisted; but all resistance was in vain.

Three days later, downcast and silent, I crossed the bar. I did not even cry; I had a fixed idea. Accursed fixed ideas! On this occasion, my idea was to repeat the name Marcella as I leaped into the ocean.

19. On Board: We were eleven passengers: an insane man accompanied by his wife, two young men traveling for pleasure, four business men, and two servants. My father had recommended me to the good offices of all, beginning with the captain, who, however, had matters of his own on board to worry about, especially his wife in the last stages of pulmonary tuberculosis.

I do not know whether the captain suspected my funereal project nor whether my father had told him about my situation; I do know that he never took his eyes off me, that he called me after him wherever he went. When it was wholly impossible for him to be with me, he took me to his wife. She remained almost all the time in a low, simple bed, coughing and promising to show me the environs of Lisbon. She was not just thin, she was transparent; it seemed impossible that she would survive each successive hour. The captain pretended not to believe that her death was imminent, perhaps chiefly in order to deceive himself. I neither knew nor wanted to know anything about her. How could I be concerned with the fate of a consumptive woman in the middle of the ocean? My world was Marcella.

One night, of a Saturday, I found a propitious opportunity to die. Cautiously I went up on deck, but there I found the captain leaning against the rail and scanning the horizon.

"A storm coming up?" I said.

"No," he replied; "no; I am drinking deep of the splendor of the night. Look: is it not heavenly!"

The style of speech belied the apparent nature of the man, rough and wholly alien to flowery phrases. I stared at him; he appeared to relish my surprise. After a few seconds, he took me by the hand and pointed to the moon, asking me why I did not compose an ode to the night. I replied that I was not a poet. The captain murmured something, stepped back two paces, put his hand in his pocket, and drew forth a very wrinkled piece of pa-

per; then, by the light of a lantern, he read a Horatian ode on the freedom of a seafaring life. He had written it himself.

"What do you think of it?"

I do not remember what I said; I remember only that he shook my hand energetically and thanked me profusely. Then he read me two sonnets, and was about to read a third, when someone came to tell him that his wife wished to speak with him. "I'll be right there," he said, and recited the third sonnet, expressively, lovingly.

I remained alone; but the captain's muse had swept the evil thoughts out of my spirit. I preferred to sleep, that is, to die temporarily.

The following day, we awoke in the midst of a tempest, which terrified us all except the insane man. He began to jump up and down and to say that his daughter was sending for him in a fine coach; the death of a daughter had been the cause of his condition. No, I shall never be able to forget that hideous figure, singing and dancing in the midst of the confusion and the howling of the hurricane, with his long, tangled hair and his eyes fairly leaping out of his face. At times he stopped, raised his bony hands in the air, made crosses with his fingers, then checkered squares, then rings, and laughed loudly and desperately. His wife was unable to take care of him; overcome by fear of death, she was praying by herself to all the saints in heaven. Finally the tempest abated. I must confess that it succeeded excellently in diverting me from the tempest in my heart. I, who had thought of going to meet death, did not dare to face it when it came to meet me.

With friendly interest, the captain asked me whether I had been afraid and whether I had not found the spectacle sublime. Naturally, the conversation turned to the subject of life at sea. The captain asked me if I did not like piscatorial idylls; I replied ingenuously that I did not know what they were.

"You shall see," he said.

And he recited a little poem, then another—an eclogue—and finally five sonnets, with which he completed his literary confidences for the day. The next day, before reciting to me, the captain explained that only for very special and compelling reasons had he chosen the profession of a sailor, for his grandmother had wanted him to be a priest, and indeed he had been something of a Latin scholar. He never became a priest but at the same time he did not abandon letters, which he considered to be his natural vocation. To prove it, he immediately recited about one hundred lines of verse. I noted something singular: the gestures he used were such that I was unable to repress my laughter, but the captain, when he recited, looked within himself with such intensity that he never noticed.

The days passed by, as did the waves and the verses, and with them the life of the consumptive woman. It was nearly ended. One day, shortly after luncheon, the captain told me that she could not last the week.

"So soon!" I exclaimed.

"She spent a very bad night."

I went to see her. I found her, in truth, almost in the last throes, but speaking still of resting in Lisbon a few days before going with me to Coimbra, for she planned to take me to the University. In great consternation, I left her and sought her husband. He was watching the waves dying against the side of the ship; I tried to console him. He thanked me, told me the story of his love, praised the loyalty and unselfishness of his wife, mentioned that he had dedicated some verses to her, and read them to me. Someone came on her behalf to call him. We both ran; it was a crisis. This day and the following one were cruel; on the third, she died. I fled the sight of her; it was repugnant to me. A half hour later, I found the captain seated on a pile of rope, with his head in his hands. I tried to say something to comfort him.

"She died like a saint," he replied; and, lest these words be attributed to weakness on his part, he stood up. He nodded his head slowly and gazed long and intently at the horizon. "Come," he said, "let us deliver her to the grave that remains forever sealed."

And indeed, a few hours later, the corpse was cast into the sea, with the usual rites. Sadness dimmed the faces of the participants; the face of the widower was like a mighty rock splintered by a great bolt of lightning. Deep silence. The sea opened its belly, received the spoil, closed again—there was a slight ripple—and the galleon went on. I stood for several minutes at the stern, my eyes

fixed on that uncertain point in the sea where one of us remained
. . . I went to the captain, to try to distract him.

"Thank you," he said, grasping my purpose; "I think that I
shall never forget your kindness. God alone can reward you as
you deserve. Poor Leocadia, remember us in heaven."

He wiped away an importunate tear with his sleeve; I sought
consolation for him in poetry. I spoke to him about the poems
that he had read to me, and I offered to have them printed. The
captain's eyes showed a little animation. "Perhaps I'll accept," he
said; "but I don't know . . . they are poor verses." I swore that
they were not. I asked him to put them all together and to give
them to me before the disembarkation.

"Poor Leocadia!" he murmured without reply. "A corpse . . .
the sea . . . the sky . . . the ship . . ."

The next day, he read to me a freshly composed dirge in which
the circumstances of his wife's death and burial were commemo-
rated. He read it in a voice quavering with emotion, and the hand
that held the paper was trembling. When he had finished, he
asked me whether the verses were worthy of the treasure that he
had lost.

"They are," I said.

"They may lack poetic inspiration," he remarked, after a moment's hesitation, "but no one can deny them sentiment—although
possibly the sentiment itself prejudices the merits . . ."

"Not in my opinion. I find the poem perfect."

"Yes, I suppose, when you consider . . . Well, after all, it's just
a few lines written by a sailor."

"By a sailor who happens to be also a poet."

He shrugged his shoulders, looked at the paper, and recited his
composition again, but this time without quavering or trembling,
emphasizing the literary qualities and bringing out the imagery
and music in the verses. When he had finished, he expressed the
opinion that it was the most finished of his works, and I agreed.
He shook my hand and predicted a great future for me.

20. I Acquire a Bachelor's Degree: A great future!

With this phrase ringing in my ears, I looked far off toward the horizon. One idea was expelling another, *i.e.*, ambition was replacing Marcella. A great future? Perhaps I would be a naturalist, a man of letters, an archeologist, a banker, a statesman, or even a bishop—any profession, provided that it entailed preeminence, reputation, a status of superiority. Ambition, like a new-born eagle, now broke through its shell and transfixed the world with its tawny, penetrating eyes. Farewell, love! Farewell, Marcella! Carefree life, days of delirium, farewell! You may have my swaddling clothes. On I go, through toil and hardship, on to glory!

These were my thoughts as I disembarked at Lisbon and set out for Coimbra. The University was waiting for me with its long list of difficult subjects. I studied them with profound mediocrity, which did not prevent my acquiring a bachelor's degree; they gave it to me with all the customary solemnity, at the end of the number of years required by law. The beautiful ceremonies and the festivities filled me with pride and, even more, with sadness at having to leave. I had won at Coimbra a great reputation as a playboy; I was a harebrained scholar, superficial, tumultuous, and capricious, fond of adventures of all kinds, engaging in practical romanticism and theoretical liberalism, with complete faith in dark eyes and written constitutions. On the day when the University certified, in sheepskin, that I had acquired a knowledge which, in truth, I had not, I confess that I felt somehow cheated, although nonetheless proud. Let me explain: the diploma was a letter of enfranchisement; if it gave me liberty, it also gave me responsibility. I put it with my other possessions, said goodbye to the banks of the Mondego, and came away rather disconsolate, but with an impulse, a curiosity, a desire to elbow other people out of the way, to exert influence, to enjoy, to live —to prolong my college days throughout my life.

21. The Muleteer: To my misfortune, the donkey on which I was riding stopped suddenly and balked. I whipped him. He bucked twice, then three times more, than once more, this last time throwing me from the saddle in such a way that my left foot remained caught in the stirrup. I tried to hold on to his belly, but the animal was frightened and started to run down the road. Or, rather, he tried to run, and actually took a couple of leaps, when a muleteer who happened to be nearby rushed to my aid in time to seize the reins and to stop the donkey, not without effort nor without danger to himself. When the beast had been subdued, I freed myself from the stirrup and stood on my feet.

"You were lucky," said the muleteer.

And he was right: if the donkey had run away, I should have been really hurt, and who can say that death would not have been the outcome. A broken head, a congestion, an internal injury of some sort, and there would have been the end of my fine education. The muleteer had perhaps saved my life; in fact, I was sure of it; I felt it in my blood. Kind muleteer! While I was regaining possession of myself, he was repairing the donkey's harness with great care and skill. I resolved to give him three of the five gold coins that I had with me; not because this was the value of my life—it would have been immeasurable—but because it was a reward worthy of the selflessness with which he had rescued me. Definitely, I would give him three of the coins.

"All ready," he said, handing me the reins.

"Not yet," I replied; "I'm still trying to pull myself together . . ."

"Why, what's the trouble?"

"Wasn't I nearly killed?"

"If the ass ran away, you might have been; but, with the help of the Lord, everything's all right now."

I went to the saddle-bags, took out an old vest in the pocket of which I kept the five gold coins, and, as I did so, wondered whether the reward was not excessive, whether two coins would not suffice. Perhaps one. In truth, one coin would be enough to give him shivers of joy. I looked at his clothes; he was a poor devil, who doubtless had never seen a gold coin. Therefore, one coin. I took it out, I saw it shine in the sunlight. The muleteer did not see it, because I had my back turned towards him; but perhaps he suspected something, for he began to talk to the donkey in a significative manner: he gave him advice, told him to be good because otherwise the "fine gentleman" might punish him, and so on—a fatherly discourse. So help me God, I even heard the smack of a kiss; it was the muleteer kissing the donkey on the forehead.

"Say!" I exclaimed.

"Please excuse me, but the devil of a beast looks at a fellow in such a knowing way . . ."

I laughed, hesitated, placed a silver crusado in his hand, mounted the donkey, and set off at a fast pace, a little troubled or, more precisely, a little uncertain about the effect of the silver coin. But at a short distance I looked back: the muleteer was bowing his thanks, and looked overjoyed. I thought that he must be so, indeed; I had paid him well, perhaps too well. I put my fingers in the vest that I was wearing and felt some copper coins; they were pennies, which I should have given to the muleteer instead of the silver crusado. For, after all, he had not thought about a reward or about the virtue of his act, he had merely yielded to a natural impulse, to his temperament, to the habits of his trade. Furthermore, the fact that he had happened to be not farther along the road nor farther back but exactly at the point where the accident occurred seemed to indicate that he had been merely an instrument of Providence. One way or the other, there was really no personal merit in his act. This thought made me miserable; I called myself wasteful, I charged the crusado mentally to the account of my prodigal past. I felt (why not tell the whole truth?), I actually felt remorse.

22. Return to Rio: Devil of a donkey, you broke completely the train of my thoughts.
Let us extend the break and omit my subsequent thoughts on the road, as well as what I did in Lisbon, in the rest of the Iberian peninsula, and in other parts of Europe—old Europe, which, at that point in its history, seemed to have become young again. No, I shall not talk about my presence at the dawn of Romanticism or about the romantic poetry that I *lived*, for I could not write it, in the hospitable bosom of Italy; of these matters, I say nothing. I should have to write a travel diary and not memoirs, such as these, in which only the substance of my life is set forth.

At the end of several years of travel, I heeded my father's plea to return. "Come," he said in his last letter; "if you do not come immediately, you will find your mother dead!" This last word was a severe blow to me. I loved my mother; still fresh in my mind were all the circumstances of the last blessing that she had given me, on board the ship. "My unhappy son, I shall never see you again," the poor woman had sobbed as she pressed me to her breast. And these words reechoed now like a prophecy come true.

I received the letter in Venice, which, for me, was still redolent with Byron's verses. I was immersed in a dream, living in the past, thinking of Venice as the Serene Republic of the Renaissance. Such was actually my state of mind. Once I happened to ask the innkeeper whether the doge was going to make a public appearance that day. "What doge, *signor mio?*" I came to myself, but I did not confess my delusion; I told him that my question was a sort of American riddle. His response was that of an experienced innkeeper: he nodded and smiled to show that he understood, and said that he was very fond of American riddles. Upon receiving the letter, I left all this—the doge, the Bridge of Sighs, the gondolas, Lord Byron, the ladies of the Rialto—I left it all and shot off like a bullet in the direction of Rio de Janeiro.

I arrived . . . But no; let us not prolong this chapter. Sometimes I forget that I am writing, and the pen moves along, eating up paper, with grave detriment to me as author. For long chapters are better suited to ponderous readers; but we are not an *in-folio* public, we are an *in-12* public, preferring little text, large margins, elegant type, gilt-edged pages, and illustrations ... especially illustrations ... No, let us not prolong the chapter.

23. Sad but Short:

I arrived. I shall not deny that, as soon as I caught sight of my native city, I felt deep emotion. This was not caused by thoughts of the place to which I owed political allegiance but by thoughts of the place where I had grown up—the street, the church steeple, the fountain on the corner, the women in mantillas, the Negroes hired out by their masters to do odd jobs—things and scenes of childhood engraved in my memory. It was nothing less than a rebirth. My spirit, like a bird, refused to be carried along with the current of the years and set its course in the direction of the spring where it knew it could find fresh, pure water, still unpolluted by the torrents of life.

All this, of course, is commonplace. Also commonplace, miserably commonplace, was the affliction of my family. My father wept as he embraced me. "Your mother cannot live," he said. It was not her old rheumatism that was killing her, it was a cancer of the stomach. She was suffering cruelly, for cancer is wholly indifferent to the virtues of the patient; when it gnaws, it gnaws; gnawing is its job. My sister Sabina, already married to Cotrim, was ready to drop with fatigue. Poor girl, she had been sleeping only three hours a night. Even Uncle João was downcast and sad. Dona Eusebia and several other ladies were there also, and they seemed to be just as sad and as eager to do what they could as were the members of the family.

"My boy!"

Pain relaxed its claws for a moment; a smile brightened the sick woman's face, on which death was beating its eternal wings.

It was less a face than a skull. Its beauty, like a bright day, had passed; nothing remained but the bones, and bones never grow thin. I could hardly recognize her; we had not seen each other for eight or nine years. Kneeling next to the bed, with her hands between mine, I remained silent, not daring to speak, because every word would have been a sob, and we were afraid she might learn that she was dying. Vain fear! She knew that she was soon to go; she told me so.

The next morning, the imminence of death was inescapable. Long was her agony, long and cruel, with a minute, cold, repetitious cruelty that filled me with pain and stupefaction. It was the first that I had seen anyone die. I knew death chiefly by hearsay; at the most, I had seen it, already petrified, in the face of a corpse on the way to the cemetery, or had thought of death all wrapped in the elaborations supplied by the professors of ancient history—the perfidious death of Caesar, the austere death of Socrates, the proud death of Cato. But this final duel between being and not being, death itself in painful, contracted, convulsive action, stripped of political and philosophical trappings, the death of a beloved person, I had never come face to face with anything like this. I did not cry; I remember well that I did not cry at all. My eyes were expressionless, stupid, my throat tight, my mind agape. What! So gentle, so submissive, so saintly a creature, who had never brought a tear of displeasure to anyone's eye, a loving mother, an immaculate wife, did she have to die this way, abused, bitten by the tenacious tooth of a pitiless disease? It all seemed obscure, incongruent, insane . . .

A sad chapter. Let us move on to a happier one.

24. Short but Happy: I was prostrate with grief. And yet my character in those days was a faithful compendium of triviality and presumption. The problem of life and death had never troubled my mind; until the day of my mother's death, I had never looked down

into the abyss of the inexplicable, for I had lacked the essential stimulus, the confusion of mind resulting from a personal catastrophe.

To tell the whole truth, my beliefs reflected those of a barber whom I had patronized in Modena and who was distinguished by the fact that he had no beliefs. He was the flower of the barbers. No matter how much time a haircut required, the customer was never bored, for the barber interspersed the strokes of his comb with a wealth of piquant sayings and racy jokes . . . He had no other philosophy. Nor did I. I do not say that the University taught me nothing; I memorized a few formulas and the vocabularies and outlines of some of the subjects. In Latin, for example, I pocketed three lines from Virgil, two from Horace, and about a dozen moral and political maxims, to pay out in the course of conversation. Of history, jurisprudence, and so on, I preserved the phraseology, the shell, the ornamentation . . .

Perhaps the reader is astonished by the frankness with which I expose and emphasize my mediocrity; let him remember that frankness is the virtue most appropriate to a defunct. In life, the watchful eye of public opinion, the conflict of interests, the struggle of greed against greed oblige a man to hide his old rags, to conceal the rips and patches, to withhold from the world the revelations that he makes to his own conscience; and the greatest reward comes when a man, in so deceiving others, manages at the same time to deceive himself, for in such a case he spares himself shame, which is a painful experience, and hypocrisy, which is a hideous vice. But in death, what a difference! what relief! what freedom! How glorious to throw away your cloak, to dump your spangles in a ditch, to unfold yourself, to strip off all your paint and ornaments, to confess plainly what you were and what you failed to be! For, after all, you have no neighbors, no friends, no enemies, no acquaintances, no strangers, no audience at all. The sharp and judicial eye of public opinion loses its power as soon as we enter the territory of death. I do not deny that it sometimes glances this way and examines and judges us, but we dead folk are not concerned about its judgment. You who still live, believe me, there is nothing in the world so monstrously vast as our indifference.

25. In Tijuca: Hold on! There goes my pen slipping to the emphatic. Let us be as modest and as simple as my life up in Tijuca during the first weeks after my mother's death.

On the seventh day, after the Mass, I put together a rifle, a few books, clothes, cigars, a young slave—the Prudencio of Chapter 11—and installed myself in an old house that belonged to us. My father had tried to dissuade me, but I would not (indeed, in my state of mind at the time, I could not) follow his wishes. Sabina wanted me to stay with her for at least two weeks; my brother-in-law almost dragged me off. He was a fine fellow, this Cotrim; he had grown from a harebrained youth into a circumspect man. At this time he was a dealer in imported goods, worked hard and unceasingly from morning till night. In the evening, seated at the window, curling his mustache, he would think of nothing but his work. He loved his wife and a son that he then had, who died several years later. People said he was avaricious.

I renounced everything; my spirit was stunned. I believe that it was then that the flower of melancholy in me began to open, this yellow, lonely, morbid flower with its subtle and inebriating perfume. " 'Tis good to be sad and say nothing." When I read these words of Shakespeare, I felt within me an echo, a delicious echo. I remember that I was sitting under a tamarind tree, with the poet's book open in my hands and my spirit as crestfallen as a sick chicken. I pressed my silent grief to my breast and experienced a curious feeling, something that might be called the voluptuousness of misery. *Voluptuousness of misery.* Memorize this phrase, reader; store it away, take it out and study it from time to time, and, if you do not succeed in understanding it, you may conclude that you have missed one of the most subtle emotions of which man is capable.

Sometimes I went hunting, sometimes I slept, sometimes I read

—I read a great deal—and sometimes I did nothing at all, just drifted from idea to idea, from fantasy to fantasy, like a vagrant butterfly or perhaps a hungry one. The hours dripped away one by one, the sun set, the shadows of night veiled mountain and city. Nobody visited me; I had expressly requested that people let me alone. One day, two days, three days, an entire week so spent, without speaking a word, was enough to drive me out of Tijuca and back to the hustle and bustle of the city. By the end of seven days my grief had abated, and the sight of trees and sky was no longer sufficient to feed my youthful spirit. Sated with solitude, I longed to live again. Into my trunk I threw the problem of life and death, the poet's melancholy, my shirts, my meditations, my neckties, and was about to close it, when Prudencio, the slave boy, told me that, on the night before, a person of my acquaintance had moved into a pink stucco house located two hundred paces from ours.

"Who?"

"Nhonhô perhaps no longer remembers Dona Eusebia . . ."

"I remember . . . Is it she?"

"She and her daughter. They came yesterday morning."

I immediately thought of the 1814 episode, and I felt ashamed; but I decided that subsequent events had justified me. Indeed, it had become impossible not to recognize the intimate relations between Villaça and the sister of the sergeant-major; even before my embarkation, people had begun to whisper mysteriously about the birth of a little girl. My uncle João wrote to me some time later that Villaça had died and had left a substantial legacy to Dona Eusebia, which had caused a lot of talk in our district. Uncle João, who loved a tasty scandal, wrote about nothing else in the letter, although it was many pages long. Events had justified me. And even if they had not, 1814 was a long way back, and so were my misdeed, Villaça, and the kiss in the thicket. Besides, no close ties existed between her and me. I reflected along these lines, and closed the trunk.

"Nhonhô is not going to visit Dona Eusebia?" asked Prudencio. "She was the one who dressed the body of my poor, dead lady."

I remembered that I had seen her, among other ladies, at the time of the death and at the burial. I had not known, however, that she had performed this final service to my mother. The slave boy was right: I decided to pay her a visit immediately, and then to go down to the city.

26. The Author Is Undecided: "Say, my boy, this isn't living!" said an unexpected voice. It was my father, who had come with two propositions in his pocket. I sat down on the trunk and welcomed him without enthusiasm. He stood there a few moments, looking at me; then he gave me his hand and said, with deep feeling, "My son, you must accept God's will."

"I have already accepted it," was my reply, and I kissed his hand.

He had not yet had luncheon; we ate together. Neither of us alluded to the sad reason for my seclusion, except once, in passing, when my father turned the conversation to the subject of the Regency and referred to the letter of condolence that one of the regents had sent him. He had the letter with him. It was badly wrinkled, perhaps because he had already read it to many other people. I think I have said that it was from one of the regents. He read it to me twice.

"I went to see him and thanked him personally for this token of consideration," said my father in conclusion, "and I think you should, too . . ."

"I?"

"Yes, you. He is an important man, taking the place of the emperor these days. Besides, I have brought you an idea, a project, or perhaps . . . yes, I'll tell you the whole story: I bring you two projects, a seat in the Chamber of Deputies and a marriage."

My father said this slowly and not all in the same tone, giving individual words a special intonation and emphasis in order to impress them on my mind. However, the projects conflicted so strongly with my feelings of the past seven days, that at first I did not fully comprehend them. My father patiently repeated them, and praised both the position and the prospective bride.

"Agreed?"

"I don't know much about politics," I said after a moment's pause. "As to getting married . . . let me go on living like the grizzly bear that I am."

"But bears get married," he replied.

"All right, find me a female bear."

My father laughed, and then began to speak seriously again. He said that I needed a political career for twenty-odd reasons, which he deduced with amazing volubility, illustrating them by reference to persons we knew. As to the prospective bride, one look at her would convince me; as soon as I saw her I would go and ask her father for her hand, immediately, without waiting even a day. He tried charm, persuasion, authority, while I remained silent, sharpening the point of a toothpick, making balls of the soft part of the bread, meditating. To tell the truth, I was neither docile nor rebellious in the face of his proposals; I was confused. Part of me said yes, that political office and a beautiful wife were advantages not to be scorned; another part said no, and the death of my mother loomed in my mind as an example of the fragility of the things of this world, of the things to which we become attached, of the family . . .

"I am not going to leave without a definite reply," said my father. "Def-i-nite!" he repeated, beating out the syllables with his finger.

He finished his coffee, sat back, and relaxed. He began to talk about various things, the Senate, the Chamber of Deputies, the Regency, a coach that he intended to buy, our house in Matacavallos . . . I remained at a corner of the table, writing aimlessly on a piece of paper with a pencil stub. I sketched a nose, a triangle, wrote a word, a phrase, a line of verse, repeated things over and over, without thinking—for example:

```
                    arma virumque cano
        A
        Arma virumque cano
                    arma virumque cano
              arma virumque
                        arma virumque cano
                    virumque
```

Automatically, all this; and yet there was a certain logic to it. For example, *virumque*, because of its first syllable, made me think of the name of the poet who had composed the words; and so, when I began to write *virumque* again, what appeared on the paper was *Virgilio*, and I continued:

```
        Vir                              Virgilio
              Virgilio        Virgilio
                    Virgilio
                                    Virgilio
```

My father, a little annoyed at my indifference, arose, came over to me, cast his eyes at the paper . . .

"Virgilio!" he exclaimed. "Why, that's *you*, my boy; the name of your bride-to-be is Virgilia."

27. Virgilia?

Virgilia? But is this not the same lady who, years later . . . ? The same. She was indeed the lady who was to be present at my demise in 1869 and who earlier, much earlier, played a large part in my emotional life. At the time when I first knew her, she was only fifteen or sixteen years old. She was possibly the boldest, and certainly the most impulsive, creature in the human race. I shall not say that she was the most beautiful, for this is not a romantic novel, in which the author gilds reality and closes his eyes to the freckles and pimples; yet the plain fact is that she had no freckles or pimples. She was pretty, spontaneous, fresh from the hands of nature, and full of that magic, precarious yet eternal, that is passed from individual to individual for the secret purposes of creation. Her complexion was fair, very fair. She was coquettish, ignorant, childish, and full of mysterious impulses. Great indolence and some devoutness—devoutness or perhaps fear; fear, I think.

There the reader has, in a few lines, the physical and psychological portrait of the person who was later to influence my life; that is how she was at sixteen. You, Virgilia, if you are still alive when these pages come to light—if you read them, beloved Virgilia, pay no attention to the difference between the words that I am using today and the words that I used when I first knew you. Please believe that I was as sincere then as now; death has made me neither hypercritical nor unjust.

"But," you will say, "how can you reconstruct the truth as of that time and express it after so many years?"

Ah, my indiscreet and grossly ignorant beloved, it is this very capacity that makes us masters of the earth, this capacity to restore the past and thus to prove the instability of our impressions and the vanity of our affections. Let Pascal say that man is a thinking reed. He is wrong; man is a thinking erratum. Each period in life is a new edition that corrects the preceding one and that in turn will be corrected by the next, until publication of the definitive edition, which the publisher donates to the worms.

28. Provided That . . . : "Virgilia?" I interrupted.

"Yes, that's your fiancée's name. An angel, my boy, an angel without wings. Imagine a girl of about this height, lively as mercury, and eyes . . . She's Dutra's daughter . . ."

"Which Dutra?"

"Counselor [*conselheiro* was an honorary title] Dutra; you

don't know him. He has a lot of political influence. Come now, do you agree?"

I did not reply immediately; for a few seconds I stared at the point of my boot. Then I said that I was prepared to consider the two things, the candidacy and the marriage, provided that . . .

"Provided that?"

"Provided that I am not obliged to accept both together. It seems to me that I can have a political career without being married and that . . ."

"Every politician should be married," said my father emphatically. "But let it be as you wish; I'm agreeable to anything. Anyway, you haven't seen her yet, and I'm sure that in this instance seeing will be believing. Besides, the girl and the seat in parliament are practically the same thing . . . I mean . . . well, you'll understand later . . . All right, I accept the condition, provided that . . ."

"Provided that . . . ?" I interrupted, imitating his voice.

"You rascal! Provided that you don't remain out here, useless, obscure, unhappy. I spent a lot of money, gave you the best care in the world, and got influential friends to do things for you, all in order to see you shine as you should, as it is appropriate for you and all us Cubases to do. You have to continue our name, continue it and make it even more illustrious. Why, I'm sixty years old, but if it were necessary for me to build a new life, I'd start right now, I wouldn't wait one minute. Fear obscurity, Braz; flee everything that isn't big. Look here, there are different ways for a man to amount to something, but the surest of all is to amount to something in other men's opinions. Don't throw away the advantages of your position, of your background . . ."

And the sorcerer went on, dangling a rattle before me, as they had done when I was a child in order to make me walk. The flower of melancholy withdrew into its bud and left the field to another flower, less yellowish and not at all morbid—the love of fame, the Braz Cubas Plaster.

29. The Visit: My father had won: I was ready to accept both public office and marriage, Virgilia and the deputyship—"two loves," my father called them, in an outburst of political tenderness. I agreed to accept them; my father embraced me energetically. At last I was acting like his own flesh and blood.

"Going down to the city with me now?"

"I'll go down tomorrow. First I have to visit Dona Eusebia . . ."

My father looked down his nose, but said nothing; he bade me farewell and left. Later in the afternoon, I went to visit Dona Eusebia. I found her scolding a colored gardener, but she left everything to come and talk with me, with an eagerness and pleasure so sincere that I quickly lost my diffidence. I think that she even hugged me, with her robust arms. She had me sit next to her on the verandah, and her happy exclamations came trippingly:

"Well now, little Braz! A man! Who would have thought it, years ago . . . A big man! And good-looking! My! You probably don't remember me very well . . ."

I told her that I did, that it would be impossible to forget so good a friend of the family. She began to speak of my mother, with many tender expressions of sentiment, so tender, indeed, that I felt very sad and very close to Dona Eusebia. She saw the sadness in my eyes and changed the subject: she asked me to tell her about my trip, my studies, my flirtations . . . "Yes, the flirtations too; just between us, I'm an old flirt myself." This brought to my mind the 1814 episode, her, Villaça, the thicket, the kiss, my announcement of it to the world; and, as I was remembering, I heard the creaking of a door, the rustle of a skirt, and:

"Mama . . . mama . . ."

30. The Flower of the Thicket: The voice and the skirt belonged to a dark young girl, who, upon seeing a stranger, hesitated at the door a few moments. Strained silence, but short. Dona Eusebia broke it with resolution and frankness:

"Come here, Eugenia," she said, "this gentleman is Mr. Cubas' son, Mr. Braz Cubas. He has been in Europe."

And, turning to me:

"My daughter Eugenia."

Eugenia, the flower of the thicket, hardly responded to my polite bow; surprised and embarrassed, she looked at me and slowly approached her mother's chair. Her mother arranged one of her braids, the end of which had become undone. "Naughty!" she said. "You can't imagine, Mr. Cubas, what kind of creature . . ." And she kissed her with so expansive a tenderness that I felt moved. I remembered my mother; also, to tell the whole truth, I felt a curious desire to become a father.

"Naughty?" I said. "She has passed the age of naughtiness."

"How old would you think she is?"

"Seventeen."

"One less."

"Sixteen. Why, then she is already a young lady!" Eugenia could not hide the satisfaction that these words gave her, but she soon regained possession of herself and became, as before, cold, erect, silent. In truth, she gave the impression of being more of a woman than she probably was: doubtless she acted her age when she was free to be herself; but, as she was at the moment, quiet, impassive, she had the sedateness and composure of a married woman. Perhaps this diminished somewhat her virginal charm. In any event, we soon began to feel at home with one another. Her mother praised her to the skies; I listened agreeably, and Eugenia smiled, with her eyes shining as if, there inside her brain, a little butterfly with gold wings and diamonds for eyes . . .

I say "there inside," for, here outside, what fluttered about was

[66]

a black butterfly [believed to be a bad omen] that had suddenly invaded the verandah and now began to beat its wings around Dona Eusebia. She cried out, jumped up, and cursed the creature excitedly and disconnectedly. "Damn you! . . . Get away, you devil! . . . Mary-Mother-of-God! . . ."

"Don't be afraid," I said; and with my handkerchief I drove the butterfly away. Dona Eusebia, breathless and a little embarrassed, sat down again. Eugenia concealed her emotion, but not without great effort; she was pale with fear. I shook hands with them and left, laughing to myself at their superstition—a philosophical laugh, objective and superior.

Later in the afternoon, I saw Dona Eusebia's daughter ride by on horseback, followed by a manservant. She waved at me with her whip handle. I flattered myself, I confess, with the idea that, after a few paces, she would turn her head to look at me again; but she did not turn.

31. The Black Butterfly:

The next day, as I was preparing to go down to the city, a butterfly flew into my room. It was as black as, and much larger than, the other one. I thought of the occurrence at Dona Eusebia's, and laughed; then I began to think about Dona Eusebia's daughter, about her fright, and about the dignity which she had nevertheless been able to preserve. After fluttering about me for a long while, the butterfly came to rest on my forehead. I brushed it off; it moved to the windowpane, and, when I chased it from there, it perched on top of an old portrait of my father. It was as black as night. Once settled, it began to move its wings gently; somehow it seemed to do so in a derisive manner, as if mocking me, and I took offense. I shrugged my shoulders and left the room; but, returning after a few minutes and finding the butterfly in the same place, I suddenly became nervous. I grabbed a towel, struck the butterfly, and it fell.

It was not dead; it was still twisting its body and moving its antennae. I felt sorry for it; I took it in the palm of my hand and placed it on the window sill. It was too late; the poor creature expired within a few seconds. I became disturbed and a little annoyed.

"Why in the devil couldn't it have been blue?" I said to myself.

And this thought—one of the most profound ever made since the discovery of butterflies—consoled me for my misdeed and reconciled me with myself. I stood there, looking at the corpse with, I confess, a certain sympathy. The butterfly had probably come out of the woods, well-fed and happy, into the sunlight of a beautiful morning. Modest in its demands on life, it had been content to fly about and exhibit its special beauty under the vast cupola of a blue sky, a sky that is always blue for those that have wings. It flew through my open window, entered my room, and found me there. I suppose it had never seen a man; therefore it did not know what a man was. It described an infinite number of circles about my body and saw that I moved, that I had eyes, arms, legs, a divine aspect, and colossal stature. Then it said to it- self, "This is probably the maker of butterflies." The idea over- whelmed it, terrified it; but fear, which is sometimes stimulating, suggested that the best way for it to please its creator was to kiss him on the forehead, and so it kissed me on the forehead. When I brushed it away, it rested on the windowpane, saw from there the portrait of my father, and quite possibly perceived a half-truth, *i. e.*, that the man in the picture was the father of the creator of butterflies; and it flew to beg his mercy.

Then a blow from a towel ended the adventure. Neither the blue sky's immensity, nor the flowers' joy, nor the green leaves' splendor could protect the creature against a face towel, a few square inches of cheap linen. Note how excellent it is to be supe- rior to butterflies! For, even if it had been blue, its life would not have been safe; I might have pierced it with a pin and kept it to delight my eyes. It was not blue. This last thought consoled me again. I placed the nail of my middle finger against my thumb, gave the cadaver a flip, and it fell into the garden. It was high time; the provident ants were already gathering around . . . Yes, I stand by my first idea: I think that it would have been better for the butterfly if it had been born blue.

32. Born Lame: I continued to prepare for my departure. I would delay no longer. I would go down to the city immediately; I would go down, even if a circumspect reader were to try to detain me by asking whether the preceding chapter is some sort of joke or just an unsavory incident . . . Alas, I did not reckon with Dona Eusebia. I was all ready to leave, when she entered my house. She had come to invite me to dinner that day. I declined; but she insisted so much, so very much, that I finally had to accept; moreover, it was the least I could do for her in view of her devotion to my mother.

Eugenia forwent all personal adornments that day, to please me. At least, I think it was to please me—unless she often went about like that. Even the gold earrings that she had worn the day before were not now to be seen hanging from her ears—two ears delicately chiseled on the head of a nymph. She wore a simple, white muslin dress, having at the top of the bodice a mother-of-pearl button instead of a brooch, and another button on each cuff to fasten the sleeve, with no bracelets whatever.

Her soul, too, seemed to be wholly without artificial adornment. No shyness in her speech, simple manners, a certain natural grace, a mature air about her, and perhaps something else—yes, something about her mouth, which was exactly like her mother's mouth and thus brought me back to the episode of 1814, and then gave me an impulse to extemporize to the daughter on the same text . . .

"Now I'm going to show you our little estate," said the mother, when we had drunk the last drop of coffee.

We left the verandah and started toward the ground behind the house. I noticed that Eugenia was limping a little, so little that I asked whether she had hurt her foot. Dona Eusebia said nothing, but her daughter replied without faltering:

"No, I was born lame."

I consigned myself to all the devils; I called myself a lout, a damned boor. Of course the mere possibility that she was a cripple should have sufficed to prevent the question. Then I remembered that, the previous day, she had approached her mother's chair very slowly and that today I had found her already seated at the dinner table. Perhaps she had been trying to conceal her defect; but then why did she confess it now? I looked at her and saw that she was sad.

I tried to erase the vestiges of my blunder. It was not difficult, for the mother was, as she had said, an old flirt, and immediately engaged me in conversation. We saw the entire estate—trees, flowers, duck pond, laundry tank, an infinitude of things, which she pointed out and explained to me, while I looked sidewise, studying Eugenia's eyes . . .

I give you my word of honor that there was nothing lame about the look with which she returned mine: it was direct and perfectly healthy; it came from black, tranquil eyes. I believe that two or three times she lowered them, a little confused; but only two or three times. Mostly she looked at me with frankness, without fear or affectation.

33. Blessed Are They That Go Not Down: The only bad thing about her was that she was lame. Eyes so clear, lips so fresh, composure so ladylike . . . and lame! This contrast made me suspect that nature is sometimes an immense mockery. Why pretty, if lame? Why lame, if pretty? These were my thoughts as I walked home in the evening, but I found no answer to the enigma. The best thing to do when you cannot solve an enigma is to throw it out the window, and that is what I did; I took hold of a towel and shooed away this other black butterfly that was fluttering about in my brain. I felt relieved and fell asleep. But sleep, which half opens the door to the mind, let the little creature come in again, and I spent the whole night wrestling with the mystery, without solving it.

In the morning it was raining, and I postponed my descent to the city; but the following morning was blue and clear, and yet I remained in Tijuca, as I did also on the third day, on the fourth day, and until the end of the week. Beautiful mornings, fresh, inviting; there below, my family calling me, and my bride-to-be, and parliament; and I doing nothing about it all, enraptured with my lame Venus. "Enraptured" is merely an effort of mine to lend splendor to my literary style; there was no rapture, but a liking, a certain physical and spiritual satisfaction. I liked her; near this unusual creature, this lame, illegitimate child, this product of heedless love, near her I had a sense of well-being, and I believe that, near me, she had an even greater sense of well-being. A simple eclogue in Tijuca.

Dona Eusebia kept an eye on us, but not too diligently; she tempered propriety with convenience. Her daughter, in this bursting forth of nature, gave me her soul in its first flower. "Are you going down to the city tomorrow?" she asked on Saturday.

"I intend to."

"Don't go."

I did not go, and I added a verse to the Gospel: "Blessed are they that go not down, for theirs is the first kiss of a maiden." As a matter of fact, Eugenia's first kiss, the first that she had ever given to a man, was on Sunday, and it was neither snatched from her nor stolen but candidly given, as a debt is paid by an honest debtor. Poor Eugenia! If you knew what thoughts were passing through my mind on that occasion! You, trembling with emotion, with your arms around my shoulders, seeing in me the husband you had been hoping for, and I looking back to 1814, to the thicket, to Villaça, and doubting that you could be false to your blood, to your origin . . .

Dona Eusebia entered the room unexpectedly, but not so suddenly that she caught us close together. I went to the window; Eugenia sat down and began to fix her braids. What charming dissimulation! What infinitely delicate art! What profound hypocrisy! And all unstudied, as natural as appetite, as natural as sleep. So much the better; Dona Eusebia suspected nothing.

34. To a Sensitive Soul:

Among the five or ten readers of this book, there is a sensitive soul who is irritated with me because of the preceding chapter, is beginning to tremble for Eugenia's fate, and perhaps . . . yes, perhaps, in his heart, is calling me a cynic. I, a cynic, sensitive soul? By Diana's thigh! [The Portuguese word for *thigh* is also the feminine form of *lame*.] Such an insult would have to be washed away with blood, if blood ever washed away anything in this world. No, sensitive soul, I was no cynic, I was merely a man; my brain was a stage on which were presented plays of all sorts—sacred drama, tragedy, romance, gay comedy, rowdy farce, morality, burlesque—creating a pandemonium, sensitive soul, a tumultuous confusion of things and of people in which everything could be seen, from the rose of Smyrna to the rue growing in your back yard and from the magnificent couch of Cleopatra to the corner of the beach where the beggar shivers in his sleep. Thoughts of every kind and of every caste mixed with one another. There you could find not only the atmosphere of the eagle and the hummingbird but also that of the frog and the snail. Withdraw, then, the unfortunate phrase that you used, sensitive soul; discipline your nerves, clean your eyeglasses—for sometimes the trouble is with one's eyeglasses—and let us be done once and for all with the flower of the thicket.

35. The Road to Damascus:

Now it happened that, after eight days, as I was on the road to Damascus, I heard a mysterious voice whispering the words of the Scripture (Acts 9:6): "Arise, and go into the city." This voice came from myself and had two origins: pity, which disarmed me before Eugenia's candor, and the fear that I would really fall in love with her and marry her. A cripple for a wife! As to the latter motive for my descent to the city, she recognized it and spoke to me about it. It was on the verandah, on a Monday afternoon, and I had just told her that the following morning I would go down. "Goodbye," she sighed, artlessly giving me her hand; "you are doing the sensible thing." And, as I said nothing, she continued, "You are doing the sensible thing in running away from the ridiculousness of marriage with me." I wanted to deny this. She moved slowly away from me, trying not to cry. I followed and swore by all the saints in heaven that I was obliged to go down but that I would never stop liking her, liking her a great deal; all this must have sounded cold and false to her, and she heard it without replying.

"Don't you believe me?" I finally asked.

"No, but I tell you that you are doing the sensible thing."

I wanted to hold her back, but the expression in her eyes was not of supplication, it was rather of command. I went down from Tijuca the next morning, partly embittered and partly pleased. I kept telling myself that it was right to obey my father, that it was desirable to embrace a political career . . . that the constitution . . . that my bride-to-be . . . that my horse . . .

36. Concerning Boots: My father, who had nearly given me up, embraced me with tenderness and gratitude. "Is it really true?" he said. "May I at last . . . ?"

I left him with these suspension marks and went to take off my boots, which were tight. Once relieved of them, I breathed deeply and stretched myself at full length, while my feet, and my whole self with them, entered a state of relative happiness. Then it occurred to me that tight boots are one of the greatest goods in the world, for, by making feet hurt, they create an opportunity to enjoy the pleasure of taking off your boots. Torture your feet, wretch, then untorture them, and there you have inexpensive happiness exactly to the taste of Epicurus and of the shoemakers. While this idea was working out on my famous trapeze, my mind's eye turned toward Tijuca and saw the young cripple disappearing on the horizon of the past, and I felt that my heart would soon take off its boots. And that is exactly what this lascivious fellow did. Four or five days later I was to enjoy that swift, ineffable, spontaneous moment of pleasure that succeeds a bitter pain, a worry, an illness . . . From this I inferred that life is the most ingenious of phenomena, for it sharpens hunger only so that it may offer an opportunity to eat, and it creates corns only because without them one cannot achieve the relief that is perfect earthly happiness. In truth, I tell you that all human wisdom is not worth a pair of tight boots.

You, my Eugenia, could never take off your boots. You labored along the road, limping in your leg and in your love life, lonely, silent, sad as a poor man's funeral, until you, too, came to this other shore . . . What I do not understand is whether the world really needed you. Who knows? Perhaps one supernumerary less would have spoiled the human tragedy.

37. At Last! At last, here is Virgilia! Before going to Counselor Dutra's house, I asked my father whether there was any preliminary understanding about the marriage.

"No understanding. Some time ago, talking with him about you, I mentioned my desire to see you a deputy; and I spoke in such a way that he promised to do something, and I think he will. As to your fiancée, she is a jewel, a flower, a star . . . She is his daughter, and I have no doubt that, if you marry her, you will become a deputy much sooner."

"Nothing more?"

"Nothing more."

And so we went to Dutra's house. He was a gem of a man, smiling, jovial, patriotic, a little irritated with social evils but hopeful that they would soon be cured. He approved of my candidacy, but said that I would have to wait a few months. And then he presented me to his wife—an estimable lady—and to his daughter, who in no respect belied my father's panegyrics. In no respect, I promise you. Reread Chapter 27. I looked at her in a way that reflected the indoctrination I had already received with respect to her; she, perhaps for a similar reason, looked at me in much the same way: our first exchange of looks was purely and simply conjugal. At the end of a month we were very close friends.

38. The Fourth Edition: "Come to dinner tomorrow," said Dutra to me one evening. I accepted the invitation.

The next afternoon, I ordered the coachman to wait for me in the Largo de São Francisco de Paula, and I went to look around town a bit. Do you still remember my Theory of Human Editions? Know, then, that I was already in the fourth edition, revised and amended, but still full of errata and barbarisms; a defect, however, for which there was some compensation in the elegant type and in the rich binding. Walking along the Rua dos Ourives on my way back to the coach, I took out my watch, and the glass fell to the pavement. I entered the first shop at hand; it was little more than a cubicle, dusty and dark.

In the rear, behind the counter, sat a woman. At first I could not clearly distinguish the features of her yellow, pockmarked face; when finally I was able to do so, I found it a most curious spectacle. One could see that she had been pretty, more than a little pretty; but premature old age and the illness had destroyed the flower of her beauty. Her pocks must have been terrible; the large projections and excavations, declivities and acclivities, that they had left gave one the impression of enormously rough sandpaper. The eyes were her best feature, and yet they had a singularly repugnant expression, which changed, however, as soon as I began to speak. As to her hair, it was a dull brown and almost as dusty as the store. On one of the fingers of her left hand gleamed a diamond. Would you believe it, posterity?—this woman was Marcella.

I did not immediately recognize her; it was difficult; but she knew me as soon as I began to talk. Her eyes sparkled, and exchanged their usual expression for another, half sweet and half sad. I saw her make a movement as if to hide or to flee; it was the instinct of vanity, and lasted only an instant. Marcella accepted the situation and smiled.

"Would you like to buy something?" she said, giving me her hand.

I did not reply. Marcella understood in a general way the cause of my silence (it was not difficult to understand), although she may have wondered which affected me more, the shock of the moment or memory of the past. She offered me a chair and, with the counter between us, talked to me for a long time about herself, the life she had led, the tears I had caused her, the financial misfortunes she had suffered, the pocks that had excavated her face, and time, which had helped the illness to hasten her downfall. In truth, she was decrepit down to her soul. She had sold everything, or almost everything. A man who had once loved her and had died in her arms had left her this goldsmith's shop; but, to cap her misfortunes, it was now little patronized, perhaps because people found it strange to see a woman in charge. Then she asked me to tell her about my life. I spent little time doing so, for, I maintained, it had been neither long nor interesting.

"Have you married?" she asked.

"Not yet," I replied drily.

Marcella looked out into the street with the dreamy expression of one who is reflecting or remembering. I let my mind turn to the past and, amid recollections and nostalgia, I asked myself why I had gone to such extremes of folly. Was not this woman the same person, the same Marcella, that I had known in 1822? Was her former beauty worth as much as one-third of my sacrifices for her? I tried to find the answer to the latter question in Marcella's face. It told me no; and at the same time her eyes told me that, then as now, there had burned in them the flame of greed. Mine simply had not been able to see it; they had been first-edition eyes.

"But why did you come in here? Did you see me from the street?" she asked, shaking off her torpor.

"No, I thought it was a watchmaker's shop; I wanted to buy a glass for this watch. I'll go elsewhere. Forgive me; I'm in a hurry."

Marcella sighed unhappily. The fact is that I felt both vexed and depressed, and I was eager to get away. Marcella, however, called a Negro boy, gave him the watch, and, over my protests, sent him to a store in the neighborhood to buy the glass. There was no escape; I sat down again. Then she said that she wanted the patronage of her old acquaintances; she added that, naturally, I would marry sooner or later, and that she could promise to let me have the finest jewels at low prices. She did not say "low prices" but used a delicate, transparent metaphor. I began to suspect that she had suffered no great misfortunes (except the illness), that she had money enough to live very comfortably, and that she was in business only to further her lust for wealth, which was like a worm gnawing at her soul. Several people subsequently told me these very same things about her.

39. The Neighbor: While I was reflecting along these lines, a short, hatless fellow came into the store, holding a four-year-old girl by the hand.

"Did you have a nice morning today?" he asked Marcella.

"So-so. Come here, Maricota."

The fellow lifted the child in his arms and lowered her on the other side of the counter.

"Go on," he said; "ask Dona Marcella if she had a nice night. She was anxious to come here but her mother couldn't dress her any earlier . . . Well, Maricota? Kiss Dona Marcella's hand . . . You're going to get the switch! . . . Ah, that's right . . . You can't imagine what she's like at home; she talks about you all day long and here she's afraid to open her mouth. Why, just yesterday . . . Shall I tell her, Maricota?"

"Don't, papa."

"Was it something naughty, then?" asked Marcella, patting the child's cheek.

"I'll tell you: her mother teaches her to say a paternoster and an Ave Maria every night to the Virgin Mary, but yesterday the little one came and asked me so sweetly . . . can you imagine what? . . . that she wanted to say her prayers to Saint Marcella."

"Poor little thing!" said Marcella, kissing her.

The fellow related some other agreeable matters and finally left with the child, not, however, before casting a questioning, or possibly suspicious, glance in my direction. I asked Marcella who he was.

"He is a watchmaker who lives near here, a fine man; his wife, too; and the little girl is nice, isn't she? They seem to be very fond of me . . . fine people."

As she spoke, there was a tremor of joy in Marcella's voice, and her face was inundated by a wave of happiness . . .

40. In the Coach: At this point the boy returned, bringing the watch with its new glass. It was high time, for I was on pins and needles to go. I gave the boy a silver coin, told Marcella that I would come back another day, and strode out. My heart was pounding; perhaps it was beating a sort of death knell. Or perhaps it could not adjust itself to the radical emotional changes that I had undergone that day. I had awakened happy; the morning was beautiful. At

breakfast, my father declaimed, in anticipation, the first speech that I would make in the Chamber of Deputies; we laughed a great deal, and so did the sun, which was exceptionally bright, and so would Virgilia when I told her about our little fantasy. And then the glass of my watch fell; I entered the first shop at hand, and suddenly the past surged up before me, kissing me, lacerating me, cross-examining me, its face etched with nostalgia and pockmarks . . .

I left the past there in the store. I hurried to the coach, which was waiting for me in the Largo de São Francisco de Paula, and ordered the coachman to drive fast. He shouted to the horses, the coach began to shake me up, the springs groaned, the wheels quickly furrowed the mud left by the recent rain, and yet everything seemed to me to be static, motionless. Is there not, at times, a certain wind, not strong or raw, but sultry and listless, that neither blows our hats from our heads nor raises women's skirts, and yet is, or at least seems to be, worse than if it merely did these things, for it depresses, weakens, and virtually dissolves the human spirit? Such a wind was blowing upon me; and I felt stifled by it, unable to escape from it, caught in the narrow pass between the past and the present, longing to leap out onto the plane of the future. If only the coach would move!

"João!" I shouted to the coachman. "Is this coach going to move or isn't it?"

"Lord, Nhonhô! We're here already at the counselor's house."

41. The Hallucination:

It was true. I hurried into the house and found Virgilia in bad humor. She had apparently been waiting for me anxiously, and her brow was clouded. Her mother, who was hard of hearing, was in the living room with her. After an exchange of polite greetings, Virgilia said drily:

"We expected you earlier."

I defended myself as best I could: I said that the horse had balked and that a friend had detained me. Suddenly my voice died on my lips, I became paralyzed with horror. Virgilia . . . could this woman be Virgilia? I stared at her, and the experience was so painful that I stepped back a pace and turned away. I looked at her again. Pocks had eaten into her face; her skin, so delicate, pink, and smooth only the day before, was now yellow and disfigured by the same scourge that had ravaged the Spanish woman's face. Her sparkling eyes had become dull; her mouth, sad; her physical attitude, tired. I concentrated my eyes on her; I took her by the hand and called her gently to me. I was not mistaken; the pocks had done their work. I think I made a gesture of disgust.

Virgilia moved away from me and sat down on the sofa. I stood motionless for a while, staring at my feet. Should I go or remain? I rejected the former alternative as wholly absurd and started toward Virgilia, who remained silent there on the sofa. Good heavens! She was once again the fresh, youthful, flowering Virgilia. In vain I sought in her face a sign of the illness; there was none; her skin was as delicate and as white as ever.

"Have you never seen me before?" asked Virgilia.

"Never so pretty."

I sat down, while Virgilia snapped her nails. After several seconds of silence, I began to talk about various things; she did not reply, did not even look at me. Except for the snapping of her nails, she was silence itself. Only once she glanced at me, but very briefly and superciliously, raising the left corner of her mouth a little and contracting her eyebrows so that they almost met; this combination gave her face an expression half comic and half tragic.

Intended as an expression of disdain, it was, however, exaggerated to the point of affectation. Within, she was suffering more than a little, although I cannot say whether from wounded feelings or from resentment; and, because pain that is concealed hurts more, Virgilia probably suffered twice as much as she should have. But let us not become involved in psychology.

42. What Aristotle Overlooked: I think that this is metaphysics rather than psychology: Start a ball rolling; it rolls along, comes in contact with another ball, transmits its motion to the other, and the second ball rolls along. Let us call the first ball Marcella; the second, Braz Cubas; and a third, Virgilia. Let us assume that Marcella, having received a fillip from the past, rolled along until it came in contact with Braz Cubas, which, in turn, yielding to the force transmitted to it, began to roll, until it bumped into Virgilia, which had been wholly alien to the first ball; and thus, by the simple transmission of a force, opposite extremes of society come into relationship with each other, and there is established something that we may call the Unity of Human Misery. How did Aristotle happen to overlook this principle?

43. "A Marchioness, for I Shall Be a Marquis": Virgilia was absolutely an imp, an angelic imp, if you wish, but still an imp, and then . . .

And then came Damião Lobo Neves, a man neither better looking, nor more elegant, nor better read, nor more charming than I, and yet it was he who, within a few weeks, snatched from me both Virgilia and the candidacy, with the breathless impetus of a Caesar. There were no jealous recriminations, no family scenes. Dutra came one day and told me that I had better wait for a more favorable breeze, because Lobo Neves had powerful influences behind him; I could do nothing but acquiesce. My downfall had begun. A week later, Virgilia smilingly asked Lobo Neves when he would become a minister of state.

"If I had my way, right now; but as others are going to have their way, perhaps a year from now."

Virgilia replied:

"Promise me that some day you'll make me a baroness?"

"No, a marchioness, for I shall be a marquis."

From that point on, I was lost. Virgilia compared the eagle with the peacock and chose the eagle, leaving the peacock with his surprise, his resentment, and three or four kisses that she had given him. Maybe five kisses; but even if it had been ten, I would have remained unsatisfied. A person's mouth is not like the hoof of Attila's horse, that made sterile the soil on which it trod; just the contrary.

44. A Cubas! These developments stunned my father and, I think, were the real cause of his death. He had built so many and such beautiful dream castles that he could not see them crumble without suffering a severe organic upset. At the beginning he could hardly believe the truth. A Cubas! A branch of the illustrious tree of the Cubases! And he repeated this with such conviction that I, already informed about our cooper's shop, forgot for a moment the inconstant lady and stopped to contemplate this curious (although by no means rare) phenomenon: a lie that gradually became accepted as true by the liar himself.

"A Cubas!" he said again the next morning at breakfast.

The meal was not a happy one. I could hardly keep awake, for I had slept little that night. Because of love? Out of the question; one does not love the same woman twice; and I, who was to love Virgilia at a later time, was now bound to her by no claim whatever except a passing fancy, obedience to my father, and considerable vanity. This last suffices to explain my sleeplessness; it was resentment, perhaps foolish, but sharp as a pinpoint, and it spent itself in cigar smoke, fists beating the air, snatches of reading, until the break of dawn, the most tranquil of dawns.

But I was young, I had the cure within myself. It was my father who could not readily support the blow. Medically speaking, he did not die of it, but undoubtedly it complicated his last illness. He died four months later—despondent, with an intense, ceaseless anxiety, a mortal disillusionment, that made him forget his cough and his rheumatism. He had one half-hour of joy in store; it was when one of the ministers of state visited him. I saw—how well I remember!—I saw his grateful smile of former times, and a light in his eyes, which was, so to speak, the last glimmer of his expiring soul. His sadness soon returned, sadness at dying without having seen me placed in a high position, as befitted me.

"A Cubas!"

He died on a May morning a few days after the minister's visit, in the presence of his two children, Sabina and me, as well as Uncle Ildefonso and my brother-in-law. Nothing could save him, not the doctors' science, nor our love, nor the great care and attention he received; he had to die and he died.

"A Cubas!"

45. Notes:
Sobs, tears, an improvised altar with saints and crucifix, black curtains on the walls, strips of black velvet framing the entrance, a man who came to dress the corpse, another man who took the measurements for the coffin; candelabra, the coffin on a table covered with gold-and-black silk with candles at the corners, invitations, guests who entered slowly with muffled step and pressed the hand of each member of the family, some of them sad, all of them serious and silent, priest, sacristan, prayers, sprinkling of holy water, the closing of the coffin with hammer and nails; six persons who remove the coffin from the table, lift it, carry it, with difficulty, down the stairs despite the cries, sobs, and new tears of the family, walk with it to the hearse, place it on the slab, strap it securely with

leather thongs; the rolling of the hearse, the rolling of the carriages one by one . . . These are notes that I took for a sad and commonplace chapter which I shall not write.

46. The Inheritance: Let the reader look upon us now, eight days after my father's death—my sister seated on a sofa; near her, Cotrim leaning on a cabinet and biting his mustache; me walking back and forth with my eyes on the floor. Deep mourning. Deep silence.

"But after all," said Cotrim, "this house can't be worth much more than thirty contos; let's say that it's worth thirty-five . . ."

"It's worth fifty," I asserted. "Sabina knows that it cost fifty-eight . . ."

"I wouldn't care if it cost seventy," replied Cotrim. "A thing is worth what you can sell it for, and your father couldn't have sold this house new for anything like fifty-eight contos. Besides, the value of real estate has gone way down during the past few years; you know that. If this house is worth fifty contos just think how much the house in Campo that you want for yourself must be worth."

"That's a different case entirely. It's an old house."

"Old!" exclaimed Sabina, raising her hands toward the ceiling. "Are you going to say that it's new?"

"Come now, brother, let's not argue," said Sabina, getting up from the sofa; "we can work out everything on a friendly basis if we are just prepared to compromise a little. For example, Cotrim doesn't want any of the slaves except papa's coachman and Paulo . . ."

"Not the coachman," I interrupted; "I'm keeping the coach and there is no reason why I should have to buy another coachman."

"All right; I'll take Paulo and Prudencio."

"Prudencio has been freed."

"Freed?"

"Two years ago."

"How nicely your father arranged all these things here in the house without telling anyone! All right, then, how about the silver? I don't suppose your father liberated the silver."

We had already spoken about it, the old silverware of the time of Dom José I, the most valuable part of the inheritance because of its fine workmanship, its antiquity, and its history; my father used to say that the Count da Cunha, when he was viceroy of Brazil, had given it as a present to my great-grandfather Luiz Cubas.

"So far as the silver is concerned," continued Cotrim, "I wouldn't raise any question about it if it weren't for your sister's wish to have it; and, after all, I think she's right. Sabina is married, she needs something presentable to put on the table. You're a bachelor, you don't entertain, you don't . . ."

"But I may get married . . ."

"What for?" interrupted Sabina.

This question was so utterly inane that for a few moments I forgot our conflict. I smiled; I took Sabina's hand, patted it gently on the palm, all so affectionately that Cotrim interpreted the gesture as one of acquiescence and thanked me.

"What do you mean?" I replied. "I'm not letting you have the silver."

"You're not?"

I shook my head.

"You may as well give up, Cotrim," said my sister to her husband. "In a few minutes he'll want the clothes off our backs; that's the only thing he hasn't asked for."

"This is really the limit. He wants the coach, he wants the coachman, he wants the silver, he wants everything. Look here, it's much quicker to haul us into court and prove with witnesses that Sabina isn't your sister, that I'm not your brother-in-law, and that God isn't God. Go ahead, and then you won't lose anything, not even a teaspoon. Oh no, my friend, you can't have everything your own way."

He was so enraged, and I was so ill prepared to yield completely, that I made him an offer of compromise; to divide the silver. He laughed, and asked me who would get the teapot and who would get the sugar bowl; and after this question he remarked that I need not worry, we could always go to court to settle our claims. Sabina had gone to the window that opened on the yard; after a moment she returned and offered to give up Paulo and the other Negro on condition that she got the silver. I was going to refuse, but Cotrim saved me the trouble.

"Never! I don't give charity!" he said.

We dined together, glumly. My uncle the canon joined us at dessert, just in time to witness a little altercation.

"My children," he said, "remember that my brother left enough bread for all."

But Cotrim:

"Sure, sure. However, the question is not about bread, it's about butter. I can't swallow dry bread."

A division of the inheritance was finally made, but it could not erase the fact that we had fought bitterly. It pained me greatly to fight with Sabina. We had been such friends! As children, we had played and quarreled together; as adults, we had talked and laughed together, we had shared the bread of pain and of joy, fraternally, like the good brother and sister that we were. But now we had fought. Our comradeship had vanished like Marcella's beauty.

47. The Recluse: Marcella, Sabina, Virgilia . . . I seemed to melt them together as if all three were merely projections of an affection within me. O arrant pen, tie a proper cravat around your literary style, put on a less sordid vest; then I shall let you come with me to my house and stretch yourself in the hammock that rocked me during the greater part of the years between my father's death and 1842. Come; and if you smell perfume, do not suppose that I scent my clothes; it is a vestige of N or Z or U—for all these capital letters

rocked their elegant degradation in my hammock. But if you desire something more than their aroma, I am sorry to have to tell you that I have kept neither portraits, nor letters, nor memories; even the emotion has vanished, and nothing remains but their initials.

I lived as a sort of recluse; once in a great while I went to a ball, or the theatre, or a speech, but I spent most of the time alone. I existed; I let myself drift with the ebb and flow of the days, now restless, now apathetic, oscillating between ambition and discouragement. I wrote on politics and dabbled in literature. I sent articles and verses to all the periodicals and even achieved a certain reputation as a polemic and as a poet. Whenever I thought of Lobo Neves, who was already a deputy, and of Virgilia, the future marchioness, I asked myself why I would not be a better deputy and a better marquis than Lobo Neves—I, who was really superior to him; and I said this while looking at the tip of my nose . . .

48. Virgilia's Cousin: "Do you know who arrived yesterday from São Paulo?"

Luiz Dutra asked me one evening.

Luiz Dutra, a cousin of Virgilia, also communed with the Muses. His verses were better, and were better received, than mine; but he needed the private approval of individuals to confirm the applause of the public. As he was shy, he never asked anyone for an opinion of his writings; but he loved to hear a word of appreciation, which enabled him to marshal new energies and to apply himself to his work with fresh impetus.

Poor Luiz Dutra! Hardly had he published something, when he would run to my house and begin to gyrate about me, looking for an opinion, a word, a gesture expressing approval of his recent production; and I would speak of a thousand different things—the latest ball in Cattete, the discussions in the legislature, coaches, horses—of everything except his verses or his prose. He would reply, at the beginning with animation, then disinterestedly, would twist the rein of the conversation toward literature, would open a book, would ask me whether I had written anything new, and I would say yes or no but would twist the rein to the other side, and he would follow me reluctantly. Finally he would balk altogether at the trend of the conversation, would become silent, and would leave in despair. My purpose was to make him lose confidence, to discourage him, and ultimately to eliminate him as a competitor. And all the while I was looking at the tip of my nose . . .

49. The Tip of the Nose: Did you ever ponder the function of the nose, beloved reader? The explanation proffered by Dr. Pangloss is that noses were created to support spectacles, and I confess that for a time I found this theory satisfactory; but one day, while I was meditating this and other obscure points of philosophy, I hit upon the true, authentic explanation.

Indeed, I had merely to remember the custom of the fakirs. The reader doubtless knows that a fakir will spend long hours looking at the tip of his nose, with the sole purpose of seeing the divine light. When he fixes his eyes on the tip of his nose, he loses the sense of external things, creates within his mind a beautiful image of himself, grasps the intangible, shakes off his earthly shackles, dissolves himself, and becomes etherealized. This sublimation of one's being, via the tip of the nose, is one of the most lofty phenomena of the spirit, and the faculty of achieving it is by no means confined to fakirs; it is universal. Every man has the need and the ability to contemplate his own nose, in order to see the divine light, and such contemplation, resulting in the subordination of the universe to one nose, establishes social equilibrium. If noses contemplated only each other, the human race would not last two centuries; indeed, it would not have survived the most primitive tribes.

I hear an objection from the reader: "How is it, then," he says, "that no one ever sees men contemplating their own noses?"

Obtuse reader, this shows that you have never been inside the brain of a hatter. A hatter walks past the store of a rival, who opened it two years ago; then it had two doors, now it has four; it promises to have six or eight before long. In the windows the rival's hats are displayed; through the doors walk the rival's customers. The hatter compares the store with his own, which is older and has only two doors; and he compares those hats with his own, for which the demand is relatively poor although the prices are the same. Naturally he is chagrined; but he walks on, his eyes looking downward or straight ahead. Then he concentrates, seeking the reasons for the other man's prosperity and his own failure, when he is really a better hatter than the other . . . At this moment, if you look closely, you will see that his eyes are fixed on the tip of his nose.

The conclusion, therefore, is that there are two major forces in society: love, which multiplies the species, and the nose, which subordinates it to the individual. Procreation, equilibrium.

50. Lobo Neves' Wife: "It was my cousin Virgilia, Lobo Neves' wife, who arrived from São Paulo," continued Luiz Dutra.

"Ah!"

"And just today I learned something, Mr. Ladies' Man."

"What?"

"That you wanted to marry her."

"My father's idea. Who told you?"

"She did, herself. I brought you into the conversation, and then she told me everything."

The next day, while I was standing in front of the door of the

Plancher printing press on the Rua do Ouvidor, I saw a beautiful woman appear in the distance. It was she, although I did not recognize her until she was only a few steps away, so greatly had she changed, nature and art having combined their forces to bring her beauty close to perfection. We nodded and smiled; she walked on and, with her husband, entered the carriage that was waiting for them; I stood there, a little stunned.

Eight days later I met her at a ball; I think we exchanged two or three words. But at another ball, given a month later at the house of a lady who had been an ornament of the salons of the First Kingdom and was still more or less ornamental in those of the Second, our contact was greater and longer, for we chatted and waltzed. The waltz is a delightful thing. We waltzed; and when I held that supple, magnificent body close to my own, I had a curious feeling, the feeling of a man who had been robbed.

"It's very warm," she said when we had finished. "Shall we go out on the terrace?"

"No, you might catch cold. Let's go to the other room."

In the other room was Lobo Neves, who paid me compliments on my political writings, adding that he would say nothing about the literary ones because he did not understand them, but the political articles were excellent, well thought out and well written. I replied with expressions of equal esteem for his accomplishments, and we parted greatly pleased with one another.

About three weeks later I received an invitation from him to a small party at his house. I went; Virgilia received me with this gracious welcome: "You're going to have to waltz with me again, you know." This did not surprise me, for I was considered an expert waltzer. We waltzed, and then we waltzed again. A book caused Francesca's downfall; a waltz caused ours. I think I pressed her hand very tightly, and she did not move it, as if she had forgotten about it, and I held her close; and everyone looked at us and at the others who were gyrating about, and saw nothing of what was happening . . . Ecstasy.

51. Mine! "Mine!" I said to myself, as another man claimed her for the next dance; and during the rest of the evening this idea was driven deep into my mind, not by a hammer but by a gimlet, which is more insidious.

"Mine!" I was saying as I approached the door of my house.

But there, as if destiny or chance or what-not was trying to provide more fodder for my possessive ecstasy, a round, yellow object gleamed on the ground before me. I stooped down; it was a gold coin, a half-dobra.

"Mine!" I repeated, laughing and putting it in my pocket.

During the night I did not think about the coin; but the next day, on remembering it, I suffered an attack of conscience, and a voice asked me how the devil a coin could be mine if I had neither inherited nor earned it but had merely found it in the street. Obviously it was not mine; it belonged to the person who had lost it, be he rich or poor, and perhaps he was poor, some laborer who now would not have enough money to buy food for his wife and children; but even if he was rich, my duty would be the same. I had to return the coin, and the best way, the only way, was through the police. I sent a letter to the chief of police, enclosing the coin and requesting him to try, by the means at his disposal, to restore it to the hands of its true owner.

I sent the letter and breakfasted contentedly, I might almost say jubilantly. My conscience had waltzed so much the evening before that she had begun to feel suffocated, unable to breathe; but the return of the half-dobra was a window on the other side of my mind; a gust of pure air blew in, and the poor lady breathed freely again. Give your conscience plenty of air!—that is all the advice you will get from me in this chapter. However, stripped of all extraneous considerations, my act was good because it expressed a scruple, a sentiment, indicative of a fastidious moral sense. That is what my lady inside told me, in an austere and yet friendly way; that is what she told me as she leaned on the sill of the open window.

"You did the right thing, Cubas; you behaved perfectly. This air is more than pure, it is balsamic, a breath from the Elysian Fields. Would you like to see what you have done, Cubas?"

And the excellent lady produced a mirror and held it before my eyes. I saw the half-dobra, round and bright, multiplying itself until there were ten, then thirty, then five hundred—thus expressing the benefits that I would derive, in both life and death, from my act of restitution. And I found complete peace of mind in the contemplation of that act, I saw myself in it, I found myself to be a good man, possibly a great man. You see what happens when one waltzes a little too much.

Thus I, Braz Cubas, discovered a sublime law, the Law of the Equivalence of Windows, and established the principle that the way to compensate for a closed window is to open another window, so that the conscience may always have plenty of air. Perhaps you do not understand these terms; perhaps you want something more concrete, a package, for example, even if it has to be a mysterious package. All right, here is your mysterious package.

52. The Mysterious Package: It happened that, some days later, as I was going to Botafogo, I stumbled on a package that was lying on the beach. To be literal, I did not stumble on it, I kicked it. Seeing a package, not large but clean and neatly wrapped, tied with stout twine, obviously something on which care had been bestowed, I did not pick it up immediately but first kicked it a little to make certain it was not empty; it resisted my foot. I cast my eyes about me; the beach was deserted; in the distance some little boys were playing, still farther away a fisherman was mending his nets. No one could see what I was doing. I bent over, picked up the package, and walked on.

I walked on, but not without misgivings. It might have been a boy's practical joke. I thought of putting the package back where I had found it, but I fingered it and rejected the idea. A little farther on, I left the road and headed for home.

"We'll see," I said as I entered my study.

And still I hesitated—out of shame, I think. The fear of a joke came again to my mind. To be sure, there was no outward sign of anything improper; but I had within me a youngster who would whistle, shout, grunt, hoot, hiss, cackle, raise the devil, if he saw me open the package and find inside a dozen dirty old handkerchiefs or two dozen rotten guavas. It was getting late; my curiosity was acute, and so must be the reader's; I opened the package and saw . . . discovered . . . counted . . . counted again no less than five contos. No less; maybe ten milreis more. Five contos in lovely bills and coins, all neatly stacked, something that you would find once in a thousand years. I wrapped them again.

At dinner, it seemed to me that one of the slave boys spoke to another with his eyes. Had they been spying on me? I questioned them discreetly, and concluded that they had not. After dinner, I went again to my study, examined the money, and had to laugh at my maternal cares lavished on five contos—I, who was so rich.

To put the whole subject out of my mind, I went that evening to the house of Lobo Neves, who had insisted that I never miss any of his wife's receptions. There I found the chief of police; I was introduced to him; he immediately remembered my letter and the half-dobra, and related the incident to the gathering. Virgilia seemed greatly pleased, and everyone in turn had to relate a similar incident, which I heard with the impatience of a hysterical woman.

That night, the next day, the entire week, I thought as little as possible about the five contos, which lay undisturbed in my desk drawer. I enjoyed talking about everything except money, especially found money. However, it was no crime to find money, it was just good luck, a blessing to be thankful for, in this case perhaps an act of Providence. For people do not lose five contos the way they lose a tobacco pouch. When one carries a package of five contos one improvises extra senses to help the five usual ones take care of it; one feels it often to make sure that the contents are still there; one does not take one's eyes off it, nor one's hands, nor one's thoughts; and if in spite of all this the package is lost on a beach, obviously there must have been . . . It would be utterly impossible to think of the finding as a crime—as a crime, as a dishonor, or as anything that could stain a man's character.

It was just a finding, a stroke of luck, like winning the grand prize in the lottery or a bet on the horses or anything else won in an honest game; and I go so far as to maintain that my good luck was merited, for otherwise I should have felt badly about it and unworthy of the rewards of Providence, and I did not feel so.

"These five contos," I said to myself three weeks later, "I must use them for a good purpose, perhaps a dowry for some poor girl or . . . I'll see . . ."

This same day I took them to the Bank of Brazil. There I was received with many gracious allusions to the half-dobra affair, news of which had spread to virtually everyone who knew me. I replied weariedly that the thing did not merit so much talk; then they praised my modesty—and, because I became annoyed, they praised it even more.

53. . . . . : Virgilia's whole being was concentrated on me—on my eyes, my life, my thoughts; she would often tell me so, and it was true.

Some plants bud and sprout quickly, others are slow and never reach full development. Our love was of the former type; it sprouted with such impetus and so much sap that in a short time it was the largest, the leafiest, and the most exuberant creature of the woods. I cannot tell you exactly how long it continued to grow. I remember, however, the night it first blossomed into flower with a kiss, if you can call it that, a kiss that she gave me, trembling—poor thing—trembling with fear because we were standing at the gate to the grounds of her husband's estate. This single kiss united us, this kiss, ardent and brief, prologue to a life of delight, of remorse, of pleasures ending in grief, of troubles blossoming into joy, of patient, systematic hypocrisy, the only restraint upon an otherwise unbridled love—a life of nervousness, of anger, of despair, of jealousy, all of them paid for in full by one hour; but another hour would come and would swallow up

the first and everything that went with it, leaving only the nervousness and the dregs, and the dregs of the dregs, which are
satiety and disgust: such was to be the book of which this kiss
was the prologue.

54. The Pendulum: I left, still feeling the kiss. I could not sleep; I stretched out

in bed and shut my eyes, but without effect. I heard the clock
strike every hour of the night. As a rule, when I was unable to
sleep, the strokes of the pendulum would annoy me greatly; their
dry ticktock, gloomy and slow, seemed to say at each stroke
that I had one second less to live. Then I would imagine an old
devil sitting between two bags, one labeled "life" and the other
"death," taking coins from the former and dropping them into
the latter, and saying:

"Another gone . . . another gone . . . another gone . . . another
gone . . ."

The strange thing about it is that, whenever the clock stopped,
I would wind it, so that I could go on counting my lost seconds.
Machines of most types change or disappear; even institutions
die; the clock is unchangeable and eternal. The last man, when
he says farewell to the cold, exhausted sun, will consult his watch
in order to know the exact time of his death.

On this night, however, I felt no annoyance; quite the contrary. Fantasies were falling over one another in my mind like a
crowd of devotees trying to see the singing angel in a religious
procession. I did not hear the seconds lost but the minutes gained.
After a certain time I heard nothing, for my psyche, sly and un-
disciplined, sneaked out the window and flew to Virgilia's house.
There he found Virgilia's psyche leaning on a window sill. They
greeted each other and began to converse. There we were in our
respective beds, in need of sleep, perhaps cold, while the two vaga-
bonds were together, repeating the venerable dialogue of Adam
and Eve.

55. The Venerable Dialogue of Adam and Eve:

Braz Cubas

. . . ?

Virgilia

. . . .

Braz Cubas

. . . .

. . . .

Virgilia

. . . . . !

Braz Cubas

. . . .

Virgilia

. . . .

. . . .

. . . .

Braz Cubas

. . . .

Virgilia

. . . . . .

Braz Cubas

. . . .

. . . .

. . . . ! . .

. . ! . . . .

. . . . !

Virgilia

. . . . ?

Braz Cubas

. . . . . . !

Virgilia

. . . . . . !

56. The Opportune Moment: How the devil can you account

for it? How can you explain the change? One day we saw each other, we considered marriage, we broke up, we went our respective ways, coldly, painlessly, for there had been no love; I was bitten a little by resentment, and that was all. Years go by, we see each other again, we take three or four turns of a waltz together, and there we are, madly in love. Virgilia's beauty, to be sure, had reached a high degree of perfection, but we were substantially the same people, and I, for my part, had become neither better looking nor more elegant. How can you explain the change?

Perhaps it is all a matter of the opportune moment. The first moment was not opportune because, even if neither of us was unripe for love, we were both unripe for *our* love: a fundamental distinction. Love is impossible unless the time is opportune for both parties. I discovered this explanation myself two years after the kiss, one day when Virgilia complained to me about the persistent attentions that she was receiving from a certain young coxcomb who used to frequent her house.

"He's so importunate!" she said, and she made an angry face.

I shuddered, I searched her face, I saw that her indignation was sincere. Then it occurred to me that perhaps at one time I had provoked that same expression on her face, and I understood how great had been my evolution. I had come all the way from importunity to opportunity.

57. Fate: Yes, we were in love. Now that all the laws of

society forbade it, now at last we were really in love. We were bound together like the two souls that the poet found in Purgatory: *"Di pari, como buoi, che vanno a giogo"*;

and yet I ought not compare us to oxen, for we were a very different kind of animal, less deliberate, more cunning, more lascivious. There we were, on our way but not knowing where we were going nor by what hidden paths we would travel—a problem that frightened me for several weeks, but whose solution I decided to leave to fate. Poor Fate! Old dispenser of human affairs, we do not hear much about you these days; humanity seems to have exiled you. Maybe you are taking on a new skin, a new face, new manners, a new name, and when we least expect you . . . I forget where I was . . . Oh yes, in hidden paths. I told myself that from now on things were in God's hands. It was our destiny to love each other; otherwise how could one account for the waltz and all the rest? Virgilia arrived at the same conclusion. One day, after she had confessed to me that she had moments of remorse, and I had told her that, if she had remorse, it was because she did not love me, Virgilia put her magnificent arms around me and murmured:

"I love you, it is heaven's will."

And she would not have said such a thing lightly; Virgilia was rather religious. She did not go to Mass on Sundays, it is true; I think she only went to church on holy days, and then only if she could obtain a seat in a reserved pew. But she prayed fervently (or at least sleepily) every night. She was afraid of thunder; upon hearing it, she would stop her ears and mumble all the prayers in the catechism. On a table in her bedroom she had a little altar of carved rosewood, perhaps eighteen inches high, with three images inside; but she never spoke about it to her friends; on the contrary, she charged those who were even moderately religious with being fanatics. For a time I suspected that she was ashamed of her beliefs and that her religion was like red flannel underwear, protective and clandestine; apparently, however, I was wrong.

58. A Confidence:

At the beginning, I was afraid of Lobo Neves. Pure imagination on my part. He adored his wife and was not ashamed to tell me so again and again; he found Virgilia to be perfection itself, a combination of fine, solid qualities, lovable, beautiful, immaculate—a model wife. And his confidences to me did not stop there. The door, at first slightly ajar, became in time wide open. One day he confessed to me that there was an open sore in his life: he had not attained great public recognition. I tried to hearten him; I told him many flattering things, which he heard with an almost religious fervor. I knew then that his ambition, although tired of beating its wings without being able to fly, was deathless. A few days later he told me about all his failures and disappointments, the bitter pills he had to swallow, his suppressed hatreds; he told me that political life was a web of jealousy, spite, intrigue, betrayal, selfishness, vanity. Apparently he was going through a crisis of dejection. I said something in an effort to cheer him.

"I know what I'm talking about," he replied despondently. "You can't imagine what I've gone through. I went into politics because I liked it, because my family wanted me to, because I was ambitious, and maybe partly out of egotism. So, you see, I had all the motives that lead a man to public service—except a taste for intrigue and treachery. I had seen the show from a seat in the orchestra, and by God it was fine! Beautiful scenery, life, movement, expert performers. I signed up with the troupe; they gave me a role that . . . But why should I bore you with all this? Maybe I'll get used to the heartache; believe me, I've spent endless days with it already. There's no real friendship, no gratitude, nothing . . . nothing . . . nothing . . ."

He became silent, deeply depressed, looking into space as if he could hear nothing but the echo of his own thoughts. After a few moments he rose and gave me his hand. "Forgive me for unburdening myself this way," he said. "The fact is that I had a little disappointment today that bit into my heart. You'll probably laugh at me for taking everything so seriously." And he uttered a dismal laugh. Then he asked me not to tell anyone what he had said; I assured him that he had said nothing unusual, nothing with which many other persons would not agree. At this point two deputies and a district leader came to see Lobo Neves. He received them with jollity, at first a bit forced but soon quite natural. After half an hour one would have thought him the happiest man in the world; he was chatting, bantering, laughing, they were all laughing.

59. An Old Friend: "Politics must be a heady wine," I said to myself as I left Lobo Neves' house; and I went my way undisturbed until, in the Rua dos Barbonos, I saw a coach. Inside was one of the ministers of state, an old schoolmate of mine. We greeted each other cordially, and the coach went its way . . .

"Why shouldn't I be a minister of state?"

This brilliant idea began to perform such wild capers that I just stood and watched it, admiringly. I forgot Lobo Neves and his opinions; I felt the spell of the jungle. I thought about that old schoolmate of mine, his running around on the hills, his fun and his mischief, I compared the boy with the man; and I asked myself why I could not do what he had done. I entered the Passeio Publico [a small park]; everything there greeted me with the same question. "Why shouldn't you be a minister, Cubas?" "Cubas, why shouldn't you be a minister of state?" A delicious sensation ran through my whole body. I sat on a bench to mull over the idea. How happy it would make Virgilia!

After a few minutes of these refreshing thoughts, I saw coming toward me a face that I had seen before. I had certainly seen it, but I could not remember where. Picture a man thirty-eight or forty years old, tall, thin, and pale. His clothes might have escaped from the Babylonian captivity; his hat was a contemporary of Gessler's. Picture also an overcoat appreciably larger than required by his flesh—or, literally, by his bones; its original black was yielding to a dull yellow, its woolly surface had nearly vanished; of the original eight buttons, only three remained. His brown cotton trousers had two large patches at the knees, and their cuffs had been eaten away by the heels of boots that lacked both pity and blacking. At his neck fluttered the ends of a cravat of two colors, both faded, tied around a collar that had not been washed for at least a week. If I remember correctly, he was also wearing a vest, a silk vest of doubtful hue, torn here and there, and unbuttoned.

"I'll bet you don't recognize me, Mr. Cubas?" he said.

"I don't remember . . ."

"I'm Borba, Quincas Borba."

I drew back in amazement . . . Would that I had the eloquence of a Bossuet or of a Vieira to describe the ravages that time had wrought! It was Quincas Borba, the delightful playfellow of my boyhood, my old schoolmate, so inventive, so rich. Quincas Borba! No; impossible. I could not bring myself to believe that this squalid figure, this grizzled beard, this oldish ragamuffin—that this whole ruin of a man was Quincas Borba. But it was. His eyes had something of their old expression, and his smile had not lost a certain derisiveness that was peculiar to it. Meanwhile, he suffered my amazement with equanimity. After a short time I looked away from him, not only because of the repulsiveness of his appearance but also because the comparison it evoked was painful to me.

"No need to tell you the story," he said finally; "you can guess it all. A life of struggle, tribulation, and misery. Do you remember, I always used to play the role of the king? What a comedown! I end up a beggar . . ."

And, raising his right hand and shrugging his shoulders with an air of indifference, he seemed resigned to the blows of fortune and maybe even content with them. Maybe content, certainly impassive. But there was in him no suggestion of Christian humility nor of philosophical acquiescence in the divine will. Misery appeared to have calloused his soul to such a point that he could no longer feel the mud of degradation. He trailed his rags as he had formerly trailed the royal purple: with a certain indolent grace.

"Look me up," I said, "I think I can do something for you."

He smiled broadly. "You're not the first to promise me something, and I'm sure you won't be the last to disappoint me. But why? All I want is money; and I want it only because I have to eat and the restaurants don't give credit. Neither do the food venders in the streets. Almost nothing, just two cents' worth of corn meal, and the damned peddlers won't even trust me for that . . . It's hell, my . . . I was going to say my friend . . . It's hell! All the devils conspire against me. For example, so far today I haven't had anything to eat."

"No?"

"No. I left home very early. Do you know where I live? On the third step of the stairs of the São Francisco Church, on the left side as you go up; no need to knock on the door. Well-ventilated home, very fresh air. Well, I left home early, and I still haven't eaten . . ."

I took out my wallet, selected a note of five milreis—the least clean—and gave it to him. As he took it his eyes sparkled. He waved the note in the air joyfully.

"*In hoc signo vinces!*" he shouted.

And then he kissed it and caressed it tenderly many times, all with such boisterous expansiveness that I felt a mixture of nausea and pity. Borba was a highly perceptive person, and he quickly understood. He became serious, grotesquely serious; he begged my pardon for his immoderate joy, saying that it was the joy of a poverty-stricken man who for many years had not seen a note of five milreis.

"Well, you can see many more of them if you wish."

"I can?" he said eagerly.

"Yes, by working."

He made a gesture of disdain. He remained silent for a few moments. Then he told me that he positively would not work. I was annoyed with such comico-tragic degradation, and prepared to go.

"Don't go until I teach you my Philosophy of Misery," he said, planting himself in my way.

60. The Embrace:

I thought that the poor devil was crazy, and I was about to run away, when he took hold of my wrist and stared at the diamond ring that I was wearing. I felt his hand tremble with acquisitiveness.

"Magnificent!" he said.

Then he began to walk around me, examining me at length.

"You take good care of your appearance," he said. "Jewels, fine clothes . . . Just compare those shoes with mine; what a difference! Naturally. I tell you, you certainly take good care of your appearance. And the ladies? How do you get along with the ladies? Are you married?"

"No . . ."

"Neither am I."

"I live on Rua . . ."

"I don't want to know where you live," Quincas Borba interrupted. "If some day we meet again, you can give me another five milreis, but please don't ask me to go to your house for it. It's a kind of pride I have . . . Goodbye now; I see that you are impatient to go."

"Goodbye!"

"And thanks. May I express my gratitude more warmly?"

And, as he said this, he embraced me with such impetus that I could not avoid him. We finally parted; I put space between us as fast as I could. My shirt was wrinkled from the embrace, and I was weary. My feeling of pity for him had yielded entirely to disgust. If he had to live in misery, it might at least have been dignified misery. However, I could not help comparing once more the man of today with the boy I had known; nor could I help facing the abyss that separates the expectations of one day from the realities of another . . .

"To the devil with all that! It must be time for dinner," I said to myself.

I put my hand in my vest pocket and did not find my watch. Borba had stolen it during the embrace.

61. A Project: I ate in sadness. It was not the loss of the watch that hurt me, it was the picture of the thief together with my recollections of the boy, and once again the comparison and the conclusion. From the soup on, the yellow, morbid flower of Chapter 25 began to open within me, and I ate rapidly in order to hurry to Virgilia's house. Virgilia represented the present; I wanted to take refuge in it from persecution by the past, for the meeting with Quincas Borba had brought before my eyes the past, not as it had really been, but larcenous, ragged, and degraded.

I left my house, but it was too early; I would have found them still at table. I thought about Quincas Borba again, and I had a desire to go back to the Passeio Publico to see if I could find him; his regeneration surged up in my mind as an absolute necessity. I went, but I did not find him. I spoke to the guard; he told me that "that fellow" came around there fairly often.

"At what time?"

"He has no regular time."

Perhaps I would find him there another day; I promised myself to return. The need to regenerate him, to persuade him to work, to restore his self-respect, filled my heart. I began to feel a well-being, a spiritual elevation . . . Night had fallen; I went to Virgilia.

62. The Pillow: I went to Virgilia; I quickly forgot Quincas Borba. Virgilia was the pillow on which I rested my soul, a soft, cool, balsamic pillow, with a cambric pillowslip bordered with fine lace. There I could find refuge from unhappiness, or from mere annoyance, or even from deep misery. And, in the last analysis, this must have been Virgilia's *raison d'être*. Five minutes sufficed to put Quincas Borba entirely out of my mind; five minutes of mutual contemplation, with her hands in mine; five minutes and a kiss. And out went the memory of Quincas Borba . . . You hideous ragamuffin, you emaciated ghost, what does it matter to me that you exist and that you frighten other people, if I have two square feet of a divine pillow on which to shut my eyes and sleep?

63. Let's Run Away!

But, alas, I could not always sleep. Three weeks after my meeting with Quincas Borba, on going to Virgilia's house—it was four o'clock in the afternoon—I found her downcast. She did not want to tell me what it was; but, as I insisted:

"I think Damião suspects something. He has been acting a little strangely . . . I don't know . . . He treats me well, all right; but his expression when he looks at me is different. I don't sleep well. Last night I woke up terrified; I had dreamed that he was about to kill me. Maybe I'm wrong, but I think he suspects . . ."

I calmed her as best I could; I said that he might have political worries. Virgilia agreed, but remained very nervous. We were in the living room, which faced the grounds where we had exchanged our first kiss. A window was open, and the air gently disturbed the curtains; I stood looking at them without seeing them. I had picked up the binoculars of my imagination. I could spy in the distance a house of our own, a life of our own, a world of our own, in which there was no Lobo Neves, no marriage, no morality, no other restraint to inhibit the free expansion of our wills. This idea intoxicated me; with the world, morality, and her husband all eliminated, we would share our house with no one but the angels.

"Virgilia," I said, "I have a proposition to make to you."

"What is it?"

"Do you love me?"

"Oh!" she sighed, putting her arms around my neck.

This reply was the patent truth; Virgilia loved me to distraction. Silent, breathing rather heavily, her arms around my neck, Virgilia looked at me a long while, her large eyes giving a strange impression of moist light. I was content to return her look and to fall in love again with her mouth, fresh as dawn and insatiable as death. There was now something magnificent about Virgilia's beauty, something grandiose that it had not had before her marriage. She was a figure carved with noble, pure craftsmanship, in Pentelic marble; as tranquilly beautiful as a statue but neither apathetic nor cold. On the contrary, she was a recapitulation of all the aspects of love; especially on this occasion, when she said, without words, everything warm and loving that the human eye can express. But time was pressing; I removed her arms from around my neck, held her by the wrists, and, gazing steadily at her, asked whether she had courage.

"To do what?"

"To run away. We'll find a place that suits us—big house or little house, whichever you wish—in the country or in some city, maybe in Europe, wherever you wish—where no one will bother us, where you'll be out of danger, where we can live just for each other . . . Will you? We must do it. Sooner or later he's bound to suspect, and then you'll be lost . . . you'll be killed . . . and he, too, because I'll kill him, I swear I will."

I stopped. Virgilia had become very pale. She let her arms fall and sat down on the sofa. For a little while she said nothing, perhaps vacillating, perhaps terrified by the idea of discovery and death. I went to her, I repeated the proposition, I told her all the advantages of a life by ourselves, without worry, without jealousy, without fear. Virgilia heard me in silence; then she said:

"Perhaps we would not really escape; he would find me and kill me just the same."

I showed her that it would not be so. The world was very big, and I had the means to permit us to live wherever there were pure air and plenty of sun; he would not even look for us; only great passions are capable of great actions, and he did not love her enough to search the world for her. Virgilia made a gesture of surprise and indignation; she murmured that her husband was very fond of her.

"Maybe," I replied; "maybe so . . ."

I went to the window and began to drum with my fingers on the sill. Virgilia called me; I remained where I was, ruminating my jealousy, itching to get my hands on her husband and to strangle him . . . Just then, Lobo Neves appeared at the gate. Do not tremble so, madam reader; rest easy, not a drop of blood shall stain this page. As soon as I saw him, I waved and said something friendly. Virgilia quickly left the room, which he entered three minutes later.

"Have you been here long?" he asked.

"No."

He seemed very serious, weighed down by something, and looked about distractedly; he often acted this way. When he saw his son Nhonhô (the future college graduate of Chapter 6) enter the room, however, he became jovial and expansive; he took him in his arms, lifted him in the air, kissed him many times. I, who hated the boy, walked away from them. Virgilia returned to the room.

"Ah!" sighed Lobo Neves, sitting down wearily on the sofa.

"Tired?" I asked.

"Very; I had to listen to two endless bores, one in the Chamber and one in the street. And we still have a third one in store," he added, looking at his wife.

"What do you mean?" asked Virgilia.

"It's a . . . no, guess!"

Virgilia sat down next to him, took one of his hands, fixed his cravat, and asked what it was.

"Nothing less than box seats."

"To hear Candiani?"

"To hear Candiani."

Virgilia clapped her hands, stood up, gave her son a kiss, all with a childish manner that did not become her. Then she asked what opera was playing, and consulted her husband in a confidential whisper about her *toilette* for the occasion, the exact location of the box, and I do not know what else.

"You're eating with us," Lobo Neves said to me.

"That's why he came," said Virgilia; "he says you have the best wine in Rio de Janeiro."

"Even so, he doesn't drink much of it."

At dinner, I proved he was wrong: I drank more than usual, although not as much as I needed. Already excited, I became more so. It was the first time that I had become really angry with Virgilia. I did not look at her during dinner; I talked about politics, the press, the cabinet, I think I would have talked about theology if I had known, or rather remembered, anything about it. Lobo Neves listened to me with great placidity and dignity, and even with a certain superior benevolence; and this also irritated me and made the dinner even longer and more distressing for me. As soon as we rose from the table, I said goodbye.

"See you soon," said Lobo Neves.

"Maybe."

And I left.

64. The Deal:
I wandered through the streets until nine o'clock, and then went home and to bed. Unable to sleep, I took refuge in reading and in working on an article that I was writing. At eleven o'clock I felt sorry I had not gone to the theatre; I looked at the clock, thought of getting dressed and going. I decided, however, that I would have arrived too late; besides, it would have been evidence of weakness. Apparently Virgilia was beginning to tire of me. And this idea made me alternately desperate and indifferent, inclined to forget and inclined to kill her. I could see her there, leaning forward in the box, attracting all eyes with her magnificent nude arms—arms that were mine, only mine—the beautiful dress that she must have been wearing, her milk-white bosom, her up-swept hair-do in the style of the day, and her diamonds, less sparkling than her eyes . . . I could see her so, and it pained me that others could see her. Then I began to undress her, to take off the combs, the jewels,

and the silks with my greedy, lascivious hands, and to make her—
I do not know whether more beautiful or more natural—to make
her mine, just mine, only mine.

The next day I could not contain myself; I went early to Virgilia's house and found her eyes red from crying.

"What happened?" I asked.

"You don't love me," was her reply; "you never had the least
love for me. Yesterday you treated me as if you hated me. If I
only knew what I'd done! But I don't know. Won't you tell me
what it was?"

"What *what* was? You did nothing."

"Nothing? You treated me worse than you'd treat a dog . . ."

At this word, I took her hands and kissed them, and two tears
burst from her eyes.

"Now, now, it's all over," I said.

I had no desire to accuse her, and, besides, of what could I accuse her? It was not her fault that her husband loved her. I told
her that she had done nothing to offend me, that naturally I was
jealous of the other man, and that I could not always look happy
when he was near. I added that he might be hiding something and
that the best way to close the door to fear and dissension was to
accept my proposal of the day before.

"I've been thinking about it," said Virgilia. "A little secluded
house with a garden, all to ourselves, hidden away on some out-
of-the-way street, isn't that it? I like the idea; but why should we
run away?"

She said this in the calm and ingenuous tone of one whose mind
is free from evil, and the smile that lifted the corners of her
mouth wore the same expression of candor. Then, walking away
from her, I replied:

"It is *you* who never loved *me*."

"I?"

"That's right; you're an egotist! You'd rather see me suffer
every day . . . You're the worst kind of egotist!"

Virgilia burst into tears, and in order not to attract attention
she held her handkerchief to her mouth, trying to stifle the sobs.
Her outburst disconcerted me; if anyone heard it, all would be
lost. I bent over her, held her wrists, whispered the sweetest

names that I called her in our most intimate moments, and pointed out the danger; fear helped to calm her.

"I can't," she said after a few moments; "I can't leave my little boy, and, if we take him, Damião will go to the ends of the earth to find me. I can't. Kill me, if you like; or leave me to die . . . Oh, God! God!"

"Quiet; they'll hear you."

"Let them hear me! It doesn't matter any more."

She was highly excited. I begged her to forget everything, to forgive me; I said that I was crazy, but that my insanity derived from my need of her and that her love would cure it. Virgilia dried her eyes and gave me her hand. We both smiled. A few minutes later, we returned to the subject of the secluded house on the out-of-the-way street . . .

65. Eyes and Ears: We were interrupted by the sound of a carriage. A slave announced that it was Baroness X. Virgilia consulted me with her eyes.

"If you have such a headache," I said, "it might be better if you didn't receive her."

"Is she still in her carriage?" Virgilia asked the slave.

"No, madam, she is at the door. She says that she must talk with you."

"Show her in."

The baroness soon entered the room. I do not know whether she expected to find me there; but no one could have seemed happier to see me.

"Bless you!" she exclaimed. "Where have you been keeping yourself that no one ever sees you any more? Why, just yesterday I looked for you in the theatre. Candiani was delightful. What a woman! Do you like Candiani? Of course you do. You men are all alike. The baron was saying yesterday, in our box, that one Italian woman is worth five Brazilian. What an insult!

And an old man's insult, the worst kind. But why weren't you there?"

"A headache."

"Go on! Some love affair, more likely; don't you think so, Virgilia? All right, my friend, but you'd better hurry, because you must be forty . . . or nearly . . . You are forty, aren't you?"

"I can't say with any degree of certainty," I replied; "but, if you'll excuse me now, I'll go take a look at my birth certificate."

"Go, go . . ." And, giving me her hand, "When shall we see you? We'll be at home Saturday. The baron has missed you."

When I got to the street, I was sorry I had left. The baroness was one of the people who were most suspicious of us. She was fifty-five years old, but had a softness, a smile, an elegance of carriage, and even a beauty of face that made her seem no more than forty. Usually she did not talk very much; she had the great art of listening to others and spying out their secrets. She would lean back in her chair, unsheathe a long, well-tempered look, and wait. The other person, not knowing what she was up to, would talk, gesticulate, adopt various facial expressions, while she just observed the person, now fixedly, now shifting her gaze, and sometimes she even looked within herself, as one could tell because she would lower her eyelids. But these eyelids were deceptive: rearranging her ideas in the light of the new information, she was still looking at the other person, reconstructing his life and dissecting his soul.

Another individual who may have suspected us was Viegas, a relative of Virgilia. He was a wreck of seventy winters, yellowish and sunken-cheeked, who suffered from a persistent rheumatism, an equally persistent asthma, and a lesion of the heart; he was a miniature hospital. His eyes, however, shone with vitality. During the first weeks, Virgilia had no fear of him; she told me that, when Viegas stared at one as if he was ferreting out one's inmost secrets, he was merely counting money to himself. He was, in truth, a great miser.

There was also Virgilia's cousin, Luiz Dutra. Because of his suspicions, I had changed my policy toward him and was now seeking to disarm him by talking to him about his verses and his prose and by introducing him to my acquaintances. When they recognized his name and seemed really pleased to know him, Luiz Dutra was exultant; and I benefited from his happiness with the expectation that he would not denounce us.

There were also two or three ladies and a few fashionable young idlers; and of course the household slaves, who found in gossip about us a sort of revenge for their servile condition. All this constituted a forest of eyes and ears, among which we had to slide with the furtiveness and cunning of snakes.

66. Legs:

While I was thinking about these people, my legs were carrying me along, street after street, until, to my surprise, I found myself at the door of the Hotel Pharoux. I was in the habit of dining there; but, as on this occasion I had not gone there deliberately, credit for my arrival belongs not to me but to my legs, which did it all themselves. Blessed legs! And yet some people treat you with indifference. Even I, until then, had a low opinion of you, and I got angry when you became tired, when you could not go beyond a certain point and left me as eager to fly and as unable to do so as a chicken with its legs tied.

On this occasion, however, you were a ray of sunshine. Yes, loyal legs, you left to my head the task of thinking about Virgilia, and you said to one another, "He has a problem on his mind, it's dinner time, so let's take him to the Pharoux. Let's split his consciousness; we'll let the lady take one part of it, but we'll take the other, so that he will go straight there, will not bump into pedestrians and carts, will tip his hat to acquaintances, and will finally arrive safe and sound at the hotel." And you carried out your project to the letter, beloved legs; in appreciation of which kindness I have now immortalized you.

67. The Little House: I dined and went home. There I found a cigar box, ostensibly from Lobo Neves; it was wrapped in silk paper and tied with pink ribbons. I understood, opened it, and found this note:

> My B . . . ,
>   They suspect us; all is lost; forget me forever. We must never see each other again. Forget your unhappy
>   V . . . a

This was a terrible blow; as soon as night fell, I hurried to Virgilia's house. Although she had changed her mind about never seeing me again, she was utterly miserable. The baroness had told her frankly that people had talked a great deal in the theatre the prior evening about my absence from Lobo Neves' box and had discussed my relationship with the family; in short, we were objects of public gossip. Virgilia said she was at her wits' end.

"The best thing to do is to run away," I suggested.

"Never," she replied, shaking her head.

I saw that it was impossible to deal separately with either of two things, neither of which she would willingly give up: her respectability and our love. Virgilia was capable of great and equal sacrifices to keep both, and flight would leave her only one. Perhaps I felt something very like resentment; but in my emotional tumult of the past two days, it quickly died. All right; let us get a little house on an out-of-the-way street.

A few days later I found one in Gambôa that was virtually made to order for us. A gem! New, freshly whitewashed, four windows in front and two on each side, brick-colored shutters, creeping vines at the corners, garden in front; mystery and seclusion. A gem!

We agreed that a certain woman, whom Virgilia knew, would move in; this woman had lived in the Dutra home with a status much like that of a poor relative and had done all the dress-making and sewing for the family. She fairly worshipped Virgilia. We would not tell her everything at the start; in time she would accept the situation.

For me this was a new phase in our love, an appearance of exclusive possession, of absolute dominion, something that would pacify my conscience and preserve decorum. I was sick and tired of the other man's curtains, his chairs, his rug, his sofa, all the things that would not let me forget our duplicity. Now I could avoid the frequent dinners, the tea every evening, and the presence of their child. The house would free me from it all; the ordinary world would end at the door. Inside, would be the infinite, an eternal, higher world, with no laws, no institutions, no baronesses, no hostile eyes or ears; only one couple, one life, one will, one affection, one private world—spiritual unity by exclusion of everything that might conflict with it.

68. The Master: Such were my reflections as I walked through Valongo after looking at the house and making arrangements to rent it. My thoughts were interrupted by the sight of a crowd, gathered around a Negro who was whipping another Negro. The victim did not try to flee; he merely groaned, "No, have mercy, master; master, have mercy!" But the other responded to each supplication with a new lash of the whip.

"Take that, devil!" he was saying. "Here's some more mercy for you, drunkard."

"Master!" groaned the victim.

"Shut your mouth, beast!"

I stopped, I looked . . . Good heavens! The whipper was none other than my slave boy Prudencio, whom my father had freed some years earlier. I approached him; he stopped immediately and kissed my hand. I asked him whether the other Negro was his slave.

"Yes, Nhonhô, he is."

"Has he done something?"

"He's a loafer and a big drunkard. Today I left him in my market-stall while I went downtown, and he left the stall and went to a saloon."

"I see; but don't whip him any more," I said. "Forgive him."

"Certainly, Nhonhô. Whatever Nhonhô wishes. Go home, drunkard."

The crowd eyed me wonderingly and whispered its conjectures. As I continued on my way, many were the reflections that passed through my mind, but I am afraid I have forgotten almost all of them; a pity, because they would have provided material for a good chapter, possibly a jolly one. I like jolly chapters; they are my weakness.

On the outside the episode I had witnessed was grim; but only on the outside. When I opened it up with the knife of rational analysis, I found a curious and profound kernel. It was Prudencio's way of ridding himself of the blows he had received—passing them on to someone else. I, as a child, had sat on his back, had put a rein in his mouth, and had beaten him mercilessly; he had groaned and suffered. Now, however, that he was free and could move his arms and legs when and as he pleased, now that he could work, relax, sleep, as he willed, unrestrained, now he rose and became top man: he bought a slave and paid to him, in full and with interest, the amount he had received from me. See how clever the rascal was!

69. A Grain of Folly: Prudencio's ingenuity brings to my mind a madman I once knew. His name was Romualdo and he thought himself Tamerlane. This was the only subject on which he was mad, and he had a curious explanation, which he gave to all skeptical inquirers.

"I am the great Tamerlane," he would say. "I used to be Romualdo, but I fell ill, and I took so much cream of tartar, so much cream of tartar, so much cream of tartar, that I became a Tartar and finally rose to be king of the Tartars. Cream of tartar, you know, can turn you into a Tartar."

Poor Romualdo! People would laugh at his reply, but probably the reader did not laugh, and the reader was right; I find nothing funny in it. When one heard it, it seemed amusing; but, set forth on paper and in connection with beatings received and transferred, it suggests this unpleasant thought: Is it possible that Romualdo and Prudencio were really doing the same thing, maybe even for the same reason—although one was mad and the other sane? An unpleasant thought. Let us return to the little house in Gambôa.

70. Dona Placida: Let us return to the little house. You would be unable to enter it today, curious reader; it became old, discolored, tumbledown, and the owner razed it. On the same site he built a new house four times as large, but I swear that it was much smaller than the first. The known world was too small for Alexander; the eaves of a roof are infinity for a swallow.

Note how democratic is the earth. Today a respectable married couple sleeps on the same bit of ground that yesterday suffered a couple living in sin. Tomorrow a priest may sleep there, then a murderer, then a blacksmith, then a poet; and, like shipwrecked persons whose lifeboat has delivered them safely to shore, they will bless this bit of ground, for it gives them the illusion of security.

Virgilia made the house a joy to see; she selected furnishings perfectly suited to the rooms and placed them with the aesthetic intuition of a gentlewoman. I brought a few books there. And everything was under the care of Dona Placida, the ostensible, and in some respects the real, lady of the house.

It was not easy for her to accept the charge of our house; she had scented our situation, and it pained her to serve in that capacity; but finally she agreed to do so. I think she cried at first and that she loathed herself for what she was doing. At least she hardly looked at me during the first two months; when she spoke to me her eyes were always lowered, and she was serious, unsmiling, sometimes obviously despondent. I wanted to win her over; I treated her with kindness and respect, and never let myself appear to be offended. With considerable effort, I won first her good will, then her confidence. When I knew I had her confidence, I trumped up a pathetic story of the great love between Virgilia and me before she married, her father's obduracy, her husband's cruelty, and I do not remember what other novelette clichés. Dona Placida accepted every page of the novelette; her conscience required her to do so. After six months, anyone who had seen all three of us together would have thought that Dona Placida was my mother-in-law.

I was not unappreciative: I established a fund of five contos— the five contos that I had found in Botafogo—for her as a bulwark against poverty in her old age. Dona Placida thanked me with tears in her eyes and thereafter prayed for me every night before an image of the Virgin that she had in her room.

71. The Defect of This Book: I am beginning to be sorry that
I ever undertook to write this book. Not that it bores me; I have nothing else to do; indeed, it is a welcome distraction from eternity. But the book is tedious, it smells of the tomb, it has a *rigor mortis* about it; a serious fault, and yet a relatively small one, for the great defect of this book is you, reader. You want to live fast, to get to the end, and the book ambles along slowly; you like straight, solid narrative and a smooth style, but this book and my style are like a pair of drunks: they stagger to the right and to

the left, they start and they stop, they mutter, they roar, they guffaw, they threaten the sky, they slip and fall . . .

And fall! Unhappy leaves of my cypress tree, you had to fall, like everything else that is lovely and beautiful; if I had eyes, I would shed a tear of remembrance for you. And this is the great advantage in being dead, that if you have no mouth with which to laugh, neither have you eyes with which to cry.

72. The Bibliomaniac: Perhaps I shall eliminate the preceding chapter. Among other reasons, there is, in the last few lines, something that might be construed as an error on my part, and I do not wish to add fuel to the fire of criticism.

Let us look into the future. Seventy years from now, a thin, sallow, gray-haired fellow, who loves nothing but books, is bent over the preceding page trying to find the error. He reads, he rereads, he reads between the lines, he takes the words apart, he picks up one syllable, then another, then a third, and one by one the rest, he looks at them inside and out, he examines them against the light, he dusts them off, he rubs them on his trouser-leg, he washes them, and all in vain; he does not find the error.

He is a bibliomaniac. He does not know the author; the name Braz Cubas does not appear in his biographical dictionaries. He came upon the book by accident in a dirty, old second-hand bookstore. He bought it for two hundred reis. He inquired, studied, hunted in other stores and in libraries, and came to the conclusion that it was the only copy in existence . . . The only copy! You who not merely love books but are, almost literally, crazy about them, you know what "the only copy" really means and you can therefore guess the ecstasy of my bibliomaniac. He would reject the crown of the Indies, the papacy, all the museums in Italy and in Holland, if he had to give up this only copy in exchange for them. And not because it is a copy of my *Memoirs*;

he would feel the same way about Laemmert's *Almanack* if it were the only copy in existence.

There he is, bent over the page, with a monocle in his right eye, wholly devoted to the noble but rugged task of ferreting out the error. He has already promised himself to write a little monograph in which he will relate the finding of the book and the discovery of the error, if there really is one hidden there. In the end, he discovers nothing and contents himself with possession of the book. He closes it, gazes at it, gazes at it again, goes to the window and holds it in the sun. The only copy! At this moment a Caesar or a Cromwell passes beneath his window, on the road to power and glory. He turns his back, closes the window, stretches in his hammock, and fingers the leaves of the book slowly, lovingly, tasting it sip by sip . . . An only copy!

73. Afternoon Snack:
The possible error made me lose another chapter. How much better it would be to tell things smoothly, without all these jolts! I have already compared my style to the progress of a drunk. If this analogy seems indecorous to you, let me offer another: my style is like the afternoon snacks I had with Virgilia in the little house in Gambôa. Wine, fruit, compotes. We would eat, to be sure, but the meal was always punctuated with sweet nothings, with tender glances, with childish whims, with an infinitude of these asides of the heart that constitute the true, uninterrupted discourse of love. Sometimes a little spat would temper the sweetness. She would leave the table and would take refuge in a corner of the sofa, or in another room where she could listen to Dona Placida's affectionate reassurances. Five or ten minutes later we would retie the thread of our conversation, as I retie the thread of the narrative from time to time, only to break it again. Not that we were afraid of conventionality; indeed, we would invite it, in the person of Dona Placida, to sit with us at the table; but she never accepted.

"You act as if you don't like me any more," Virgilia said to her one day.

"Mary-Mother-of-God!" exclaimed the good woman, raising her hands in the air. "Not like Yayá! Then whom in the world would I like?"

And, taking Virgilia's hands, she looked fixedly into her eyes, until her own eyes watered. Virgilia put her arms about her; I slipped a silver coin into the pocket of her dress.

74. The Personal History of Dona Placida:

Never repent your acts of generosity; the silver coin gained me Dona Placida's complete confidence and thus made possible this chapter. One day when I found her alone in the house we began to talk, and she told me in a few words her personal history . . . She was the natural child of the sacristan of a cathedral and of a woman who made cakes and candy on order. At the age of ten she lost her father. By then she had already begun to grate cocoanuts and to do all sorts of other work compatible with her age. At fifteen or sixteen she married a tailor, who died of consumption a few years later, leaving her with a two-year-old daughter. The young widow had also to take care of her mother, who was worn out from a lifetime of work. Thus she had to support three people. She made cakes and candy on order; she sewed industriously day and night for three or four stores; on the side, she tutored several children in the district for one milreis per month. Thus the years passed away, but not her beauty, for she had never had any. From time to time she had a few minor flirtations; also some would-be seducers, whom she rejected.

"If I could have found another husband," she told me, "believe me, I would have married again; but nobody wanted to marry me."

One of the would-be seducers managed to get into her good

graces; but, as his intentions were no more honorable than those of the others, she sent him, too, on his way and, after doing so, cried a long time. She went on sewing and stirring the pots. Her mother was peevish by temperament, by years, and by financial necessity; she continually tried to mortify Dona Placida into accepting a borrowed or occasional "husband" from among those who sought this status. And she shouted:

"Do you want to be better than your mother? I don't know where you get these highflown notions. My fine friend, life doesn't give you things on a silver platter; you can't eat air. Who do you think you are? Fine young fellows like Polycarpo at the tavern, poor thing . . . Are you waiting for a high-society beau?"

Dona Placida swore to me that she was not waiting for a high-society beau. It was her nature. She wanted to be married. She knew very well that her mother had not been, and she knew some women who had only lovers; but it was her nature and she wanted to be married. And she wanted the same thing for her daughter. She worked very hard, burning her fingers on the stove and her eyes at the lamp, in order that they might eat without falling into sin. She grew thin, she became sick, she lost her mother, she buried her by public subscription, and she continued to work. Her daughter was fourteen, but frail, and did nothing except flirt with the cheap fellows who hung around her window. Dona Placida took great precautions, even making the girl go with her when she went to deliver things she had sewn. The store people looked knowingly and winked at each other, certain that she had brought her along in the hope of catching a husband or something else. Some made wisecracks or called the girl endearing names; some even offered the mother money . . .

She stopped a moment, but soon continued:

"My daughter ran away with a fellow—I don't know his name and don't want to know it. She left me all alone and so sad, so sad, that I thought I would die. I had no one else in the world, and I was sick and almost an old woman. About then, I became acquainted with Yayá's family: fine people, who gave me work and had me live at their house. I was there many months, a year, more than a year, sewing and helping out. I left when Yayá got married. Then I made a living however God let me. Look at my fingers, look at these hands . . ." And she showed me her calloused, cracked hands, the tips of her fingers pricked by a thousand needles. "They didn't get this way by accident, sir; only God knows what I went through . . . But then Yayá helped me, and you did, sir, too . . . I was afraid I'd end up in the street, begging . . ."

As she said this last word, Dona Placida shuddered. Then, as if coming to herself, she seemed to consider the impropriety of having told her story to the lover of a married woman, and she began to laugh, to retract, to call herself crazy, full of "high-flown notions" as her mother had said. Finally, as I remained silent, she withdrew from the room. I remained there, looking at my boots.

75. To Myself: As some of my readers may have skipped the preceding chapter, let me observe that one must read it in order to understand what I said to myself just after Dona Placida left the room. I said the following:

"And so the cathedral sacristan, helping at Mass one day, saw the woman come in who was to be his collaborator in producing Dona Placida. He saw her on other days, perhaps over a period of several weeks; he liked her; he said something flattering to her, he touched her foot with his, while lighting the altars on holy days. She liked him, they drew near to each other, they fell in love. From this conjunction of vagrant lusts, issued Dona Placida. Probably Dona Placida did not speak when she was born, but if she did, she might have said to the authors of her days, 'Here I am. Why did you summon me?' And the sacristan and his lady naturally would have replied, 'We summoned you so that you would burn your fingers on pots and your eyes in sewing; so that you would eat little or nothing, rush around, become sick and then get well so that you might become sick again; sad today, desperate tomorrow, finally resigned, but always with your hands on the pot and your eyes on the sewing, until you wind up in the gutter or in a hospital. That is why we summoned you, in a moment of love.' "

76. The Fertilizer: My conscience attacked me, accused me of having overcome Dona Placida's integrity, of having consigned her to an indecent role after a long life of hard work and privation. An intermediary is no better than the concubine herself, and I had lowered her to this office by means of money and kindness. So spoke my conscience; and for ten minutes I could find no reply. It added that I had taken advantage of the ex-seamstress's love for Virgilia, of her gratitude, and of her poverty. It referred to Dona Placida's resistance at first, to her tears during the early days, her sad face, her silence, her lowered eyes, and to my Machiavellian tact in the face of all this. And it shook me in an irritated and nervous manner.

I agreed with the facts alleged by my conscience, but I alleged in reply that now Dona Placida would not have to resort to beggary, and that this compensated her for the rest. If it had not been for my illicit love, probably Dona Placida would have faced the same miserable old age as so many other human creatures. From this observation one may reason that vice is often the fertilizing manure of virtue. Which does not prevent virtue from being a fragrant and healthy flower. My conscience agreed, and I went to open the door for Virgilia.

77. In Error: Virgilia entered, calm and smiling. Time had cured her fear and her sense of guilt. How sweet it had been during the early days to see her enter, trembling and ashamed! She had come in a coach, her face veiled,

[123]

wrapping herself in a large shawl that concealed the curves of her figure. The first time, she had thrown herself on the sofa, breathless, blushing, looking at the floor; and, on my word, never before or since have I found her so beautiful, perhaps because on no other occasion did I feel so deeply flattered.

Now, however, as I was saying, the fear and the shame were ended; our meetings entered the period of normality. The intensity of our love had not altered; the difference was that our flame had lost the madness of the early days and had become a shaft of light, tranquil and steady, as in marriage.

"I am very angry with you," she said as she sat down.

"Why?"

"Because you didn't come yesterday as you said you would. Damião asked again and again whether I didn't think you'd come at least for tea. What happened?"

I had indeed failed to keep my promise, and the fault was entirely Virgilia's. A matter of jealousy. This magnificent woman knew the reason very well but wanted to hear me confess it. The evening before, at the baroness's house, she had danced twice with the same coxcomb, after standing with him near a window for several minutes listening to his gallantries. She had been so happy, so expansive, so glad to be desired! When she had discovered, between my eyebrows, an interrogatory wrinkle, she had not started nor become suddenly serious; but she had cast the coxcomb and his gallantries into the sea. She had come to me, taken my arm, and led me to the other room, where there had been fewer people; there she had complained to me of fatigue and had said many other things in the childish manner that she affected on certain occasions. I had heard her in almost complete silence.

Now, sitting on the sofa in our little house, it was hard for me to bring myself to answer her question, but finally I confessed the reason for my absence . . . Eternal stars, I never saw a more amazed expression on a face! Mouth agape, eyebrows arched, visible, almost tangible stupefaction—this was Virgilia's first reply. She shook her head, with a smile of pity and tenderness that completely confused me.

And she went to take off her hat, as light and gay as a little girl home from school. Then she came to me and, with one finger, tapped me several times on the forehead, saying, "Take that . . . and that . . . and that"; and I could do nothing but laugh, and everything ended in merriment. Obviously I had been in error.

78. The Governorship:
One day, several months later, Lobo Neves came home and said that he might receive the governorship of a province. He and I both looked at Virgilia and saw her face pale. He asked:

"Don't you like the idea, Virgilia?"

She shook her head.

"I don't like it very much," was her reply.

Nothing more was said; but in the evening Lobo Neves talked again about the project, a little more resolutely than in the afternoon. Two days later he informed his wife that the governorship was definitely his. Virgilia could not hide her repugnance. Lobo Neves talked about political considerations.

"I can't refuse what they offer me; it's a good thing for our future and for the prestige of our family, my love, because, remember, I promised to make you a marchioness and so far you're not even a baroness. You say that I am ambitious. I am indeed, and you must not tie stones to my wings."

Virgilia was all at sea. The following day I found her despondent, waiting for me in the house in Gambôa. She had told everything to Dona Placida, who was seeking to console her. I was as despondent as Virgilia.

"You must go with us," she said.

"Are you mad? It would be foolhardy."

"But then what . . . ?"

"Then we must defeat the whole project."

"That's impossible."

"Has he already accepted?"

"I think so."

I rose, threw my hat on a chair, and began to pace up and down, not knowing what to do. I thought a long time and found no way out of our predicament. Finally, however, I walked over to Virgilia, who had remained seated, and took both her hands in mine. Dona Placida went to the window.

"My whole life is in these little hands," I said; "you are responsible for it. Do what you think best."

Virgilia made a worried gesture. I leaned against the cabinet, facing her. Several moments of silence went by; we heard only the barking of a dog and possibly the sound of waves breaking on the beach. Virgilia stared at the floor with lusterless eyes, her hands resting limply on her lap, her fingers interlaced, in an attitude of supreme hopelessness. Seeing her so dejected for any other reason, I would surely have thrown myself at her feet, would have comforted her with my tenderness, would have guided her with my mind; now, however, it was necessary to force her to make the effort on her own, to make the sacrifice, to take responsibility for our life together, and therefore it was necessary for me to deprive her of my help, to leave her, to go out; this is exactly what I did.

"I repeat, my happiness is in your hands," I said.

Virgilia wanted to hold me back, but I was already out the door. I heard a bursting into tears, and I tell you that I was on the point of turning back so that I might dispel them with a kiss; but I mastered myself.

79. Compromise: If I had to relate in detail what I suffered during the next few hours, I should never finish. I vacillated between wanting and not wanting, between the pity that drew me toward Virgilia's house and another sentiment—egotism, let us suppose—that kept saying,

"Don't go; leave her alone with the problem, leave her alone so that she herself may resolve it in favor of love." The two forces were equally strong, each fighting tenaciously and neither willing to yield. Sometimes I felt a little pinch of remorse; it seemed to me that I was abusing the weakness of a woman who loved me and who, for my sake, was living in sin without any sacrifice or risk on my part. But when I was about to capitulate, along came egotism repeating its advice, and I remained irresolute and miserable, eager to see her but afraid that I would then have to share the responsibility for the solution.

Finally I found a compromise between egotism and pity: I would go and see her only in her house, in the presence of her husband, not to tell her anything but only to await her decision. Thus I could reconcile the two forces. Now, as I write this, it seems to me that the compromise was a fraud, that this pity was really a form of egotism, and that my desire to go and console Virgilia was prompted by my own suffering.

80. The Secretaryship:

And so, the next evening, I went to Lobo Neves' house. They were both there, Virgilia very sad, he very jovial. I am sure that she felt a certain relief when our eyes met, full of questions and tenderness. Lobo Neves talked to me about the governorship, the local difficulties in the province, his hopes, his plans. He was so happy, so eager! Virgilia was pretending to read a book, but from time to time she glanced at me above the page, inquisitive and anxious.

"The trouble," said Lobo Neves suddenly, "is that I haven't yet found a secretary."

"No?"

"No, but I have an idea."

"Ah!"

"An idea . . . How would you like to take a trip to the North?"

I do not remember what I said.

"You're rich," he continued, "you don't need the homeopathic salary; but if you want to make me happy, you'll come along with me as secretary."

My mind stepped back warily, as if it had seen a snake. I looked hard into Lobo Neves' face to see if I could catch some sign of a hidden thought . . . His glance was straight and open; the placid expression on his face was natural, not forced, and suggested joy rather than machinations. I breathed easier. I lacked courage to look toward Virgilia; I could feel her looking at me over the book, asking me the same thing that her husband had asked, and I said yes, I would go. In truth, our being governor, governor's wife, and secretary would resolve things along administrative lines.

81. The Reconciliation: On my leaving Lobo Neves' house, however, a shadow of doubt crossed my mind; I wondered whether the arrangement would not recklessly endanger Virgilia's reputation, whether there was not some other reasonable means of reconciling Gambôa with the Government. I found none. When I got out of bed the next day, my mind was made up: I would accept the appointment. At noon a servant came to tell me that a lady wearing a veil was awaiting me in the living room. I hurried there. It was my sister Sabina.

"We mustn't go on this way," she said; "once and for all, let's make peace with each other. Our family is dying out; we shouldn't act like enemies."

"I agree, with all my heart, sister!" I cried, holding out my arms to her.

I sat her next to me. I talked to her about her husband, his business, their daughter, everything. And everything, according to Sabina, was going well; the daughter was as beautiful as love itself. Cotrim would come and show her to me if I was agreeable.

"What do you mean! Why, I'm going to call on you to see the young lady."

"Really?"

"Word of honor."

"So much the better," said Sabina, smiling. "It's high time we stopped all this nonsense."

I found her a little stouter and perhaps more youthful. She was about thirty years old and looked twenty. Affable, charming, no embarrassment, no resentment. We gazed at each other, holding hands, talking of everything and of nothing, like two lovers. My infancy, fresh, naughty, and towheaded, was rising before me; the years were falling away like cards that I had played with as a child, and I saw our house, our family, our parties. With some effort, I was able to control my feelings; but a barber in the neighborhood decided then to invade my memory with the drone of his violin, and this voice—for until then the memory had been mute—this voice from the past, nasal and nostalgic, stirred me so deeply that . . .

Her eyes were dry. Sabina had not inherited the morbid, yellow flower. What did it matter? She was my sister, my blood, a part of my mother, and I told her so, earnestly, tenderly . . . Suddenly I heard a knock; I opened the door; I saw an angel about five years old.

"Come in, Sarah," said Sabina.

It was my niece. I lifted her and kissed her many times; the child, frightened, pushed my shoulder with her little hand, twisting her body to get away . . . At this moment I saw a hat at the door and then a man, none other than Cotrim. I was so deeply touched that I left the child and threw myself into the father's arms. Perhaps this effusion disconcerted him a little; he seemed embarrassed. But he soon got over it. In a short time we were talking like old friends. No allusion to the past, many plans for the future, promises to dine at each other's house. I explained that this exchange of dinners might suffer a short interruption because I was thinking of taking a trip North. Sabina looked at Cotrim, Cotrim looked at Sabina; they agreed that my idea did not make sense. What in the devil could I find in the North? Ought I not continue my brilliant career here in the capital, where I outshone all the other young men of the time? For, in truth, none of them could be compared to me; he, Cotrim, had watched my progress from a distance and, in spite of our ridiculous quarrel, he had always taken an interest, even pride, in my triumphs. He heard what they were saying about me in the streets, in the salons; it was a symphony of praise and admiration. And to abandon all this in order to spend a few months in the provinces, unnecessarily, without serious purpose? Unless it was a matter of politics . . .

"That's exactly what it is," I said.

"Even so, you ought not go," he replied after a moment's pause.

And then, after another pause, "Anyway, come to our house for dinner today."

"With pleasure; but tomorrow or soon after, you must dine with me."

"I don't know, I don't know," objected Sabina; "a bachelor's house . . . You ought to get married, brother. And I want a niece, understand?"

Cotrim checked her with a gesture which I did not exactly comprehend. No matter; the reconciliation of a family is much more important than an enigmatic gesture.

82. A Matter of Botany: Let the melancholy say what they will, life is sweet. This is what I thought as I watched Sabina, her husband, and the child bustling down the stairs and saying affectionate things to me, who, from the head of the stairs, said equally affectionate things in return. Yes, it was sweet. I was to go away with a fine woman who loved me and with her husband who trusted me, and my family and I had become reconciled. What more could I expect of twenty-four hours?

This same day, in an effort to create the proper public attitude toward my adventure, I began to spread the news that I might go to the North as provincial secretary in order to further certain political purposes of a personal nature. I said this in the Rua do Ouvidor and, the next day, repeated it in the Pharoux and in the theatre. Connecting my nomination with that of Lobo Neves, which was already being bruited although not yet confirmed, some people smiled maliciously, others slapped him on the shoulder as if to congratulate him. In the theatre, a lady remarked to me that I was carrying a bit far my love for sculpture—a not too subtle allusion to Virgilia's beautiful figure.

But the boldest reference made to the subject in my presence was a remark dropped three days later in Sabina's house by an elderly surgeon named Garcez. He was small, trivial in speech, and much given to gossip, and would doubtless go on to the age of seventy or even eighty or ninety years without ever acquiring that dignified composure that should be the finest characteristic of an elderly person. A ridiculous old age is the last and perhaps the saddest surprise of human nature.

"This time, I hope, you'll read Cicero," he said to me, upon learning of the proposed trip.

"Cicero!" exclaimed Sabina.

"Why not? Your brother is a great Latin scholar. He translates Virgil at a glance. But make sure it's Virgil, not Virgilia . . . don't get mixed up . . ."

And he uttered a loud, nasty, silly laugh. Sabina looked at me, afraid of what I might say or do; but, when she saw me smile, she smiled too and turned elsewhere. The other people looked at me with curiosity, indulgence, and sympathy; obviously the intimation they had just heard was nothing new to them. My love affair was better known than I had supposed. I smiled a quick, fugitive little smile, and then became as talkative as a magpie.

Virgilia was a beautiful sin, and it is so easy to confess a beautiful sin! At first I had always frowned when I heard an allusion to our relationship; although, on my word of honor, the allusion had always given me a bland and satisfied feeling. Once, however, I smiled, and thereafter I continued to do so. I do not know whether anyone can explain this phenomenon. I explain it as follows: the smile was always there, but at the beginning it had been internal—in the bud, so to speak; as time went on, it blossomed forth into flower and became visible to everyone. A simple matter of botany.

83. Thirteen: Cotrim interrupted my agreeable thoughts and led me to a window. "Do you want me to tell you something?" he asked. "Don't accept this position; it's senseless, it's dangerous."

"Why?"

"You know very well why," he replied. "Here in the capital a thing like this is lost in the crowd—so many people, so many interests; but in the provinces it's a different story. And in the case of political personalities, it would really be mad; as soon as the opposition newspapers got wind of the thing, they would print it in headlines, and then would come the jokes, insinuations, nicknames . . ."

"But I don't understand . . ."

"You understand, you understand . . . You must think me a pretty poor friend if you try to hide from me what everybody knows. I've known about it for months. I repeat, don't make such a trip; put up with her absence, it's better that way, and avoid a big scandal or even worse . . ."

He said this and walked away. I stood there staring at a lamp in the corner, an old oil lamp, sad, dim, and curved like a question mark. What ought I do? It was Hamlet's old problem: "Whether 'tis nobler," and so on. In other words, to embark or not to embark: that was the question. But the lamp did not give me the answer. Cotrim's words echoed in my ears very differently from the words of Garcez. Perhaps Cotrim was right; but could I give Virgilia up?

Sabina came to me and asked what I was thinking about. I replied that I was not thinking of anything, that I was tired and was going home. Sabina said nothing for a moment; then, "I know what you need: a wife. Just wait, I'm going to find a nice girl for you."

I left, oppressed and disoriented. Heart and soul, I had been all set to go, and here this doorman, Propriety, suddenly blocked the entrance and insisted on seeing my invitation. I consigned Propriety to the devil, and with him the constitution, the legislature, the ministry, everything.

The next day I opened a political journal and read the news that, by a decree of the thirteenth, Lobo Neves and I had been appointed president and secretary, respectively, of the province of ——. I wrote immediately to Virgilia and, two hours later, went to Gambôa. Poor Dona Placida! She was greatly distressed. She asked whether we would forget our old servant, whether we would be gone very long, and whether the province was far away. I tried to console her, but I, too, needed consolation; Cotrim's argument troubled me. Soon Virgilia arrived, as light and gay as a swallow; however, on seeing how sad I looked, she became serious.

"What's happened?"

"I'm wavering," I said. "I don't know whether I ought to accept . . ."

Virgilia plumped down on the couch, laughing.

"Why?" she said.

"It's not wise, it will make everything too obvious . . ."

"But we're not going."

"What do you mean?"

She told me that her husband was going to refuse the appointment, and for a motive which he had confided only to her, begging her to keep it very secret. "It's puerile," she observed, "it's ridiculous; but it's good enough for me." He had told her that the decree bore the date of the thirteenth and that for him this number signified death. His father had died on a thirteenth, thirteen days after a dinner for thirteen persons. The house in which his mother had died was number thirteen. *Et cetera*. It was a prophetic number. He could not say such things to the minister; he would tell them that he had private reasons for not accepting.

This sacrifice to a number amazed me, as it must amaze the reader; but Lobo Neves was very ambitious, and so the sacrifice must have been made in all sincerity.

84. The Conflict:

Fateful number, do you remember how often I blessed you? Thus the red-haired virgins of Thebes must have blessed the red-maned mare who substituted for them in Pelopidas's sacrifice—the gallant mare who died there, covered with flowers, without a word of loving remembrance from anyone. Well, I give you a word of loving remembrance, sacred mare, not only in token of your passing but also because, among the young ladies whom you saved, there may well have figured an ancestor of the Cubases' . . . Fateful number, you were our salvation. Her husband did not confess to me the real cause of his action; he told me that some private matters made acceptance impossible, and the serious, credulous expression on my face did honor to the art of dissimulation. His problem of dissimulation was more difficult; one could see that he was profoundly sad. Absorbed in his thoughts, he spoke little; he remained at home almost all the time, and read. At times he received visitors, and on these occasions he talked and laughed a great deal, noisily and affectedly. Two things weighed on his mind: his ambition, which a superstition had defeated, and doubt, perhaps even remorse, but a remorse that would have come again if the situation had occurred again, for the depth of his superstition had not diminished. He questioned the superstition without rejecting it. This persistence of a feeling, even when it was repugnant to the individual who felt it, was a phenomenon worthy of attention. But I preferred the pure ingenuousness of Dona Placida when she confessed that she could not bear to look at a shoe lying bottom up.

"What's wrong with it?" I asked her.

"It's bad luck," was her reply.

Just this bare statement, nothing more, and for her it had the authority of the Seven Sages. "It's bad luck." They told her this when she was a child, with no further explanation, and she was satisfied that some misfortune or other had to follow. The case was somewhat different when a finger was pointed at a star; in this case she knew perfectly well the nature of the bad luck that it would bring: namely, a wart.

But, wart or no wart, the sacrifice involved in not pointing at a star is small compared with the sacrifice of a provincial governorship. One can put up with a superstition that costs little or nothing; but it becomes insupportable when it can take away part of a man's life. It must have become insupportable to Lobo Neves when to his burden there were added doubt and the fear of having been a fool. And he suffered still another misfortune: the minister did not believe he had private reasons, but attributed to political machinations Lobo Neves' refusal of the appointment —a conclusion which he found consistent with certain impressions he had received. He treated Lobo Neves badly, communicated his distrust to his associates; incidents occurred; and finally, in the course of time, the ex-governor-elect went over to the opposition party.

85. The Top of the Mountain: He who escapes a mortal danger loves life with a new intensity. As I had been on the verge of losing her, I now began to love Virgilia with much greater ardor, and the same thing happened to her love for me. Thus the governorship had no effect on us other than to give new life to our affection; it was the tonic that made us enjoy more than ever the taste of our love and made it more than ever precious to us. In the first few days after the episode, we liked to imagine the grief that our separation would have caused us, the sadness that would have grown as the distance between us grew;

and, like children who, when a playmate makes a "face," run to take refuge on their mothers' laps, we would flee the supposed danger and would take refuge in each other's arms.

"Virgilia darling!"

"My love!"

"You're mine, aren't you?"

"Yours, yours . . ."

And thus we resumed the thread of our adventure, as Scheherazade had resumed the thread of her tales. This, I think, was the best tale in the book of our love; it was the top of the mountain, from which, for some time, we looked upon the valleys of the east and of the west, and above us the sky, peaceful and blue. When this time had gone, we began to descend the slope, sometimes holding hands and sometimes not, but always going down, down . . .

86. The Mystery: One day, on the way down, I noticed something different about her, perhaps a certain touch of melancholy, and I asked her what was wrong. She said nothing, merely made a gesture of weariness. I persisted, and she told me that . . . A subtle fluid ran through my whole body: a powerful, rapid, strange feeling which I cannot transfer to this paper. I took her hands in mine, drew her gently toward me, and kissed her on the forehead with the delicacy of a zephyr and the solemnity of an Abraham. She trembled a little, took my head between the palms of her hands, looked deep into my eyes, and then caressed me as if I were a child . . . There is a mystery here; let us give the reader time to solve it.

87. Geology: About this time, a misfortune occurred: Viegas died. He appeared briefly, you will remember, in an earlier part of this book, with his seventy years choked by asthma and racked by rheumatism, not to mention his lesion of the heart. He was one of the perspicacious individuals who first suspected our adventure. Virgilia nourished the hope that this elderly relative, close as the tomb in money matters, would take care of her son's future with a legacy. If her husband had similar thoughts, he hid or repressed them. To be fair to him, there was in Lobo Neves a certain basic dignity, a stratum of rock that resisted the impact of daily commerce. As to the other strata, the upper ones of loose earth and sand—life, which is an eternal torrent, shifted them about at will. If the reader still remembers Chapter 23, he will note that this is the second time that I have compared life to a torrent; but he will note also that this time I added an adjective—eternal. And God alone knows the power of an adjective, especially in new, tropical countries.

New also is the study of man in terms of spiritual geology. Yes, these strata that life changes, preserves, or dissolves, in accordance with their power of resistance—these strata merit a chapter of their own, which I shall not write, because I do not like to delay the story. I shall say only that the most honest man I ever met was one Jacob Medeiros or Jacob Valladares—I do not exactly remember his name. Perhaps it was Jacob Rodrigues; anyway, Jacob. He was honesty personified. He could have become rich by a small violation of one of his minor scruples, but would not; he let no less than four hundred contos slide through his fingers. His honesty was so exemplary that it became petty and irritating. One day, when he and I were alone in his house enjoying an agreeable conversation, a servant announced that Dr. B., a tiresome fellow, had come to call on him. Jacob ordered the servant to say that he was not at home.

"It won't work," shouted a voice from the hallway; "I'm inside already."

And, indeed, Dr. B. soon appeared at the door of the room. Jacob went to greet him, saying he had thought it was a different person and not Dr. B., and adding that he was greatly pleased with the visit—which gave us an hour and a half of mortal boredom, and so short a period only because Jacob consulted his watch, causing Dr. B. to ask him whether he was going out.

"With my wife," said Jacob.

Dr. B. retired, and we breathed again. After a few breaths, I called Jacob's attention to the fact that he had just told four lies in the space of less than two hours: the first, by saying he was not at home; the second, by pretending to be happy with the importunate fellow's visit; the third, by saying that he was going out; the fourth, by adding that his wife was going, too. Jacob reflected a moment and then confessed the justice of my observation, but he excused himself on the ground that absolute truth is incompatible with an advanced state of society and that peace and order can only be achieved at the cost of reciprocal deceit . . . Ah, now I remember: his name was Jacob Tavares.

88. The Invalid: Needless to say, I refuted with the most elementary arguments this pernicious doctrine; but my observation of his falsehoods embarrassed him so greatly that he fought until the end, showing a certain false intensity of conviction, perhaps the better to soothe his conscience.

To get back to the more serious matter of Virgilia and her hopes of a legacy: Wanting her husband's scruples, she betrayed these hopes by the attention and the caresses that she gave her elderly relative; they deserved a codicil at the very least. To tell the truth, she fawned upon him. I have observed that women's adulation is different from men's. The latter comes close to servility; the former takes the guise of affection. Her body graciously bent over the object of adulation, her soft speech, even her physical fragility give to a woman's adulation a certain appropriateness, an aspect of legitimacy. The age of the person is unimportant; the woman inevitably becomes to him a sort of mother or sister—or nurse, another feminine office in which the most skilful man will always lack a certain basic quality.

These were my thoughts as I watched Virgilia showering her graciousness on the old man. She would go to receive him at the door; chatting and laughing, she would take his hat and cane, would give him her arm, and would lead him to a chair—or rather to *the* chair, "Viegas's chair," overstuffed and of special design for the elderly infirm. She would hasten to shut the nearest window if there was a breeze; or to open it if the day was warm, but with great care, making certain that he was not in a draught.

"Do you feel a little stronger today, darling?"

"Bah! I had a terrible night: this devilish asthma didn't let up for a second."

And he would puff and pant, recovering little by little from the fatigue caused by coming in and climbing the stairs. She would sit on a stool close to him, with her hands on his knees. Meanwhile, Nhonhô would come into the living room, without his customary jumping; in Viegas's presence he was always gentle, well-behaved, and serious. Viegas liked him greatly.

"Come here, Nhonhô," he would say; and, with considerable difficulty, he would put his hand in his ample pocket, would take out a little box of lozenges, would put one in his mouth, and would give one to the little boy. Anti-asthma lozenges. Nhonhô said they were delicious.

All this was repeated each time, with minor variations.

As Viegas liked to play at draughts, Virgilia would have a game or two with him, waiting patiently while he moved the checkers with his weak, slow hand. Then again, they would go downstairs and take a walk in the garden; she would give him her arm, but he sometimes refused it on the ground that he was sturdy and fully capable of walking a league. They would walk, sit down, walk again, talk about various things: family matters, drawing room gossip, a house that he was planning to build as his residence—a house in the new style, for the one in which he was living dated from the reign of Dom João VI, like some that may be seen even today, I believe, in the São Christovam district, with their stout columns in front. He had already employed a well-known architect to prepare the plans for the new house. Ah! then, then indeed, Virgilia would see what good taste an old man could have.

As one might have supposed, he spoke slowly and with difficulty, interrupted from time to time by a spell of heavy breathing, which was disagreeable both to him and to persons who were with him. Now and then he suffered an attack of coughing; bent over, groaning, he raised his handkerchief to his mouth, coughed, and examined the handkerchief for blood. When the attack had passed, he returned to the plan of the new house, which was to have such and such rooms, a terrace, a coach house—altogether a joy!

89. In Extremis: "I'm going to spend tomorrow at Viegas's house," she said to me one day. "Poor fellow, he has nobody . . ."

Viegas had finally become bedridden. His daughter, who was married, had fallen ill and therefore could not keep him company. Virgilia used to visit him from time to time.

I took advantage of the circumstance to spend a good part of the day with her. It was two o'clock in the afternoon when I arrived. Viegas was coughing so violently that it made my chest burn; between attacks, he bargained with a thin fellow over the price of a house. The fellow offered thirty contos. Viegas demanded forty. The buyer talked fast, like a man who is afraid he will miss the train, but Viegas would not yield; he refused first the thirty contos, then two more, then still three more, and finally suffered a violent attack that rendered him speechless for fifteen minutes. The buyer was very solicitous, rearranged his pillows, and offered him thirty-six contos.

"Never!" groaned the sick man.

He asked for a bundle of papers on the writing table; having insufficient strength to remove the rubber band that held the papers together, he asked me to remove it, and I did so. They were the bills and accounts for the construction of the house: the mason's bills, the carpenter's bills, the painter's bills; bills for wallpaper for the living room, for the dining room, for the bedrooms, for the library, for the study; bills for metal fixtures; the cost of the land. He opened them, one by one, with his trembling hands, and asked me to read them; I read them.

"Look here: twelve hundred, wallpaper at twelve hundred a roll. French hinges . . . You see, you are practically getting it free," he concluded after I had read the last item.

"Well . . . but . . ."

"Forty contos; I will not let you have it for less. Why, the interest alone . . . just consider the amount of the interest payments . . ."

These last words were coughed rather than spoken, in spurts, syllable by syllable, as if they were little pieces of disintegrated lungs. His burning eyes were rolling in their deep orbits; they reminded me of two lamps in the early dawn. Through the sheet, the skeleton of his body was outlined, with protruding points at his knees and feet. His yellow, sagging, wrinkled skin covered the bones of an expressionless face. A white cotton nightcap covered his scalp, shaved close by the passage of time.

"Well . . . ," said the thin fellow.

I made a gesture to tell him not to continue, and he said nothing for a few moments. The sick man was staring at the ceiling, silent, breathing deeply. Virgilia turned pale, arose, walked to the window. She suspected the imminence of death, and was afraid. I tried to speak of other things. The thin fellow told a funny story and then returned to the principal subject, raising his offer.

"Thirty-eight contos," he said.

"Hnhn . . . ?" grunted the sick man.

The thin fellow approached the bed, took his hand, and felt how cold it was. I came close to the sick man, asked him whether he felt any pain, whether he wanted a cup of wine.

"No . . . no . . . f . . . for . . . f . . . f . . ."

He had an attack of coughing, and it was his last. In a short time he expired, to the great disappointment of the thin fellow, who told me later that he had been on the point of offering the forty contos; but it was too late.

90. The Old Colloquy between Cain and Adam:

Nothing. No testamentary remembrance whatever, not even a lozenge, to prevent his appearing utterly ungrateful. Nothing. Virgilia confessed to me that she was furious, not because of the personal slight to her but only because she was thinking of her boy; she said this rather guardedly, as she knew that I did not like the boy very much, nor, for that matter, at all. I suggested that she try not to think about it. It would be best to forget the defunct, who had really been nothing but a half-wit and a miserable miser, and to think of pleasant things: our child, for example . . .

There I go giving away the solution of the mystery, that sweet mystery of several weeks before, when Virgilia had acted strangely. A child! A being derived from my own being! This was the exclusive subject of my thoughts. Public opinion, the husband's jealousy, Viegas's death, gave me no concern. Nothing interested me—neither political conflicts, nor revolutions, nor earthquakes, nothing. I had thoughts for only that anonymous embryo—of obscure parentage to be sure, but a secret voice kept telling me, "It's your child." My child! And I repeated these two words again and again with a peculiar voluptuousness and all sorts of pride. I felt that I had just become a man.

Best of all were the talks we had together, the embryo and I, especially about the future. He really loved me, the cute rascal; he would pat my cheeks with his fat little hands. And then he would appear in academic cap and gown (for of course I planned to have him go through law school) and would deliver a speech in the Chamber of Deputies. And his father, sitting there in the gallery, would listen with tears in his eyes. Then he would become a youngster in school, his slate and books under his arm, or would fall back into his cradle—only to rise from it again a full-grown man. I tried in vain to establish his age and his external appearance: in my mind's eye his size and his mien varied momentarily: he sucked at the breast, he wrote, he waltzed, he was the infinite within the limits of a fifteen-minute daydream—baby and deputy, schoolboy and man about town.

Sometimes when I was with Virgilia I would forget the whole world, including her. She would shake me, would reproach me for my silence, and would say that apparently I no longer cared for her. The truth is that I was talking with the embryo. It was the old colloquy between Cain and Adam, a conversation without words, between one life and another, between one mystery and another.

91. An Extraordinary Letter: About this time I received the following extraordinary letter:

My dear Braz Cubas,

Some time ago, in the Passeio Publico, I borrowed a watch from you. It gives me satisfaction to return it with this letter. To be sure, it is not the same watch but another—I shall not say a better, but one at least equal in quality to the first. "*Que voulez-vous, monseigneur?*" as Figaro would say. "*C'est la misère!*" Many things have happened since our meeting; I shall relate them to you in detail if your door is open to me. I no longer wear those decrepit boots nor that infamous coat with its tails lost in the twilight of the past. I have vacated my step on the stairs of the São Francisco Church. And I dine regularly.

Apart from all this, I should like, one of these days, to expound to you a work of mine, the fruit of long study: a new system of philosophy that not only describes and explains the origin and the end of things but also carries ethics far beyond Zeno and Seneca, whose stoicism is a mere plaything by comparison with my concept of the good life. The practical effects of my system are revolutionary: it purifies the human spirit, eliminates sorrow, insures happiness, and glorifies our nation. I call it Humanitism, after *Humanitas*, the basic principle behind all phenomena. My first notion about a name for the system revealed my own fatuity; it was to call it Borbism, after Borba—a designation as egotistical as it would be ill-mannered and noisome. Furthermore, it would be less expressive. As you shall see, my dear Braz Cubas, my work is really monumental; and if there is anything that can make me forget the bitterness of life it is the satisfaction of having finally captured truth and happiness. I have them in my hands, these two fugitives; after so many centuries of struggle, inquiry, discovery, systems of thought, and failures, here they are at last in man's hands. Goodbye for the present, my dear Braz Cubas. Affectionate regards from

Your old friend,

Joaquim Borba dos Santos

I read this letter without fully understanding it. The letter was accompanied by a little jewelry box containing a fine watch; engraved upon it were my initials and the following words: "A remembrance from your old friend Quincas." I turned again to the letter, reread it slowly and attentively. The return of the watch excluded all possibility of a hoax; the letter's lucidity, serenity, convictions—although it was also a little prideful, to be sure—seemed to eliminate any suspicion of insanity. Apparently Quincas Borba had inherited money from one of his relatives in Minas, and wealth had restored his earlier dignity. Perhaps I ought not go quite so far: there are things that cannot be restored in their entirety; but partial regeneration is quite possible. I put away the letter and the watch, and awaited the philosophy.

92. An Extraordinary Man: Never fear, I shall soon have done

with extraordinary things, and we shall then resume the narrative proper.

I had no sooner put away the letter and the watch when a short, thin man came looking for me with a note from Cotrim, inviting me to dinner. The bearer of the note was married to a sister of Cotrim, had arrived from the North a few days earlier, was named Damasceno, and had taken part in the bloodless revolution of 1831. He told me all this in the first five minutes. He had left Rio de Janeiro because he disagreed with the policies established by the regent, who was an ass, almost as big an ass as the ministers that served under him. Besides, another revolution was on its way.

At this point, although the political ideas he expressed were somewhat tangled, I managed to formulate a notion of the sort of government he desired: it was a dictatorship tempered—not, as some would have it, by the spirit of the people—but by the rifles of the National Guard. I was unable to discover whether he preferred a single dictator or an oligarchy.

He expressed opinions about various matters, among them the development of the slave trade and the expulsion of the English. He greatly enjoyed the theatre; upon his arrival, he had gone immediately to the São Pedro Theatre, where he had seen an excellent drama, *Maria Joanna*, and a very interesting comedy, *Kettly, or the Return to Switzerland*. Also, he had liked Deperini very much, in *Sappho* or in *Anne Boleyn*, he did not exactly remember which. But Candiani! Yes, sir, she was really hunkydory. Now he wanted to hear *Ernani*, which his daughter often sang at the piano. "*Ernani, Ernani, involami . . .*," he trilled, and rose to his feet. In the North, all these things were just echoes. His daughter was dying to hear all the operas. She had a very sweet little voice. And wonderful taste in music. Oh, he had been so anxious to come back to Rio de Janeiro. He had already wandered through the whole city, remembering this place and that, sometimes feeling as if he was going to cry. He would never go away again. He had been very seasick during the trip as, indeed, had been all the passengers except an Englishman . . . the devil take the English! This country would never be right until every last one of them had been thrown out. After all, what could England do to us? If he could find a few people of good will to help him, he could rid the country of all the Goddamns in one night . . . Thank God, he was a patriot—and he beat his chest; his patriotism need surprise no one, for he came of a good family: he was a descendant of a very patriotic old pioneer leader. Yes, sir! He was not just one of these nobodies. If the right occasion arose, he would show the stuff he was made of . . .

But it was getting late, and I said that I should be delighted to accept the invitation to dinner and that I looked forward to a continuation of our conversation at that time. I took him to the door of the living room; he stopped a moment and said that he liked me very much. When he had got married, I had been in Europe. He had known my father, a fine man; in fact, they had both danced at a glorious ball at the Praia Grande . . . Ah, the good old days! We would talk again, it was getting late, he had to take my reply to Cotrim. He left; I shut the door after him . . .

93. The Dinner: The dinner at Cotrim's was torture for me. Fortunately, Sabina seated me next to Damasceno's daughter, Dona Eulalia or, more familiarly, Nhan-lóló, a most pleasing young lady. She was a little shy at first, but only at first. She wanted elegance of manner, but was compensated for this shortcoming by her eyes, which were superbly beautiful. Indeed, they had only one defect: they stared at me continually, except when they were compelled to look at her plate—and this was seldom, as Nhan-lóló ate very little. After dinner, she sang; her voice was, as her father had said, very sweet.

Nevertheless I left early. Sabina went with me to the door and asked me how I liked Damasceno's daughter.

"So-so."

"Don't you find her charming?" said Sabina. "She needs a little more time in Rio. But what a grand person, really a pearl! She'd make you a fine wife."

"I don't like pearls."

"Don't be so blasé. How long do you want to hold out? Until you're past-ripe and ready to drop? Well, my dear, whether you like it or not, you're going to marry Nhan-lóló."

And she tapped me on the cheek with her fingers, as gentle as a dove but at the same time resolute and menacing. Great God! Was this the purpose of our reconciliation? The thought disturbed me, but a mysterious voice was calling me to Lobo Neves' house; I said farewell to Sabina and her threats.

94. The Real Reason: "And how is dear mama to-night?" As always upon hearing an allusion to the coming event, Virgilia pouted. She was alone at a window, looking at the moon, and had greeted me joyfully; but when I spoke these words, she pouted. My anticipatory paternal endearments annoyed her, and so, on this occasion, I did not repeat them; for to me she had become a consecrated person, a sacred ampulla. At first I assumed that the foetus, thrusting itself into our adventure, had brought back her consciousness of sin. I was wrong. Virgilia had never been more expansive. She had never seemed less worried about people or about her husband. There was no sign of remorse. It occurred to me also that the pregnancy might be pure fiction, a device to hold me, and that it now began to trouble her, especially as she could not hope to impose it on me for very long. This hypothesis was by no means absurd; my sweet Virgilia used sometimes to prevaricate, and how charmingly!

That night I discovered the real reason. It was fear of childbirth and annoyance with the state of pregnancy. She had suffered greatly with the birth of her first child; and anticipation of the coming delivery, with its crisis of life and death, made her shiver like a man before the gallows. As to her annoyance, it had to do with the enforced deprivation of social pleasures to which she was accustomed.

This was surely the reason for her attitude. I gave her to understand that I knew, and even reprimanded her a little in the name of my rights as a father. Virgilia stared at me; then she looked away and smiled incredulously.

95. The Blossoms of Yesteryear: Where are they now,

the blossoms of yesteryear? One afternoon the castle of my paternal fantasies crumbled to dust. The embryo went away, at that stage at which a Laplace and a turtle look very much alike. I received the news from Lobo Neves, who then left me in the living room and accompanied the doctor to the chamber of the frustrated mother. I leaned against the window and looked out at the grounds behind the house, where the orange trees were turning green.

96. The Anonymous Letter: Someone touched me on the shoul-

der. It was Lobo Neves. For a few moments we stood facing each other, mute, inconsolable. I broke the silence by asking about Virgilia, and we talked for about half an hour. Then a servant brought him a letter; he read it, turned very pale, and folded it with trembling hands. I believe he made a gesture as if about to throw himself upon me, but my memory is not quite clear on this point. What I do remember clearly is that during the following weeks he was cold and taciturn in my presence.

At our first meeting in Gambôa after her illness, Virgilia told me what had happened. As soon as her condition had permitted it, Lobo Neves had shown her the letter. It was anonymous and it denounced us. It did not tell everything; it did not mention, for example, our meetings outside; it merely advised him of our intimacy and added that everyone suspected the truth. Virgilia had read the letter and had said indignantly that it was an infamous calumny.

"Calumny?" asked Lobo Neves.

"An infamous one."

Her husband breathed more easily; but he looked again at the letter, and every word in it wagged a finger from side to side in token of the negative, every syllable cried down his wife's indignation. This man, usually fearless, was now the weakest of creatures. Perhaps his imagination showed him, in the distance, the well-known eye of public opinion looking at him sarcastically, as if it was thinking of a joke at his expense; perhaps an invisible mouth was whispering in his ear the obscene insinuations that he had heard or had himself said on other occasions about other persons. He insisted that his wife confess everything and promised that he would forgive her. Virgilia knew then that she was safe. She pretended to be annoyed with his insistence. She swore that she had heard from me nothing but amenities and words of respect. The letter must have been written by some disappointed beau. And she mentioned some—one who for three months had openly shown her attention, one who had written her a letter, and a number of others. She cited them by name, with all the circumstances, studying the while her husband's eyes; and finally said that, in order to nip any gossip in the bud, she would treat me in such a way that I would never come there again.

When she had told me all this, I felt troubled, not by the additional precautions that would thenceforth be necessary, which might require me to absent myself entirely from Lobo Neves' house, but by Virgilia's moral insensitivity, by her lack of emotion, of fear, and even of remorse. Virgilia observed my concern, raised my head with her hands (for I had been staring at the floor), and said with a certain bitterness:

"I wonder if you deserve the sacrifices I make for you."

I said nothing. It would have been idle to explain that a little despair and terror might have restored to our situation the delightfully caustic flavor it had once had. Yet, if I had told her, it is by no means impossible that, by patient artifice, she would have achieved the desiderated touch of despair and terror. I said nothing. She tapped nervously on the floor. I came close to her and kissed her on the forehead. She recoiled as if she had been kissed by a corpse.

97. Between Lips and Forehead: I am afraid
—or, more accurately, I hope—that the reader is trembling. The last word of the preceding chapter was intended to bring to his mind a number of unpleasant thoughts appropriate to the occasion. Let us take a good look at the tableau: a little house in Gambôa, two people who have loved each other a long time, one bending over the other and kissing her on the forehead, the other recoiling as if she had felt the touch of an ambulatory corpse. There in the meagre interval between lips and forehead, between the just-before and the just-after of a kiss, there is ample space for many things: the contraction of a resentment, the wrinkled brow of distrust, the pale and somnolent nose of satiety . . .

98. Deleted: We parted pleasantly enough that afternoon.
I dined alone, completely reconciled to the situation. The anonymous letter had brought back the salt of mystery and the pepper of danger; and, after all, it was a good

thing that Virgilia, in the midst of the crisis, had not lost her self-possession. After dinner, I went to the São Pedro; an elaborate piece of theatre was on display, with Estella, as usual, wresting tears from the audience. I entered, ran my eye along the boxes, and saw in one of them Damasceno and family. The daughter was dressed elegantly and expensively—a fact hard to explain, for her father earned barely enough to run into debt.

During intermission, I visited them in their box. Damasceno and his wife greeted me profusely—he with words, she with smiles. As for Nhan-lóló, she did not take her eyes from me. She seemed prettier than on the day of the dinner. I found in her a certain ethereal softness combined with earthy substantiality—a vague phrase, to be sure, but perhaps suitable to a chapter that cannot be other than vague. In truth, I do not know how to communicate to you the feeling of elevation that I experienced near this maiden, nor my guilty self-identification with Tartuffe as I contemplated the way her fine dress fell over her knee, chastely covering it and yet suggesting its smooth roundness. This contemplation led me to the discovery of a subtle point, namely, nature's need of human clothing as a condition necessary to the development of our species. In a world in which extra-sexual functions and problems claim a great part of the individual's attention, habitual nudity would tend to dull the senses and to retard sexual activity, whereas clothing, by concealing nature, sharpens the appetites, increases them, and hence permits civilization to survive and to progress.

I have half a mind to delete this chapter. Some may find it offensive. Yet, after all, these are my memoirs, prudish reader, not yours. And the truth is that near this pleasing young lady I was possessed by an indefinable and ambivalent urge. She represented for me Pascal's duality of human nature, *l'ange et la bête*, with this difference: the Jansenist did not recognize the possible simultaneity of the two, whereas here they were together, coexistent— *l'ange* speaking of heavenly things, and *la bête* insisting . . . Yes, I shall definitely delete this chapter.

99. In the Pit:
In the pit of the theatre, I ran into Lobo Neves talking with some friends. We spoke together briefly; we were ill at ease and cool to each other. But in the intermission, a few minutes before the curtain was to rise, we met in a corridor where there was no one else. He came to me, affable and smiling, led me by the arm to one of the little rooms behind the orchestra boxes, and talked at great length. He seemed completely at ease. I asked about his wife; he replied that she was well, but quickly turned the conversation to other subjects. He was expansive, almost gay. Perhaps you would like to explain the change; as for me, I shall take refuge in Damasceno, who is observing me from the door of his box.

I heard nothing during the second act, neither the words of the actors nor the applause of the audience. I leaned back in my chair. Snatches of Lobo Neves' conversation ran through my mind, I considered his general manner, and I concluded that the new situation was better than the old. We still had Gambôa, and this was sufficient for our purposes. My visits to the other house had apparently aroused or increased someone's jealousy, with results that might have been disastrous. As a matter of fact, we did not need to see each other every day; an occasional respite might introduce a little longing into our affair. Further, I was past forty and amounted to nothing, not even an alderman. I had to accomplish something soon—for Virgilia's sake if for no other reason; it would make her proud to see my name in headlines . . . I think that, about this time, the audience broke into applause, but I cannot swear to it; I was thinking of something else.

O crowd, whose love I coveted until the day of my death, this is how I avenged myself for your indifference: I let you buzz all around me, without hearing you. My attitude may be compared to that of Aeschylus' Prometheus toward his tormentors. Did you think you could chain me to the rock of your triviality, of your agitation over the inconsequential? Yours are fragile chains, my friend. With a Gulliver-like flexing of my muscle, I could break them at will.

To meditate in solitude is a common thing. But for truly exquisite voluptuousness, a man must isolate himself in the midst of a sea of gestures and words, of nerves and passions; he must declare himself an alien, remote and inaccessible. The worst that they can say, when he returns to himself—*i. e.*, when he returns to others than himself—is that he has come down from his ivory tower; and what is this secret and luminous tower in the mind's architecture but the disdainful affirmation of one's spiritual freedom? Blessed be the Lord, what an impressive closing for a chapter!

100. Probably True: If most people were not superficial and unperceptive, I should

not feel obliged to remind the reader that when I affirm certain laws of nature or of human nature it is because I have found them to be true beyond peradventure of doubt; if there is any doubt whatever, I confine myself to an assertion of probability. An example of a law in the "probable" class provides the substance of the present chapter, which I recommend to all persons who have a taste for the study of social phenomena.

Very probably there is a regular and perhaps periodic interaction between political events and private lives. It is something like the tides at the Flamengo beach or at other beaches where the water is rough. A wave inundates part of the beach and in so doing becomes, as it were, a separate thing, apart from the sea; but then this very water returns to the sea and augments a new wave, which in turn, and so on. Now you have the basic principle and a more or less explicative analogy; let us examine a specific application.

On a previous page, we learned that Lobo Neves refused an appointment as governor of a province because the decree was dated the thirteenth—a serious act, whose consequence was a break between the administration and Virgilia's husband. Thus, the private fact of a numeromantic superstition produced a political breach. We shall see how, some time later, a political event caused the separation of two individuals.

It would be inconsistent with the general method of this book if I were immediately to set forth this latter phenomenon. I shall content myself here with the fact that, four months after our meeting in the theatre, Lobo Neves returned to, and was welcomed back by, the administration—a fact which the reader will need to bear in mind if he is to appreciate my thought in all its subtlety.

101. The Dalmatian Revolution: It was Virgilia who
told me about her husband's political about-face, one October morning between eleven o'clock and noon. She spoke of meetings, conferences, a speech . . .

"And so you're probably going to become a baroness after all," I interrupted.

She lowered the corners of her mouth and shook her head, but her gesture was given the lie by a facial expression that somehow suggested desire and hope. It occurred to me that the imperial communication might lead her back to the path of virtue, not out of any deep respect that she had for virtue but out of gratitude to her husband. For she loved nobility with all her heart. Indeed, one of the chief annoyances in my life at that time was the appearance, on our little stage, of a highly polished if somewhat impoverished diplomatic representative—a member, let us say, of the Dalmatian legation—Count B.V., who flirted with Virgilia for three months. A genuine nobleman by birth, he was beginning to turn Virgilia's head. (Incidentally, she liked the atmosphere of diplomacy and would probably have made a very successful diplomat herself.) I do not know what would have become of me if a revolution had not overthrown the Dalmatian government and purged all the Dalmatian embassies. The revolution was extremely bloody. Every ship from Europe brought newspapers describing the horrors and counting the heads as they rolled. Everyone was trembling with indignation and pity . . . But not I. In my heart I blessed this tragedy for removing a pebble from my shoe. And besides, Dalmatia was so far away.

102. To Forget for a Moment: Shortly thereafter, this very

man, who had been so pleased with his rival's departure, did something that . . . No, I shall not tell about it on this page. Let this chapter serve to let me forget my shame for a moment. It was so unkind, so ungentlemanly, so wholly inexplicable . . .

103. A Case of Forgetfulness: "No, Mr. Braz, you mustn't do

a thing like this. You must never do it."

Dona Placida was right. No gentleman arrives one hour late for an appointment with a lady. I rushed in, panting, but Virgilia was gone. Dona Placida told me that she had waited a long time, had become angry, had cried, had sworn never to see me again, and other things, all of which our housekeeper related with tears in her voice, begging me not to abandon Yayá, because it would be a terribly unfair thing to do to a girl who had sacrificed everything for me. I explained that it had all been a misunderstanding as to the time we were to meet . . . But it had not been. It had been a simple case of forgetfulness. Some conversation, some story or other that someone had been telling me, something had made me forget.

Poor Dona Placida, she was so worried! She walked about, shaking her head, sighing noisily, and occasionally looking out the window. Poor Dona Placida! With what patience and art she would tuck in the blankets and blow warmth upon the cheeks of our love! With what fertile imagination she would try to find ways to make our hours together more pleasant, to drive away every trace of tedium! Flowers, sweets—the wonderful sweets of an earlier time—and much laughter and caresses, laughter and caresses that increased from day to day, as if she was trying frantically to make our adventure permanent or to bring back the atmosphere of our first months in Gambôa. Our housekeeper and confidante omitted nothing, not even prevarication, for she would tell each of us about sighs and expressions of longing by the other which in truth she had not witnessed; nothing, not even slander, for she once told Virgilia that I had a new love. "You know I could never like another woman," was my reply when Virgilia asked me about it. And these words alone, with no protest or reproof, disposed completely of the matter. It made Dona Placida despondent.

To come back to the episode of my tardiness: "All right," I said after about a quarter hour, "we'll have to make Virgilia understand that I was not at fault. How would you like to take her a letter right now?"

"She must be very sad, poor thing! I never wished death to any human creature, but if some day you, sir, and Yayá can get married, then you'll see what a heavenly angel she is!"

I remember that I averted my face and stared at the floor. I recommend this gesture to any person who has no ready reply or who is afraid to look the other person in the eye. In such cases, some prefer to recite a stanza of the *Lusiad*, others whistle *Norma*. I stick to the gesture that I have mentioned; it is simpler and requires less effort.

Three days later I explained it all to Virgilia. She was probably a little puzzled when I asked her forgiveness for the tears I had caused her to shed. Perhaps in my heart I suspected that the tears had really been Dona Placida's. It may well be that, upon seeing Virgilia disappointed, Dona Placida had wept and that, by an optical illusion, her tears seemed to be flowing from Virgilia's eyes. Anyway, all was explained but neither forgiven nor forgotten. Virgilia said a lot of strong things to me, threatened me with separation, and then began to laud her husband. He was a wonderful man, a paragon of considerateness and affection, far superior to me. While she said this, I sat with my elbows on my knees and stared at the floor, where a fly was dragging an ant, which was biting the fly's leg. Poor fly! Poor ant!

Virgilia stopped in front of me. "Why don't you say something?"

"What can I say? I've explained everything, but you insist on getting angry. What can I say? Do you know what I think? I think you're fed up, that you're sick and tired of me, that you're looking for an excuse to break it up . . ."

"Exactly!"

She put on her hat. Her hands were trembling with rage . . . "Goodbye, Dona Placida," she shouted toward the interior of the house. Then she went to the door, slipped open the bolt, and was about to go. I seized her by the waist. "All right, all right," I said. Virgilia still tried to leave. I held her back, asked her not to go, said that we should both forget the whole thing. Finally she turned away from the door and let herself drop on the sofa. I sat next to her, said many gentle things, many humble things. I do not care to decide whether our lips were a hair's breadth apart or whether they were closer together; it is a moot point. What I do remember definitely is that during the excitement one of Virgilia's earrings fell, that I leaned over to pick it up, and that the fly, with the ant on its leg, climbed onto the earring. Then, with the delicacy so characteristic of a man of our century, I caught these two unhappy creatures in the palm of my hand. I considered the distance from my hand to the planet Saturn and asked myself what interest there could possibly be in this miserable and minute entomological episode. If you think that I was about to perform a barbarity, you are mistaken, for what I did was to ask Virgilia for a hairpin in order to separate the two insects; but the fly perceived my intention, opened its wings, and fled away. Poor fly! Poor ant! And God saw that it was good, as the Scripture saith.

104. It Was He! I returned Virgilia's hairpin. She placed it carefully and prepared to leave. It was late: the clock had already struck three. All was forgiven and forgotten. Dona Placida, who was watching for the right opportunity for an inconspicuous exit by Virgilia, suddenly shut the window and exclaimed:

"Mary-Mother-of-God! Here comes Yayá's husband!"

Our terror was brief but intense. Virgilia turned the color of the lace on her dress and ran to hide in the bedroom. Dona Placida, having closed the window, hurried to lock the door. I awaited Lobo Neves' arrival. This brief moment passed. Virgilia regained possession of herself, pushed me into the bedroom, sat down in a corner of the living room, and told Dona Placida to go back to the window.

It was he. Dona Placida opened the door and greeted him with many exclamations of surprise: "Mr. Lobo Neves! To think that you would come here to honor your old servant's house! Please, please, come in. Guess who's here . . . You know already, that's why you came . . . Yayá, come here."

Virgilia ran eagerly toward her husband. I was watching through the keyhole. Lobo Neves, pale, came in slowly and quietly; there was no explosion. He glanced about.

"Of all things!" exclaimed Virgilia.

"I was passing by, I saw Dona Placida at the window, and I came to pay my compliments."

"Thank you very much," replied Dona Placida. "And they say that nobody cares about old women. Just look, I think Yayá is really jealous." And, putting her arm around her, "This little angel never forgot her old Placida. Sweet thing, she has her mother's face exactly . . . Sit down, Mr. Lobo Neves . . ."

"I can't stay."

"Are you going home?" said Virgilia. "Let's go together."

"Yes, I am."

"Where's my hat, Dona Placida?"

"Here it is."

Dona Placida brought a mirror and opened it for Virgilia, who put on her hat, tied the ribbons, and fixed her hair, speaking all the while to her husband, who remained silent. Our loyal old housekeeper kept on prattling; it was her way of hiding the trembling of her body.

By this time, Virgilia was in complete control. "Goodbye, Dona Placida. Don't forget to come, now." Dona Placida promised not to forget, and opened the door.

105. The Equivalence of Windows: Dona Placida

shut the door and let herself drop into a chair. I immediately left the bedroom and started toward the door with the purpose of going out into the street and snatching Virgilia away from her husband. At least that is what I said I would do, and it is well that I said it, for Dona Placida held me back by the arm. At one time I tended toward the notion that I had said this merely so that she would hold me back; but further reflection makes it quite clear that, after ten minutes in the bedroom, the most genuine and natural impulse would have been exactly the one I expressed. This follows from that famous Law of the Equivalence of Windows that I had the satisfaction of discovering and formulating in Chapter 51. My conscience needed air. The bedroom was a closed window; with my gesture and its avowed purpose I opened another window and breathed freely again.

106. A Dangerous Game: I breathed freely and sat down. The room

resounded with Dona Placida's lamentations. I said nothing. I was wondering whether it would not have been better for me to have shut Virgilia in the bedroom and to have remained in the living room. But I soon decided that it would have been worse; it would have confirmed his suspicion and there would have been a bloody scene. It was better this way. But later? What would happen in Virgilia's house? Would her husband kill her? Would he strike her? Would he lock her in? Would he throw her out? These questions were moving slowly through my mind like the black commas and periods that move through the field of vision of eyes that are fatigued or sick. They came and went, ugly and tragic, and I could not put my finger on one of them and say, "It's you and no other."

Suddenly I saw a dark form. It was Dona Placida, who had put on her black mantilla and was offering to go to Lobo Neves' house to obtain what news she could. I said that it would be dangerous, for a visit at this time might stimulate his suspicions.

"Don't worry," she interrupted. "I'll know what to do. If he's there, I won't go in."

She left. I remained there, wondering what would happen, both immediately and in the more distant future. I concluded that I was playing a very dangerous game, and I asked myself whether it was not time for me to move along. I felt a longing for marriage, a desire to channel my life. Why not? There still were regions that my heart had not explored; in particular, I felt by no means incapable of a chaste love, a pure, austere love. After all, amorous adventures are only the giddy, torrential part of life, *i. e.*, the exceptional part. I was fed up with adventures. Perhaps I was even pricked a little by remorse. I sat back and surrendered myself to my imagination. I saw myself with my wife, my adorable wife, and we were both looking at a baby asleep on its nurse's lap. We were all at the far end of our private park, which was shady and very green, and through the trees we could spy a patch of blue sky, very blue . . .

107. A Note from Virgilia: "Nothing happened. However, he defi-

nitely suspects. He is very serious and does not talk. Now he has gone out. He smiled only once, at Nhonhô, after staring at him intensely for a long time. He does not mistreat me, but pays little attention to me. I don't know what is going to happen. With God's help, this may blow over. For the present, extreme caution."

108. Beyond Understanding: There you have real drama,

Shakespearian tragedy in a nutshell. That little scrap of crumpled paper, parts of it almost illegible, is a document worthy of careful analysis, which, however, I shall bestow upon it neither in this chapter, nor in the following one, nor, probably, anywhere else in the book. If I did so, perhaps I should deprive the reader of the pleasure of noting for himself the coldness and perspicacity in these few hastily written lines; and, behind Virgilia's words, the tempest in the mind of another person, the repressed rage, the despair that must decide whether to dissolve itself in blood, in tears, or in the mud of dishonor.

As for me, if I tell you that I read the note three or four times that day, believe me, for it is true. Even if I tell you that I reread it the next day, both before and after breakfast, you may believe me, for it is the pure and simple truth. But if I tell you that the note drove me to despair, or anything of the sort, you may entertain a little doubt and may insist on proof. For I was unable, indeed I am still unable, to understand exactly what my feeling was at the time. It was fear, yet it was not fear; it was pity, yet it was not pity; it was vanity, yet it was not vanity; and

it was love without love, *i. e.*, without ecstasy. And all this together was a vague and complicated mixture that you surely cannot begin to understand any more than I could. Let us drop the
whole matter.

109. The Philosopher: The reader knows that I read the letter both before
and after breakfast. He therefore knows that I breakfasted. It remains only to inform him that this was one of the most frugal
breakfasts of my life: an egg, a slice of bread, a cup of tea. I have
all but forgotten many important things, but this breakfast stands
out vividly in my mind. The principal reason might have been
my misfortune associated with the letter; but it was not this. The
principal reason was a thought expressed to me that day by
Quincas Borba. He paid me a visit and said, among other things,
that one need not be frugal in order to understand Humanitism
and certainly not in order to practice it; that this philosophy was
wholly amicable to the pleasures of life, including those of the
table, the theatre, and love; and that, indeed, frugality might indicate a certain tendency towards asceticism, which was the ultimate expression of human madness.

"Look at St. John," he continued. "He grew thin living on
grasshoppers in the desert, instead of strengthening himself with
good food in the city in order to make Pharasaism grow thin in
the Synagogue."

God deliver me from the task of repeating Quincas Borba's
personal history, which he told me on that sad occasion; for although interesting, it was long and complicated. And if I omit
his history, perhaps I shall be permitted also to dispense with the
description of his person, which was very different from the one
that had approached me in the Passeio Publico. I shall say only
that, if clothes make the man, this man was not Quincas Borba;
he was a judge without robe, a general without uniform, a busi-

nessman without deficit. I noted the perfect tailoring of his coat, the whiteness of his shirt, the polish of his boots. His voice, which had been hoarse and snuffling in the Passeio Publico, seemed to have been restored to its earlier sonority. His gestures, without losing their vivacity, had become less spasmodic, more orderly. But I do not wish to describe him *in toto*. If I began to speak of such matters as the gold stud in his shirt and the rich quality of his boots, I should become involved in interminable detail. Suffice it to say that his boots were of patent leather and that he had inherited a substantial number of contos from an aunt in Barbacena. My mind, on this occasion, was like a shuttle-cock. Quincas Borba's story hit it into the air; when it was about to fall, Virgilia's note hit it and sent it soaring; it came down, received a stiff blow from the Passeio Publico episode, and up it went again. I was not meant for complex situations. This pulling and pushing between different mental attitudes put me off balance. I wanted to wrap Quincas Borba, Lobo Neves, and Virgilia's note in one over-all philosophy and send them as a gift to Aristotle. Nevertheless, I found our philosopher's story more than a little instructive. I admired particularly the talent for acute observation which he evidenced in his description of the origin and growth of his degradation, the internal struggles, the gradual capitulation, and the use he made of his degraded condition.

"Consider this," he observed: "the very first night that I spent on the São Francisco stairs, I slept the whole night through, as if it had been the most gentle feather bed. And why? Because I had gradually proceeded from a straw-mattressed bed to a plain wooden cot, from my own room to a jail cell, from jail to the street . . ."

Finally, he wanted to expound his philosophy to me; but I begged off. "I have something on my mind today and can't give it the concentrated attention it deserves. Come soon and explain it to me. I'm always at home." Quincas Borba smiled with, I thought, a suggestion of malice. Perhaps he knew about my adventure, although he said nothing—except, at the door as he was about to leave:

"Come join me in Humanitism; it is a great lap with room enough for every soul in the world, the eternal sea into which I dove, to rise again with Truth in my hand. The Greeks looked for Truth in a well. Petty, my friend, how pitifully petty! In a well, of all places! And of course they didn't find it. Greeks, anti-Greeks, sub-Greeks, the whole long procession of mankind leaned over the well to watch Truth come out, but it just wasn't there. They used ropes and buckets; the more daring even went down to the bottom of the well and brought up a frog. I went directly to the sea. Come join me in Humanitism."

110. Thirty-one:

A week later, Lobo Neves was appointed governor of a province. I clung to the hope that the decree would be dated the thirteenth. However, it was dated the thirty-first, and the digits, by this simple transposition, lost their influence. How deep are the forces that control our lives!

111. The Wall:

As it is my practice here to conceal nothing, I shall relate on this page the episode of the wall. Virgilia and Lobo Neves were soon to sail. Entering Dona Placida's house, I saw on the table a folded piece of paper. It was a note from Virgilia. It said that she would be waiting for me in the garden at sundown, without fail. It concluded, "The wall is low on the side toward the little path."

I made a gesture of displeasure. The letter seemed to me extraordinarily audacious, ill-considered, and even ridiculous. It not only invited scandal, it invited it together with laughter and sneers. I pictured myself leaping over the wall and caught in the act by an officer of the law, who led me off to jail. "The wall is low . . ." And what if it was low? Obviously Virgilia did not know what she was doing; perhaps by now she wished she had not sent the note. I looked at it, a small piece of paper, wrinkled but inflexible. I felt an urge to tear it in thirty thousand pieces and to throw it to the wind as the last vestige of my adventure; but I did not do so. Self-love, shame at the thought of fleeing from danger . . . There was no way out; I would have to go.

"Tell her I'll go."

"Where?" asked Dona Placida.

"Where she said she would wait for me."

"She said nothing to me."

"In this note."

Dona Placida stared. "But this piece of paper, I found it this morning in your drawer and I thought that . . ."

I felt a queer sensation. I reread the paper and looked at it a long time; it was, indeed, an old note that Virgilia had sent me in the early days of our love, and I had leaped the cooperatively low wall and had met her in the garden. I had put the note away and . . . I felt a queer sensation.

112. Public Opinion: This was fated to be a day of ambivalence. A few hours after the episode of the note, I met Lobo Neves on the Rua do Ouvidor. We talked about the governorship and about politics. He took advantage of the opportunity presented by the first passer-by that he knew to leave me, after an elaborate exchange of compliments. I remember that he was constrained but that he made an effort to appear at ease. It seemed to me at the time (and I beg my critic's pardon if he finds this idea a little remote), it seemed to me that he was afraid, not of me, not of himself, not of the law, not of his conscience, but of public opinion. It was this anonymous tribunal, in which every member both prosecutes and judges, that imposed limits upon the exercise of Lobo Neves' free will. Very probably he no longer loved his wife. I

believe (and here again I beg the critic's indulgence), I believe that he would have been quite ready to leave her had it not been for public opinion, which would have dragged his life through every street in the city. It would have conducted a minute and thorough inquest, would have collected all the circumstances, antecedents, and surmises, and would have repeated them wherever idle people met. This terrifying public opinion, with its bedroom curiosity, alone prevented a separation. At the same time, it made revenge wholly impossible, for revenge would have meant divulgation. He could not even appear resentful toward me without being compelled to seek a separation. He had to simulate the very ignorance that he had once really enjoyed and, consequently, the old sentiments consistent with such ignorance.

That it was difficult for him, I do not doubt. In those days the strain showed in his face. But time callouses the sensibilities and dims the memory; doubtless the years would blunt the thorns, remoteness would blur the factual contours, a shadow of retrospective doubt would cover the nudity of reality, and public opinion would occupy itself with other scandals. His son, as he grew, would try to realize the father's ambitions, and the father would direct to him all his affection. This, plus activity in the world, public prestige, then old age, illness, decline, death, a religious service, a biographical obituary, and the book of life would be closed. Not a trace of blood on any of its pages.

113. The Solder: If there is any point to the preceding chapter, it is that public opinion serves as an excellent solder of domestic institutions. Possibly I shall develop this thought before the end of the book; possibly, also, I shall let you mull it over without my help. In any event, I consider public opinion an excellent solder not only in domestic matters but in politics as well. Some bilious metaphysicians have taken the extreme position that public opinion issues from the irresponsible minds of the dull and the mediocre; but obvi-

ously, even if so radical a concept did not carry with it its own refutation, the most superficial consideration of the salutary effects of public opinion would suffice to establish it as the supremely superfine product of the flower of mankind, namely, the greater number.

114. End of a Dialogue: "Yes, tomorrow. Are you going to see us off?"

"Are you mad? It's out of the question."

"Then goodbye!"

"Goodbye!"

"Don't forget Dona Placida. Go see her once in a while. Poor thing! She came yesterday to say goodbye. She cried and said I would never see her again . . . She's a good creature, isn't she?"

"She certainly is."

"If we need to write, we can do it through her. And so goodbye for . . ."

"Perhaps two years?"

"Two years! Why, he says we'll be back after the elections."

"Yes? Then let's just say 'so long' . . . They're looking at us."

"Who?"

"Over there on the sofa. Let's separate."

"It's very hard."

"But we must. Goodbye, Virgilia!"

"So long. Goodbye!"

115. Luncheon: I did not see her off; but at the scheduled departure time I felt something that may be described as a mixture, in approximately equal parts, of loneliness and relief. This confession need not irritate the

reader. To titillate the reader's taste for the dramatic, I ought to suffer deep despair, shed some tears, and certainly not eat. This would be romantic but not biographical. The pure fact is that I lunched much as on other days, nourishing my heart with memories and my stomach with Mr. Prudhon's delicacies . . .

Old contemporaries of mine, do you by any chance remember this master chef of the Hotel Pharoux, who, according to the proprietor, had exercised his profession in the famous Véry and Véfour restaurants of Paris and in the palaces of Count Molé and of the Duke de la Rochefoucauld? He was world-famous. He came to Rio along with the polka . . . The polka, the Tivoli, the strangers' ball, the Casino—there you have some of the impressive memories of our time; but above them all one remembers Mr. Prudhon and his remarkable titbits.

They were really delicious, and this morning the devil of a man seemed to guess that I had suffered a misfortune. Never before had his art and his science so conspired to produce a masterful entrée. What refinement of seasoning! What tenderness! What beauty of form! One ate it with one's mouth, one's nose, and one's eyes. I have not preserved the bill for that feast, but it was high. After all, I had to bury my love magnificently. There it went, across the sea in both space and time, and there I remained at a table, with my forty-odd years . . . forty-odd vagrant, empty years. I remained behind, never again to see my love, no matter if Virgilia returned (and she did return), for at dusk one seeks in vain the fresh exhalations of morning.

116. Old Letters: The last chapter left me so sad that I had half a mind not to write this one, but to rest a while, to purge my spirit of the melancholy that had saturated it, and to continue a little later. But no, perhaps you are pressed for time.

Virgilia's departure gave me a taste of what it is like to be a widower. I spent most of my time at home, harpooning flies—like Domitian, if Suetonius is not lying—but harpooning them in my own way, *i. e.*, with my eyes. At the end of a large living room, stretched out in a hammock with an open book in my hands, I harpooned them, one by one. This was all: memories, a little boredom, and much day-dreaming.

During this period my uncle the canon died; item, two cousins. I was not greatly moved. I took them to the cemetery like a man taking money to the bank. Or rather like one taking letters to the post office: I affixed stamps, dropped the letters in the box, and left it to the mailman to deliver them to the right party. It was about this time that my niece Venancia, Cotrim's daughter, was born. Some died, others were born; I went on harpooning flies.

Now and then I bustled about. I would take a bureau drawer full of old letters—from friends, relatives, girls (including Marcella)—would spill them onto a table, would open and read them all, and would recompose the past . . . Unenlightened reader, if you do not keep the letters of your youth you will never enjoy the pleasure of seeing yourself, far off in the flatteringly dim light, with a three-cornered hat, seven-league boots, and curled mustachios, dancing at a ball to the music of Anacreontic pipes. By all means, save the letters of your youth.

Or, if you do not like the figure of the three-cornered hat, I shall use an expression of an old sailor who used to come to Cotrim's house. I shall say that, if you save the letters of your youth, you will be able to "sing a yearning." It seems that our sailors give this name to songs about the land that are sung only at sea. It would be hard to find a more poetic expression of nostalgia.

117. Humanitism:

However, two forces—and a third to be taken up in the next chapter —impelled me to return to a more active life: Sabina and Quincas Borba. My sister conducted a whirlwind campaign for the conjugal candidacy of Nhan-lóló. Before I knew it, there I was with the young lady almost in my arms. As to Quincas Borba, he finally initiated me into the mysteries of Humanitism, a system of philosophy destined to destroy all prior systems.

"Humanity," he said, "the basic principle of everything, is nothing but man himself manifested through all individual men. Considered historically, Humanity has known three phases: the *static*, prior to all creation; the *expansive*, which is the beginning of things; the *dispersive*, which is the appearance of men; and there will be one more, the *contractive*, which is the reabsorption of men and of things in Humanity. The phase of *expansion*, which brought the initiation of the universe, also brought to Humanity the suggestion that it might experience and enjoy this universe; hence the phase of *dispersion*, which is nothing more than the multiple personification of the original substance."

As I was not certain that I had fully grasped his meaning, Quincas Borba patiently developed both the details and the grand contours of his system. He explained to me that Humanitism was akin to Brahmanism in one respect, to wit, the distribution of men through the various parts of Humanity's anatomy; but what in the religion of India had only a narrow theological and political significance constituted in Humanitism the great law of personal value. Thus, to descend from the chest or from the kidneys of Humanity is to be a strong man; it is a very different thing to descend, say, from the hair or from the tip of the nose. Hence the need to cultivate and to temper one's muscles. Hercules was simply an anticipatory symbol of Humanitism. In this connection, Quincas Borba expressed the opinion that paganism might have achieved Truth if it had not impeded its progress by a lot of frivolously carnal and romantic myths. Nothing of the sort will happen to Humanitism. In this new church there is no easy happiness and no puerile sadness or joy. Love, for example, becomes a sacrament; reproduction, a ritual. As life is the greatest good in the world, and there is not a beggar who does not prefer misery to death (itself nothing but a delightful influx of Humanity), it follows that the act by which life is transmitted, far from being an occasion for gayety or carnal joy, is the supreme hour

[170]

of spiritual Mass. For, in truth, there is only one genuine misfortune: not to be born.

"Suppose, for example, that I had never been born," continued Quincas Borba; "I would not now have the pleasure of talking with you, of eating this potato, of going to the theatre—in a word, the pleasure of *living*. You will observe that I do not make man merely a vehicle of Humanitism. No, he is at once vehicle, coachman, and passenger. He is Humanity itself in miniature; hence the necessity for self-love. Do you want a demonstration of my system's superiority? Consider envy. Every moralist, whether Greek or Turk, Christian or Mussulman, thunders against envy. From Idumea to Tijuca, everyone agrees that envy is bad. Well, we must reject ancient prejudices on this subject, we must forget the hollow rhetoric of the past, and we must study objectively this salutary and noble sentiment called envy. As every man is Humanity in miniature, obviously no man is fundamentally opposed to another man, however much appearances may suggest the contrary. Thus, the hangman who executes the condemned may excite the indignation of poets, but in substance he is Humanity correcting in Humanity a breach of Humanity's law. I say that the same principle applies to a man who in private aggression disembowels one of his fellows: he is manifesting the fundamental force of Humanity. There is nothing to prevent (and there are cases of this) his being disemboweled in turn. If you have been able to follow me, you will understand that envy is nothing but a fighting admiration, and, as fighting or struggle is the great function of the human race, all bellicose feelings tend toward its welfare. From this it follows that envy is a virtue."

I was completely dumbfounded. The lucidity of the exposition, the rigor of the logic, the irrefutability of the conclusions —it all appeared so overwhelmingly wonderful and so revolutionary that I asked for a few minutes in which to digest the new philosophy. Quincas Borba could not conceal his satisfaction. He was serenely gnawing a chicken wing. I offered a few minor objections to his argument, but they were so weak that he took only a minute or two to crush them utterly.

"To grasp the meaning of my system," he concluded, "it is important never to forget the universal principle, shared by and summed up in every man. Just consider: war, which to many persons seems to be a calamity, is really a desirable activity—a snap of Humanity's fingers, so to speak. Hunger (and he sucked the chicken wing philosophically), hunger is a discipline to which Humanity subjects its own viscera. But the sublimity of my system really requires no better documentation than this very chicken. It was fed on corn that was planted, let us say, by an African imported from Angola. This African was born, grew up, was sold; a ship brought him here, a ship built of wood cut in the forest by ten or twelve men and driven by sails that eight or ten men wove, not to mention the rope and the rest of the nautical apparatus. Thus, this chicken, on which I have just lunched, is the result of a multitude of efforts and struggles carried on for the sole ultimate purpose of satisfying my appetite."

Between the cheese and the coffee, Quincas Borba showed me that his system would destroy pain. According to Humanitism, pain is pure illusion. When the child is threatened with corporeal punishment, it shuts its eyes and trembles even before it is actually struck; this *predisposition* to pain creates an allusion which each man inherits and in turn transmits. Intellectual acceptance of the system will not, of itself, immediately expel pain; it is, however, an indispensable beginning. Natural evolution will take care of the rest. Once man is fully convinced that he is Humanity itself, he has only to make his thoughts revert to the original substance in order to avoid every painful sensation or sentiment. However, evolution toward this goal will probably be so slow that one must allow several thousands of years for it.

A few days later, Quincas Borba read me his great work. It consisted of four manuscript volumes of one hundred pages each, in a fine hand and with numerous quotations from the Latin. The final volume was a political treatise based upon Humanitism; it was perhaps the most tiresome part of the work, although conceived with amazing logical precision. Even when society was reorganized in accordance with his scheme, war, revolution, murder, misery, hunger, and disease would by no means disappear; but as these "scourges," erroneously so called, were nothing but external manifestations of the internal substance and therefore of little influence on man except as a diversion from monotony, it was clear that their existence did not stand in the way of human happiness. But even if we accepted the old-fashioned notion about the effects of these "scourges," the system would remain unshaken for two reasons: first, as Humanity is the absolute creative substance, every individual ought to be delighted to sacrifice himself to the principle from which he descends; second, the "scourges" do not detract from our dominion over the earth, which, with everything in and about it—the stars, the breezes, the exotic date-palm, and the common garden rhubarb—was created solely for our pleasure. "Pangloss," he said as he closed the book, "was not so great a fool as Voltaire thought."

118. The Third Force:

The third force that drove me to the hurly-burly of an active life was the desire to shine before men. I had no vocation for a hermit's life. The crowd drew me, applause wooed me. If the idea of the plaster had come to me at that time, who knows, I might have achieved fame. But it did not come. All that came was the desire to get myself head-over-heels involved in something, in anything.

119. Parenthetical:

I should like here to set down parenthetically a half dozen maxims that I composed at this time. They are yawns born of boredom, but perhaps some aspiring essayist will find use for them as epigraphs.

* * *

One endures with patience the pain in the other fellow's stomach.

*

* *

We kill time; time buries us.

*

* *

A coachman-philosopher used to say that the desire to ride in carriages would be greatly diminished if everyone could afford to ride in carriages.

*

* *

Believe in yourself, but do not always refuse to believe in others.

*

* *

"Nothing could be more ridiculous than the childish delight that savages take in piercing a lip and adorning it with a piece of wood," said the jeweler.

*

* *

Do not feel badly if your kindness is rewarded with ingratitude: it is better to fall from your dream clouds than from a third-story window.

120. Compelle Intrare: "No, my friend, whether you like it or not, you've got to get married," said Sabina. "What a wonderful future! A childless old bachelor."

Childless! The idea of having children suddenly took complete possession of me; it ran through my veins like a mysterious fluid. Yes, I was really meant to be a father. A bachelor's life had certain advantages, to be sure, but they were unsubstantial and cost too much in loneliness. Childless! No, it was something to avoid at all costs. I would accept everything, even Damasceno as father-in-law.

As I had great confidence in Quincas Borba's judgment, I went to him and told him all about my paternal yearnings. The philosopher listened and beamed. He declared that Humanity was stirring in my breast; he encouraged me to marry; he informed me that additional converts to Humanitism were knocking at his door; etc. *Compelle intrare*, as Jesus said. And before we parted he proved that the Gospel was nothing but a prefiguration of Humanitism erroneously interpreted by the churchmen.

121. Down the Hill: Three months later everything was moving along beautifully.

The fluid, Sabina, the girl's eyes, her father's hopes, all were impelling me toward matrimony. I thought of Virgília from time to time, and a black devil would come and hold before my eyes a mirror in which I saw her, far off, undone in tears; but then another devil, a rose-colored one, would come along with another mirror, in which I saw the tender, angelic face of Nhan-lóló.

I say nothing about my years, for I did not feel them. I cast them aside, on a certain Sunday when I attended Mass in the chapel on Livramento Hill. As Damasceno and family lived in Cajueiros, I often accompanied them to Mass. At that time there were no houses on the hill except at the very top, where the little palace and its chapel were situated. On this certain Sunday, as I was coming down the hill with Nhan-lóló on my arm, I found myself dropping two years here, four there, five a little farther on, so that, when I arrived at the bottom, I was only twenty years old and as light and gay as one expects a twenty-year-old to be. If you want to know the exact circumstances under which this dropping of years took place, simply read on to the end of the chapter.

We were coming from Mass—she, her father, and I. Halfway down the hill we spied a group of men. Damasceno knew immediately what was going on and ran ahead excitedly; we followed. And this is what we saw: men of every age, size, and color, some in shirt-sleeves, some with jackets, others in tattered coats, in various attitudes—squatting, bending forward with hands on knees, sitting on stones, leaning against the fence—but all with eyes fixed on the center of the circle and with their souls hanging out of their eyes.

"What is it?" asked Nhan-lóló.

I signaled her to hold her question a moment. I wormed through the crowd, and they made way without looking at me. Their eyes were glued to the space in the center, where a cock-fight was in progress. I saw the two antagonists, sharp-spurred roosters with fiery eyes and pointed beaks. Their crests were bloody, their breasts almost featherless, and they were tired, but they fought on, pecking, clawing, trembling with rage. Oblivious to everything else in the world, Damasceno was concentrating his attention on the duel. In vain I told him that we had better move on; he did not answer, he did not even hear.

Nhan-lóló pulled me gently by the arm and said we ought to go. I accepted this counsel, and we continued down the hill. I have already told you that the hill was without habitation; I have also said that we were coming from Mass; and, as I have not said that it was raining, you may assume that the weather was favorable. The sun was delightful. And strong. So strong that I opened the parasol, held it high on the handle so that it would be close to our heads, and inclined it at such a concealing angle that I was able to add a page to Quincas Borba's philosophy: Humanity osculated Humanity . . . These were the circumstances under which my years fell away.

At the bottom of the hill we waited for Damasceno. After a few minutes he came along, surrounded by the men who had wagered on the fight and discussing it with them. One of them, the stakeholder, was distributing a handful of small, dirty bills to the winners, who experienced the double joy of victory and wealth. As to the cocks, they were carried under the arms of their respective owners. The crest of one of them was so torn and bloody that I thought he must have been the loser. But I was wrong; the loser had no crest at all. Both were open-beaked, breathing with difficulty, utterly exhausted. The spectators, on the contrary, were lively and happy, despite the strong emotions with which they had watched the struggle. They were talking about the history of the antagonists, especially their pugilistic exploits. I walked on, annoyed. Nhan-lóló walked next to me, ashamed.

122. A Lofty Purpose: Nhan-lóló was ashamed of her father. The ease with which he had become one of the group had brought into sharp relief his old habits and social ties, and Nhan-lóló had already begun to fear that I would think him unworthy to be my father-in-law.

She had been analyzing and studying my manners and her own, and one could see the consequent changes that she had made in herself. The drawing-room life of elegance and polish attracted her, chiefly because it seemed to her to offer the environment in which we could most surely adjust ourselves to each other. Nhan-lóló observed and imitated, and gradually developed a certain social intuition. She did everything possible to conceal the inferiority of her family background, and her father's gross conduct on the occasion of the cockfight saddened her greatly. I tried to divert her with fashionable talk and amusing stories, but in vain. Her dejection was so profound and so clearly expressed in her face and attitude that I began to attribute to Nhan-lóló an active purpose to separate her cause from her father's in my mind. This seemed to me a commendable and even a lofty purpose; it established another bond between us.

"There is no alternative," I said to myself; "I must pluck this flower from the swamp."

123. The Real Cotrim: In spite of my forty-odd years, I determined not to propose marriage without first speaking to Cotrim, for I strongly desired harmony within the family. He heard me and replied that he did not permit himself to express opinions about matters concerning his relatives. Some people might attribute a personal motive to him if by chance he were to praise Nhan-lóló's rare virtues; therefore, he would say nothing. Moreover: he was certain that his niece entertained a true passion for me, yet if she were to consult him his advice would be against the marriage. I was not to think that he disliked me; he recognized my good qualities—he never grew tired of singing their praises, which was only right; and so far as Nhan-lóló was concerned, he could not deny that she would make an excellent wife; but between recognition of these facts and advice to marry there yawned a wide abyss.

"I wash my hands of the responsibility," he concluded.

"But only the other day you were saying that I ought to marry."

"That's another question. I think that it is important for you to marry, especially as you have political aspirations. In politics, bachelorhood is a handicap. But as to your choice of a bride, I do not wish to influence you in any way, and I ought not do so; my relationship to one of the parties involved deprives me of this privilege. It seems to me that Sabina went too far in talking to you about marriage with Nhan-lóló; but in any case she is not a blood relative of the girl, as I am. And yet . . . but no . . . I prefer to keep this thought unspoken."

"What is it?"

"No. I have nothing to say."

These scruples may appear inordinate to anyone who does not recognize the deep and fierce sense of honor in Cotrim's character. In the years following the settlement of my father's estate, I too was unjust to him. Now I understand that he was one man in a thousand. They used to call him avaricious, and perhaps they were right; but avarice is only an exaggerated form of a virtue, and with virtues as with budgets it is better to have an excess than a deficit. As his manner was very sharp, he had enemies, who accused him of barbarity. The only fact alleged to support this charge was that he frequently committed slaves to the dungeon and that they were always dripping blood when released; but, apart from the fact that he did this only to fugitives and incorrigibles, one must remember that, as he had long been engaged in smuggling slaves into the country, he had become accustomed to long-established methods of treatment that were somewhat harsher than those practised in the regular slave trade, and one cannot honestly attribute to a man's basic character something that is obviously the result of a social pattern. Further, although he may have owed kindness to some, he owed money to none.

The proof of Cotrim's good heart is seen in the love he bore his children and in the grief he suffered when, a few months later, his daughter Sarah died; an irrefutable proof, it seems to me, and by no means the only one. He was treasurer of a fraternal organization and a member of various philanthropic brotherhoods. He was even a paid-up life member of one of these—a fact that is hardly consistent with the alleged avarice. True, his generosity in this case did not fall on barren ground: the brotherhood (of which he was one of the trustees) ordered his portrait to be painted in oil.

Naturally, he was not perfect. For example, after making a charitable contribution he always sent out a press release about it —a reprehensible or at least not praiseworthy practice, I agree. But he explained his conduct on the ground that good deeds, if made public, rouse people to do likewise—an argument to which one cannot deny a certain force. I even believe, to his very great credit, that he made these contributions with no purpose other than to awaken the latent philanthropy in men, a goal to whose achievement the publicity was a condition *sine qua non*.

124. Interposition:

What separates life from death? Only the shortest of bridges. (I do not claim originality for this thought, but it is a true one and I have expressed it in succinct and picturesque form. As I say, however, it is not original.) Nevertheless, if I did not interpose this chapter, the reader might suffer a great shock. To hop from a character study to an epitaph may be realistic and even commonplace, but the reader probably would not have taken refuge in this book if he had not wished to escape the realistic and the commonplace.

125. Epitaph:

HERE LIES

DONA EULALIA DAMASCENA DE BRITO

SHE DIED

AT THE AGE OF NINETEEN YEARS

REMEMBER HER IN YOUR PRAYERS

126. Disconsolation:

The epitaph tells all. The details about her illness, her agony, her family's grief, the funeral, would add nothing important. It is enough to know that she died. I might add that it was during the first epidemic of yellow fever. I attended the funeral. It made me sad but it did not cause me to cry; from this I concluded that I had not really loved her.

See the errors to which a misunderstanding of basic principles may lead: I was offended by the blindness of the epidemic which, killing at random, took away, among others, a young lady who was to have been my wife. I did not understand the need for the epidemic, much less the need for that particular death. I even think that this death seemed more absurd to me than all the others together. However, Quincas Borba explained to me that epidemics are useful to the species although fatal to a certain number of individuals. He showed me that, however horrible the spectacle may be, the greater part of the population survives and can continue to subsist. He went so far as to ask me whether, in the midst of the turmoil, I did not feel a secret joy at having escaped the claws of the pestilence; but this question was so absurd that I did not dignify it with a reply.

As I have not related the death, I shall also omit the seventh-day Mass. A fortnight later I was talking with Damasceno, who was still deeply sad and inconsolable. He said that the great sorrow with which God had punished him was increased by the sorrow that man had inflicted upon him. He did not explain. Three weeks later he returned to the subject and confided in me that, in the throes of the irreparable tragedy, he had hoped for the consolation that the presence of friends can give. Only twelve people, and three-fourths of them friends of Cotrim, accompanied his daughter's coffin to the cemetery. And he had sent out eighty invitations. I expressed the opinion that there were so many deaths during the epidemic that one might well excuse the apparent neglect. Damasceno shook his head sadly and incredulously.

"No," he groaned, "they let me down."

Cotrim, who was present, said:

"Those came who had a genuine interest in you and in us. The eighty would have come only as a formality, would have talked about the inertia of the government, about patent medicines, about the price of real estate, or about each other . . ."

Damasceno listened in silence, shook his head again, and sighed:

"But they should at least have come."

127. Formality:

It is a wonderful advantage to have been endowed by heaven with the gift of seeing the relationship between things that are apparently unrelated. I had this gift, and even today I am grateful for it from the bottom of my grave.

In truth, an ordinary man who heard that last remark by Damasceno would not bring it to mind when, some time later, he happened to glance at a picture of six Turkish ladies. But I did. The picture was of six modern ladies of Constantinople in street clothes, their faces hidden, not by thick cloth that really concealed, but by the most tenuous veils, which pretended to reveal only the eyes but actually revealed the whole face. I found amusing this clever Mussulman coquetry that thus hides the face —and satisfies custom—but does not hide it—and divulges beauty. Apparently there is no connection between the Turkish ladies and Damasceno; but if you have a profound and perspicacious mind (and I strongly suspect that you will not deny this), you will understand that in both cases there may be discerned a constant and tender companion of social man . . .

Sweet Formality, you are the true staff of life, the balsam that heals the heart, the tie that binds man to man and earth to heaven. You dry a father's tears; you win the indulgence of a prophet. If in the former case grief is assuaged, and in the latter conscience is appeased, to whom but you do they owe these benefits? High esteem, passing by with a mere nod, does not speak to the soul; but indifference, bowing and tipping its hat, creates a most delightful impression. The reason is that, contrary to an absurd old saying, it is not the letter that kills; the letter gives life; it is the spirit that causes doubt, interpretation, controversy, and therefore struggle and death. So, long live sweet Formality, to the glory of Mohammed and the peace of mind of Damasceno.

128. In the Chamber of Deputies: And please note that I

saw the Turkish picture two years after Damasceno made his remark, and that I saw it in the Chamber of Deputies, in the midst of a great buzz of conversation, while a deputy was discussing a report of the Budget Commission. I too was a deputy. For anyone who has read this book till now, it is unnecessary for me to describe my satisfaction, and for other persons it would be futile for me to do so. I was a deputy and, as I leaned back in my chair, I saw the Turkish picture between a colleague who was telling a joke and another who was drawing a profile of the speaker in pencil on the back of an envelope. The speaker was Lobo Neves. The sea of life had brought us to the same shore like two bottles from a shipwreck, he managing to contain his resentment, I containing, one would perhaps expect, my remorse; and I use this provisional, problematic, suspensive form of expression in order to be able to point out that in truth I contained nothing whatever except an ambition to become a minister of state.

129. No Remorse: I suffered no remorse. If I had the necessary laboratory equipment, I

should analyze remorse into its elements and should thus discover why Achilles paraded his adversary's cadaver around the walls of Troy and why Lady Macbeth paraded her spot of blood around the room. But I have no laboratory equipment, and, as I said, I had no remorse; all I had was a desire to become a minister of state. However, if you must know, I should like to have been neither Achilles nor Lady Macbeth; but if I had to choose between them, I should choose to be Achilles, to achieve a great triumph, to hear Priam's supplications, to win a glorious reputation among both the military and the literary. But I did not hear Priam's supplications, I heard Lobo Neves' speech, and I felt no remorse.

[183]

130. To Insert in Chapter 129: My first opportunity to

speak to Virgilia after the end of the governorship came at a ball in 1855. She was wearing a strikingly beautiful gown of grogram and was exhibiting the same pair of shoulders as in the old days. She lacked the freshness of those days but was still beautiful, with an autumnal beauty that seemed to be most impressive in the evening. I remember that we spoke a great deal. The past was in our minds but we did not directly allude to it. A remotely suggestive remark, a glance, and nothing more. Shortly after, she left. I watched her go down the stairs, and I do not know by what trick of cerebral ventriloquism (philologists will, I hope, forgive the use of so barbarous a phrase) I found myself murmuring this deeply retrospective word:

"Magnificent!"

This chapter is to be inserted between the first two sentences of Chapter 129.

131. Concerning a Calumny: When the cerebro-ventriloquial proc-

ess had produced this word—which expressed a mere opinion and not remorse—I felt someone's hand on my shoulder. I turned. It was an old friend, a naval officer, jovial and somewhat unrestrained in speech and manner. He smiled maliciously and said:

"You gay dog, you! Memories of the past, eh?"

"Long live the past!"

"I suppose you've been taken back in your old job."

"Get out of here!" I said in mock anger, threatening him with my hand.

I confess that this dialogue was an indiscretion—especially the last reply. And I confess it with a certain pleasure, because it is women that have the reputation for indiscretion in speech, and I do not wish to finish the book without rectifying this false notion. In the case of a reference to their amorous adventures, I have known men to smile, to deny half-heartedly, to reply with a monosyllable, etc., whereas their partners in guilt not only said nothing to give themselves away but swore by all the saints that it was a malicious slander. The reason for this difference is that a woman (except where such motives as that in Chapter 101 exist) gives herself for love's sake, whether it be romantic love or the purely physical love experienced by certain ladies in ancient Rome, for example, and by women among the Polynesians, Laplanders, Kaffirs, and possibly one or two other ethnic groups; but a man—and I speak only of men in a cultured and elegant society—adds vanity to the sentiment of love. In addition (and I am referring always to love involving infidelity), a woman feels that she is false to her duty and therefore devotes great energy and skill to dissimulation; but the man, considering himself the irresistible cause of the affair and the vanquisher of the other man, becomes rightfully proud. Before long, however, he adopts another attitude, less stiff and less secretive than pride, the attitude of fatuous vanity, the conspicuous badge of amorous merit.

But whether or not my explanation is true, I wish to record on this page, for reference through the centuries to come, that woman's proverbial indiscretion is a fraud invented by men. With respect at least to the revelation of their love affairs, women are as silent as the tomb. It is true, of course, that they often give themselves away by gestures and glances. Perhaps that is what Margaret of Navarre, a great lady and fine wit, had in mind when she coined the following metaphor: "Even the best-trained dog cannot stifle his bark forever."

132. Not Profound:

In connection with this maxim by the Queen of Navarre, I am put in mind of the customary way, among our people, of inquiring about the cause of another person's anger: "Say, who killed your little doggies?" It is as if one were to ask, "Who robbed you of your love, of your secret joys, *etc.*?" Please note that this chapter is not intended to be profound.

133. Helvetius' Theory: We were at the point at which the naval officer had extorted a confession of my affair with Virgilia. The episode serves to illustrate and perhaps amend Helvetius' theory that self-interest is the mainspring of human action. My interest dictated silence. Confession of the old love affair might have aroused a dormant hatred, started a scandal, or, at the very least, given me a reputation for indiscretion in speech. So it was in my interest to say nothing; and, considering Helvetius' theory on a superficial level, that is what one would have expected me to do. But, in an earlier chapter, I stated the motive of this sort of indiscretion: men are governed less by considerations of ultimate safety than by vanity, which is more intimate, more immediate. The decision to avoid a future danger comes from the intellect and rests upon a syllogism; vanity springs spontaneously from instinct, from the viscera. Conclusion: Helvetius' law applies in my case, but the self-interest that guided me was not based upon a real calculation of consequent pleasure and pain but upon an emotional judgment of hidden origin.

134. Fifty Years: I have not yet told you, but I tell you now, that when Virgilia went down the stairs and the naval officer touched me on the shoulder, I was fifty years old. Therefore it was my life that went down the stairs, or at least the best part of it, a part full of pleasure, agitation, fear, cloaked in dissimulation and duplicity, but still the best part of my life, if we must speak the language of ordinary men. If, however, we choose a more elevated, more philosophical level, the best part of my life was still to come, as I shall have the honor of relating in the few remaining pages of this book.

Fifty years! Perhaps I need not have told you. Perhaps you noted that my literary style is less gay, less spirited than in the early years. On this occasion, after my dialogue with the naval officer, who put on his cape and left, I became a little heavy-hearted. I returned to the salon, danced a polka, intoxicated myself with the lights, the flowers, the beautiful eyes, and the light hum of conversation. And I became young again. But half an hour later when I left the ball at four o'clock in the morning, what do you think was waiting for me in my carriage? My fifty years. There they were, uninvited—not benumbed with cold nor rheumatic, but dozing off their weariness, eager for home and bed. Then (and you can see to what extremes a sleepy man's imagination may go), then I heard a bat, perched on the roof, saying, "Mr. Braz Cubas, your rejuvenation lay in the salon, in the lights, in the silk dresses . . ."

135. Oblivion: I fear that if any female reader has got this far she will now shut the book and refuse to read the rest. For her, all interest in my life disappeared with the love interest. Fifty years! Not yet invalidism, but certainly not robustness. Come ten more and I shall understand the significance of something that an Englishman once said: "The problem is no longer to find someone who remembers my parents; it is to find someone who remembers me."

I shall write the great name in capital letters: OBLIVION! In all justice, let us bestow what honors we can upon so despised and yet so worthy a personage—a guest who may arrive late but who never fails to come. He calls upon the lady who shone in the dawn of the present reign, but more poignant is his relationship with the lady who exhibited her charms in their flower during Paraná's ministry, for she is still so close to the days of her triumphs that she has a feeling that others have stolen her carriage and are riding in it. If she is worthy of herself, she will not persist in trying to arouse dead or dying memories; she will not seek in today's glance the same warmth that she found in yesterday's, when other persons, nimble and hearty, were starting on the great parade. *Tempora mutantur*. She understands what this whirlwind is about, she knows that it is sweeping the leaves from the grove and old rags from the road, with neither exception nor pity, and if she has a little philosophy she will not envy but will feel compassion for those who took her carriage, for they too will have to alight and will find the faithful footman OBLIVION at the door. A spectacle whose purpose is to divert the planet Saturn, which would otherwise, I suppose, be utterly bored.

136. Unnecessary: And, if I am not greatly mistaken, I have just written an utterly unnecessary chapter.

137. The Shako: No, I am wrong; for it sums up the thoughts that I expressed the next day to Quincas Borba. I added that I felt spiritually defeated. But the philosopher, with his supramundane insight, scolded me for letting myself slide down the fatal slope of melancholy.

"My dear Braz Cubas, don't let yourself suffer from these old-fashioned vapors. What the devil, you have to be a man! Be strong! Fight! Conquer! Shine! Influence! Dominate! Fifty years is an age for wisdom and politics. Courage, Braz Cubas; don't turn ninny on me. Why should you be bothered by the fact that everything moves along? Try to taste life, to enjoy it; and try to understand that the worst philosophy of all is that of the cry-baby who lies down at the edge of the river and bewails the incessant flow of the water. The function of the river is to flow on; adjust yourself to this law of nature and try to take advantage of it."

Even little things, as you see, are cleared up by the authority with which a great philosopher can speak. Quincas Borba's words had the magic effect of dispelling my moral and mental torpor. All right, I would really take up politics seriously; there was still time. Until then I had not taken part in the debates. I had been courting a position in the Cabinet by means of servility, teas, work on commissions, and astute voting; but the position did not come. I should have to take the platform.

I began slowly. Three days after my talk with Quincas Borba, during a discussion of the budget of the Department of Justice, I took advantage of the opportunity to inquire modestly of the Minister whether he did not think it desirable to diminish the size of the shakos worn by the National Guard. The subject was not one of great scope, but at the same time I pointed out that it was not unworthy of a statesman's consideration; and I cited Philopemen, who ordered replacement of his troops' bucklers because they were too small and of their lances because they were too light—a fact which history found quite consistent with the gravity of its pages. The shakos of our National Guard had to be reduced in size, not only because they were inelegant but also because they were unhygienic. In parades on sunny days the excessive heat produced by them could well prove fatal. Hippocrates laid down the rule that one should always keep his head cool; it was cruel to force a citizen of the nation, solely because he wore a uniform, to risk his health, his life, and consequently the future of his family. The Chamber and the administration had to remember that the National Guard was the bulwark of liberty and independence and that the citizen, called to serve gratuitously, frequently, and laboriously, had a right to expect us to minimize his burden by decreeing that his uniform be light and comfortable. Moreover, the heavy shako then in use weighed down the citizens' heads, and the fatherland needed citizens who could raise their heads high and serene in the face of tyranny. And I concluded with this idea: The weeping willow, which bends its branches to the ground, grows in the cemetery; the palm tree, erect and firm, grows in the garden and in the city square.

The speech was variously received. As to form, eloquence, literary quality, and philosophical implications, there was only one opinion: everyone told me that in these respects it was perfect and that no one else had ever succeeded in deriving so many thoughts from a shako. But many considered the speech deplorable from a political point of view; some went so far as to call it a parliamentary disaster. I was informed that others believed me to have joined the opposition party; the opposition deputies accepted this conclusion and began to talk about introducing a motion for a vote of lack of confidence in the administration. I vigorously denied the charge of apostasy, which was not only erroneous but also calumnious, for I had conspicuously supported the Cabinet in all its proposals. I added that the need to reduce the size of the shako was not so urgent that its satisfaction could not be delayed a few years; that in any case I should be willing to compromise on the extent of the reduction and would be content with three-quarters of an inch or possibly a little less; and, finally, that even if no action was taken on my proposal, I had done my duty by introducing it.

Quincas Borba, however, made no concessions whatever. "I'm no politician," he told me at dinner. "I don't know whether you did the wise thing or not, but I do know that you made an excellent speech." And then he referred to the brilliance of certain passages, to the beauty of the imagery, and to the strength of some of the arguments—all, however, with that moderation that is so characteristic of a great philosopher. Then he took the argument upon himself and impugned the present shako with such force and lucidity that he finally convinced me that it really ought to be made smaller.

138. To a Critic: My dear critic:

Several pages back, after stating that I was fifty years old, I said, "Perhaps you noted that my literary style is less gay, less spirited than in the early years." Maybe you find this sentence difficult to understand in the light of my present condition. But the sentence and the condition are quite reconcilable, for I do not mean by the former to suggest that I am older than when I began to write the book. Death does not age one. The meaning of the sentence rests upon the fact that in writing each phase of the story of my life I feel the corresponding emotion or attitude, which is of course reflected in my style. Good God, do I have to explain everything!

139. How I Did Not Become a Minister of State:

. . . .
. . . .
. . . .
. . . .
. . . .

140. Which Explains the Preceding Chapter:

Some things are better said without words—for example, the subject of the preceding chapter. Other frustrated aspirants to high office will understand. If, as has been maintained, the passion for power is stronger than all others, try to imagine the depression, the grief, the despair that I felt on the day I lost my seat in the Chamber of Deputies. All my hopes were gone; my political career was over. Quincas Borba, by philosophical ratiocination, found that my ambition was not a real passion for power but merely a whim, a desire to amuse myself. In his opinion, this desire, although weaker than the passion for power, is, if unsatisfied, even more troubling to the mind; it is much like the desire that women have for beautiful combs and lace. A Cromwell or a Bonaparte, by the very fact that he is consumed by the passion for power, lets nothing stand in his way and inevitably, by hook or by crook, gets what he wants. My desire was different: it lacked strength and therefore lacked certainty of success. My desire, according to Humanitism . . .

"To the devil with you and your Humanitism," I broke in. "I'm fed up with philosophies that don't get me anywhere."

In the case of a philosophy so vast and so profound as Humanitism, this interruption amounted to unpardonable insolence. However, Quincas Borba was not disturbed. They brought us coffee. It was one o'clock in the afternoon; we were in my study, a lovely room that opened onto the grounds behind the house. Good books, *objets d'art*—including a bronze Voltaire, which on this occasion seemed to smile with exaggerated sarcasm—fine chairs, and out-of-doors the sun, which Quincas Borba, whether punning at my expense or poetizing I don't know, called one of nature's ministers. There was a cool breeze, and the sky was blue. In each of the three windows hung a bird cage whose tenant trilled a rustic opera. Everything took on the appearance of a conspiracy of things against man. And, although I was in *my* room, looking at *my* grounds, seated in *my* chair, listening to *my* birds, close to *my* books, illuminated by *my* sun, I could not rid myself of a longing for that other chair that was not mine.

141. The Dogs:
"Well, what are you going to do now?" asked Quincas Borba as he placed his empty cup on a window sill.

"I don't know. I'll probably move to Tijuca and hide. I'm ashamed. Such dreams, my dear Borba, such dreams, and I am nothing."

"Nothing!" he interrupted with a gesture of protest.

To distract me, Quincas Borba invited me to take a stroll with him. We set out in the direction of the Engenho Velho and philosophized as we went. I shall never forget the benefits I derived from this walk. The word of that great man was the fountain of wisdom. He told me that I must not flee from battle; if they shut the doors of the Chamber in my face, I could start a newspaper. He even used a slang expression, showing that the language of philosophy can sometimes be enriched by the idiom of the common people. Start a paper, he advised, and "give them hell."

"A magnificent idea! I'll found a newspaper. I'll smash them, I'll . . ."

"You'll fight. Maybe you'll smash them and maybe you won't; the main thing is to fight. Life is struggle. A life without fighting is a dead sea in the universal organism."

In a short while we came upon a dogfight, which, to an ordinary man, would have no philosophic significance whatever. Quincas Borba made me stop and observe the two dogs. He noted that near them there was a bone, the motive of the war, and called my attention to the fact that there was no meat on the bone. Just a plain, bare bone. With fury in their eyes, the dogs growled and bit each other . . . Quincas Borba put his cane under his arm and seemed to be in ecstasy.

"How beautiful this is!" he would say from time to time.

I wanted to drag him away, but was unable to do so. He was rooted to the spot and resumed our walk only when the fight had completely ended and one of the dogs, badly chewed up, took his hunger elsewhere. I noted that Quincas Borba was joyful, although he contained his joy, as became a great philosopher. He spoke again of the beauty of the spectacle and reminded me of the motive of the struggle, *i. e.*, the satisfaction of hunger; but he added that privation of food was not in itself important for the broad purposes of philosophy. In some parts of the world the spectacle is more grandiose: human creatures fight with dogs for bones and for other even less appetizing dishes—a struggle greatly complicated by the use of human intelligence with all the accumulation of wisdom that man has received through the centuries, *etc.*

142. The Confidential Request: "How much lies hidden in a minuet!" said someone or other. How much lies hidden in a dogfight! But I was no servile or timid disciple, afraid to express reasonable doubts. As we walked along, I said that I was not exactly clear about the reason for the philosophic approval of a fight between men and dogs for a bone. He replied with remarkable patience:

"It is more logical for men to fight with men for it, because the antagonists are more evenly matched. But can we deny that the spectacle of men battling with dogs for a bone also has a certain grandeur? Locusts have been eaten voluntarily, as in the case of

John the Baptist; Ezekiel ate even worse things. We may therefore conclude that the range of the humanly edible is wider than is commonly supposed. We have only then to ask whether it is preferable to fight for a bone in response to a natural need or to forgo it in obedience to a religious summons. Religious enthusiasm is subject to change, but hunger is as eternal as life and death."

We were now at the door of my house. A servant gave me a letter, saying that it was from a lady. We went in, and Quincas Borba, with the discretion appropriate to a philosopher, studied the names of the books in one of the bookcases while I read the letter, which was from Virgilia:

> My good friend,
>   Dona Placida is very ill. I shall be grateful if you will do something for her. She lives in Escadinhas Alley. See if you can get her into the Misericordia Hospital.
>
> Your sincere friend,
V

The letter was not in Virgilia's neat and precise hand; the writing was coarse and irregular. The V of the signature was really a scrawl with no very obvious alphabetical intention. If the letter had been discovered it would have been very difficult to prove that she was the author. I read and reread it. Poor Dona Placida! But I had given her the five contos of the Botafogo beach and I could not understand.

"You'll soon understand," said Quincas Borba, taking a book from the bookcase.

"What?" I asked in amazement.

"You'll soon understand that it is only I who tell you the truth. Pascal is one of my intellectual grandfathers, and, although my philosophy is worth more than his, I cannot deny that he was a great man. Now, what does he say on this page?" And hat on head, cane under his arm, he pointed to a passage with his finger. "What does he say? He says, 'Were the Universe to crush him, man would still be more noble than that which has slain him, because he knows that he dies . . . The Universe knows nothing of this.' Do you see the analogy? The man who fights with a dog for a bone has a great advantage, for he knows he is hungry; and it is this that makes the struggle so impressive. 'Knows that he dies' is a profound phrase, but I believe that mine is still more profound: 'knows he is hungry.' For the fact of death limits, so to speak, the human understanding; and the consciousness that one is dying lasts only a brief moment and never comes back, but hunger comes back again and again and may remain in consciousness a considerable length of time. With all due modesty, I believe that Pascal's thought is inferior to mine, but I do not deny that it deserves to be called great nor that he himself was a great man."

143. I Won't Go: While he was putting the book back in the bookcase, I reread the letter.

At dinner, as I spoke little, chewed without being able to swallow, stared at a corner of the room, at the end of the table, at a plate, at a chair, at an imaginary fly, he said to me, "Is something wrong? I'll bet it's that letter." The fact is that I felt annoyed with and inconvenienced by Virgilia's request. I had given Dona Placida five contos; I greatly doubt that anyone else would have been so generous. Five contos! What had she done with them? Doubtless she had wasted them on big parties and now she wanted to get into the Misericordia, and I was elected to take her there! Why must a dying person be taken to a hospital? You can die anywhere. Besides, I did not know, or did not remember, Escadinhas Alley; it sounded like some dark, crowded corner of the city. I would have to find it, suffer the curiosity of the neighbors, knock at the door, *etc*. What a nuisance! I won't go.

144. A Limited Purpose: But that good counselor the Night advised me to gratify, as a matter of courtesy, my former mistress's desires.

"One must pay one's debts graciously," I said as I got out of bed.

After breakfast I went to Dona Placida's house. I found a heap of bones covered with rags and stretched out on an old, nauseatingly dirty cot. I gave her some money. The next day I had her taken to the Misericordia, where she died a week later. No, that is not quite accurate. She did not die; one morning she simply failed to wake, and thus departed from life the same way that she had entered it—surreptitiously. Once again I asked myself, as I had in Chapter 75, whether it was for this that the sacristan of the cathedral and his lady, in a moment of love, had brought Dona Placida into the world. But then I remembered that, if it had not been for Dona Placida, perhaps my affair with Virgilia would have been interrupted or even terminated just as it was getting under way. This, perhaps, was the purpose of Dona Placida's life. A limited, relative purpose, I agree; but what the devil is absolute in this world?

145. Mere Repetition: As to the five contos, it is hardly worth writing that a stone-cutter of the neighborhood pretended to be in love with Dona Placida, succeeded in awakening her affection or her vanity, and married her; after a few months he said that he needed capital for a business venture, sold the bonds, and fled with the money. It is hardly worth writing. It is the case of Quincas Borba's dogs all over again. Mere repetition of a chapter.

146. The Platform: I should have to start a newspaper. I prepared its editorial platform, which was a political application of Humanitism. However, as Quincas Borba had not yet published the book (which he continually corrected and rewrote, year after year), we agreed to make no reference to Humanitism. Quincas Borba insisted only on a signed statement, simple and unostentatious, that certain new

principles, here applied to politics, had been derived from his book, which had not yet been published.

It was the best platform one could possibly imagine: it promised to cure the ills of society, to destroy misrule, to promote liberty and security; it appealed to business and to labor; it quoted Guizot and Ledru-Rollin; and it ended with this threat, which Quincas Borba found paltry and provincial: "The new doctrines that we espouse must inevitably overthrow the present administration." I may say that, under the political circumstances of the time, the platform seemed to me to be a masterpiece. As to the threat at the end, which Quincas Borba found paltry, I showed him that it was saturated with Humanitism, and he finally agreed with me. For Humanitism is alien to nothing: Napoleon's wars and a fight between two nanny goats would, under our system, be equally sublime, with the sole difference that Napoleon's soldiers knew, and nanny goats apparently do not know, of the possibility of death. Now, I merely applied our philosophic formula to the circumstances, *i.e.*, to the desirability of overthrowing the administration: Humanity wished to replace Humanity for the welfare of Humanity.

"You are my beloved disciple, my caliph," cried Quincas Borba with a note of affection that I had never before heard in his voice. "I may say with the great Mohammed that even if the sun and the moon oppose me, I shall never retreat. Just think, my dear Braz Cubas, we have really found eternal Truth, the Truth that existed before the phenomenal world and that will go on forever, for it is beyond time."

147. My Folly: I sent the press a modest announcement that in a few weeks an opposition newspaper, edited by Mr. Braz Cubas, would begin publication. Quincas Borba, to whom I read the announcement before sending it, took my pen and, in an outburst of humanitistic brotherliness, wrote these words after my name: "one of the most glorious members of the preceding Chamber."

The next day Cotrim paid me a visit. He was a little upset but tried to hide this fact and to appear calm and even happy. He had seen the announcement of the newspaper and thought that, as a relative and as a friend, he ought to dissuade me from going through with it. It would be a mistake, a fatal mistake. He pointed out that it would place me in a difficult situation and that I would lose my chance of re-election. In his opinion, the present administration was excellent, and even if I did not agree I would have to admit that it would probably remain in power a long time. What could I gain by making an enemy of it? He knew that some of the ministers liked me; perhaps there would be a vacancy and . . . I interrupted to say that I had carefully considered the step I was going to take and that there was no possibility of my retreating. I suggested that he read the platform, but he vigorously refused, saying that he wanted no part of my folly.

"It's folly," he repeated. "Just think it over for a few days and you'll see that it's folly."

That night in the theatre, Sabina said the same thing. She left her daughter with Cotrim and took me to the corridor behind the boxes.

"Brother Braz, do you know what you're doing?" she asked in a tone of tribulation. "Why do you want to provoke the government needlessly, when you could . . ."

I explained to her that it would not be proper for me to beg for a seat in Parliament; that my idea was to overthrow the administration because I thought it unable to solve the problems of the day and because it violated certain basic philosophical principles. I promised always to use polite language; it might at times be energetic, but never violent. Sabina tapped her finger tips with her fan, shook her head, and came back to the subject with alternate supplications and threats. I said no, and no, and no. She accused me of preferring the advice of outsiders to hers and her husband's. "All right, do what you wish," she concluded; "we have fulfilled our duty to you." She turned her back and returned to the box.

148. An Insoluble Problem: I published the first issue of the newspaper. Twenty-four hours later there appeared in other newspapers a statement by Cotrim that, although he was not a member of any of the political parties into which the nation was divided, he considered it necessary to state categorically that he had played no part, direct or indirect, and exercised no influence whatever, in relation to the newspaper of his brother-in-law, Mr. Braz Cubas, whose ideas and political behavior he wholly repudiated; and that, in his opinion, the present ministry (or any other composed of men of comparable ability) was fully qualified to promote the public welfare.

I could hardly believe my eyes. I rubbed them once or twice and reread the puzzling, inopportune, and gratuitous statement. If he was not interested in political parties, what importance could there be for him in so commonplace a thing as the publication of a newspaper? All the citizens who approve or disapprove of a ministry do not rush into print with statements on the subject, and there is no need for them to do so. Indeed, there was mystery in Cotrim's intrusion as well as in his personal aggressiveness toward me. From the time of our reconciliation until this episode, our relations had been amicable and candid—no quarrels, no unpleasantness, nothing. On the contrary, the record was one of favors bestowed; for example, when I was a deputy I was able to get him a contract to supply the naval arsenal, and he had told me only a few weeks prior to the publication of my newspaper that the contract had already netted him two hundred contos. Would one not have expected the memory of this favor to have restrained him from a public attack on his benefactor? The motive behind his statement must have been very strong to drive him to both impropriety and ingratitude. The problem was insoluble . . .

149. Theory of Benefits: ... So insoluble that even
Quincas Borba was perplexed, although he studied it long and carefully. "The devil with it!" he concluded. "Some problems are not worth five minutes' thought."

As to the charge of ingratitude on Cotrim's part, Quincas Borba rejected it entirely, not as untrue but on the ground that to anticipate gratitude is wholly inconsistent with philosophic principles.

"You cannot deny," he said, "that the pleasure of the benefactor is always greater than that of the beneficiary. What is a benefit? It is an act that eliminates a certain privation previously suffered by the beneficiary. Once this result has been produced, that is, once the privation has ended, the organism returns to its prior state of indifference. Suppose that you have made your trouser waistband too tight; to terminate the discomfort you unbutton the waistband, enjoy the feeling of relief for a moment, and then you return to a state of indifference and you don't even remember the labors of your fingers that brought you the relief. As nothing positive and lasting has been created, memory soon fades, for, like a plant, it must have roots in the soil and cannot hover unsupported in the air. However, if the beneficiary can hope for other favors from the same source, he will always remember the first favor; but this fact, one of the most significant from a philosophic point of view, is explained by the memory of the privation or, to put it another way, by the privation itself persisting in memory, which brings back the old pain and counsels that the beneficiary take precautions always to have a remedy at hand. I do not say that there have not been cases in which, even without these circumstances, the memory of a kindness, together with a more or less intense feeling of affection for the benefactor, has persisted; but these are aberrations and have no importance in the eyes of a philosopher."

"But," I replied, "if there is no reason why the memory of a kindness should persist in the mind of the beneficiary, there is even less reason why it should do so in the mind of the benefactor. I wish you would explain this point."

"I should have thought it self-evident," replied Quincas Borba. "The persistence of the benefit in the benefactor's memory follows from the very nature of a benefit and of its effects. Firstly, there is the feeling of having done a good deed and, by deduction, the consciousness that one is capable of good deeds; in the second place, one enjoys the conviction that he is superior to another creature, that is, to the beneficiary, superior in personal status and in the resources at his command—and, according to the best opinions, this feeling of superiority is one of the most legitimately agreeable feelings that the human organism can experience. Erasmus, who said some excellent things in his *Praise of Folly*, called attention to the complacency with which two donkeys scratch each other. I am far from rejecting this observation of Erasmus', but I shall add something that he omitted: that if one of the donkeys scratches the other better than the other scratches him, the eyes of the more expert scratcher will betray a pronounced feeling of special satisfaction. Why does a pretty woman look in the mirror so often? Because, upon doing so, she experiences a feeling of superiority over the many women who are less pretty or absolutely ugly. One's conscience is much the same: if it considers itself beautiful, it looks at itself again and again. Remorse is nothing but the wry face that a conscience makes when it sees itself hideous. Don't forget, everything that exists is simply an irradiation of Humanity; and therefore a benefit and all its effects, including the benefactor's pride, are wholly admirable phenomena."

150. Rotation and Revolution: Every enterprise, every

personal attachment, every age in history goes through the same cycle as a human life. The first issue of my newspaper filled my soul with a vast dawn, crowned me with laurel, gave me back the lightness of youth. Six months later the hour of old age struck, and two weeks later the hour of death, which was as clandestine as Dona Placida's. On the morning following the night in which it died in its sleep, I breathed heavily, like a man who has walked a long road. And so, if I tell you that a human life feeds other subsidiary lives, all more or less ephemeral, as the body feeds its parasites, I believe that I am not saying something altogether absurd. But, not to trust my point to a figure that may be found obscure or otherwise inadequate, I prefer an astronomical metaphor: in the wheel of the great mystery, man both rotates and revolves; he has his days—unequal, like Jupiter's—and of these he makes up his year of uncertain length.

At the moment when I finished my journalistic rotation, Lobo Neves completed his revolution. He died with his foot on the ministerial stairs. For several weeks it had been bruited that he would receive the appointment, and the gossip had filled me with vexation and envy. The news of his death gave me relief, peace of mind, and two or three minutes of pleasure. Pleasure is a strong word in this context, but I swear that it expresses the literal truth.

I went to the funeral. In the mortuary parlor I found Virgilia standing near the bier, sobbing. She raised her head, and I saw that she was really crying. When the funeral party was about to leave, she clung to the coffin. They took her to an inner room. I tell you, she shed real tears. I went to the cemetery. I could hardly speak; I had a lump in my throat, or maybe in my conscience. At the cemetery, when I dropped my shovelful of lime on the coffin at the bottom of the grave, the dull thud of the lime gave me a shudder—fleeting but disagreeable. The day was as heavy as lead; it even looked like lead. The cemetery, the black clothes . . .

151. Philosophy of Epitaphs: I walked away from the others and pretended to read epitaphs. I like epitaphs; among civilized people they are an expression of a secret and pious egoism that leads men to try to rescue from death at least a shred of the soul that has passed on, with the expectation that the same will be

done for them. Hence, perhaps, the inconsolable sadness of persons whose friends and relatives have been buried in the paupers' field; it seems to them that they partake by anticipation in the permanent anonymity.

152. Vespasian's Revenue: They had all gone; only my carriage

still awaited its owner. I lit a cigar and rode off. I could not get the burial ceremony out of my eyes nor Virgilia's sobs out of my ears. The sobs troubled me especially, for they had the vague and mysterious sound of a problem. In deep sincerity Virgilia had betrayed her husband, and now, in equally deep sincerity, she wept for him. It all seemed hopelessly inconsistent to me. But as I arrived home and was alighting from the carriage, I began to see the explanation. Merciful Nature! Your tax on grief is like Vespasian's revenue: it is collected indiscriminately from good sources and evil, and nothing about it suggests the ethical acceptability or unacceptability of its origin. Morality may perchance condemn my accomplice; but you, my impartial friend, you will not condemn so long as you receive punctually your payment in tears. Merciful, thrice merciful Nature!

153. The Psychiatrist: I am beginning to become morbid and had better sleep

a little. I slept, dreamed I was a nabob, and woke thinking I should like to become one. Sometimes I used to imagine such changes in region, status, and creed. A few days earlier I had thought of the possibility of a social, religious, and political revolution that would make the Archbishop of Canterbury a tax collector in Petropolis, and I had cogitated and calculated for hours to determine whether the publican would destroy the archbishop or whether the archbishop would cast out the publican, and what part, if any, of the archbishop could persist in the tax collector, what part, if any, of the tax collector could live within the archbishop, *etc*. Apparently insoluble questions, but actually quite soluble, once you accept the fact that in an archbishop there may be two archbishops—the administrator and the man of God. In any event, I wanted to be a nabob.

Jokingly, I told my ambition to Quincas Borba, who looked at me warily and a little sorrowfully and then had the graciousness to inform me that I was crazy. At first I laughed; but the high conviction with which he spoke frightened me. The only reply I could think of making to Quincas Borba's statement was that I did not feel crazy, but, as the insane do not generally know they are insane, the reply would have been without force.

Judge for yourself whether there be any truth in the popular belief that philosophers scorn the amenities of life: the very next day Quincas Borba sent me a psychiatrist. I knew the man, understood his mission, and became terrified. However, he conducted himself with the greatest delicacy and tact, and said good-bye so pleasantly that I was encouraged to ask whether he had found me really insane.

"No," he said, smiling. "You're saner than most."

"Then Quincas Borba was wrong?"

"Quite." And after a pause, "The shoe belongs rather on the other foot. If you're his friend . . . I wonder if you can't find some diversion for him . . . something that will . . ."

"Good heavens! Do you really think . . .? A man of such intellect, a philosopher!"

"Intellectuals are not immune."

You can imagine my distress. Seeing the effect of his words, the psychiatrist understood that I was a good friend of Quincas Borba and tried to minimize the seriousness of the matter. He observed that it might amount to nothing, and added that a little grain of folly, far from being injurious, actually gave a certain spice to life. As I rejected this opinion with horror, the psychiatrist smiled and told me something very interesting—so interesting that it deserves nothing less than a separate chapter.

154. The Ships of Piraeus: "Doubtless," said the psychiatrist, "you remember that famous Athenian madman who thought that all
the ships that came into the harbor of Piraeus belonged to him.
He was a pauper, who probably didn't even have a tub to sleep
in; but his imaginary ownership of the ships was worth more
than all the drachmas in Greece. Believe me, there is in every one
of us an Athenian madman; and anyone who says that he never
owned, in his mind, a schooner or two, is lying."

"Even you?" I asked.

"Even I."

"I, too?"

"You, too. And your servant, if that man beating the rugs at
the window is your servant."

In truth, it was one of my servants. We watched him as we sat
talking in the garden. The psychiatrist remarked that the servant
had opened wide all the windows, that he had lifted the curtains,
that he had exposed as much as possible of the richly furnished
living room so that persons outside the house could see it, and
concluded:

"This servant of yours has the same state of mind as the Athenian: he thinks the ships are his. He is enjoying a delusion that
makes him, for an hour, the happiest man in the world."

155. A Loyal Thought: "If the psychiatrist is
right," I said to myself,
"there is little reason to feel sorry for Quincas Borba. Insanity is
a matter of degree. Nevertheless, I ought to take care of him and
guard his mind against any new, alien follies that may try to in-
filtrate."

156. Pride of Servitude: Quincas Borba differed with the psychiatrist

about my servant. "One may, by way of analogy," said he, "attribute to your servant the Athenian's delusion; but analogies are not based on scientific observation nor do they prove anything deductively. What your servant has is a noble sentiment in perfect accord with the laws of Humanitism: the pride of servitude. He tries to show that he is the servant of a rich man, of a man of taste." He called my attention to the coachmen on great estates, who are prouder than their masters; to the hotel servants, whose attentions to each guest depend upon his apparent social status; *etc.* And he concluded that in each case there was an expression of that delicate and noble sentiment, the pride of servitude—absolute proof that man, even when he shines shoes, can be sublime.

157. The Most Brilliant Phase: "It's you who are sublime,"

I cried, throwing my arms about his neck.

It was impossible to believe that so profound a mind could be touched with insanity. I told him this after my embrace and ridiculed the psychiatrist's suspicion. I cannot describe Quincas Borba's reaction; I remember that he trembled and turned very pale.

It was about this time that Cotrim and I became reconciled once more, although I still did not know the cause of his break with me. A timely reconciliation, for solitude was weighing heavily upon me, and my life had become boredom of the worst sort, the boredom of the idle. A short time later, he invited me to join the Third Order of a brotherhood—which I did not do without first consulting Quincas Borba.

"Go ahead, if you wish," said he, "but on a temporary basis. I'm thinking of adding to my philosophy a theological and liturgical part. Humanitism must be also a religion, the religion of the future, the only true religion. Christianity is all right for women and beggars, and other religions are no better: they all are tainted by vulgarity or weakness. The Mohammedan paradise is as unsatisfactory as the Christian paradise, and Buddha's nirvana is nothing more than a heaven for paralytics. You'll see what kind of religion Humanitism can produce. The final absorption, the *contractive* phase, is the reconstitution of substance, not its annihilation, *etc*. Accept the invitation, but never forget that you are my caliph."

And now please observe my modesty: I joined the Third Order of ***, I carried out certain good works, it was the most brilliant phase of my career; but I shall say nothing about it, I shall not relate the nature of my works, nor what I did for the poor and the sick, nor the recompense I received—I shall say absolutely nothing.

Perhaps social economy would gain something if I were to show why each and every external reward is worth little in comparison with the immediate subjective reward; but I swore to keep silent on this subject. Moreover, the phenomena of the conscience are hard to analyze; and, to explain one of these phenomena, I should have to explain all those that are related to it and should end by writing a chapter on psychology. I shall merely state that it was the most brilliant phase of my life. The scenes I saw were sad; they had the monotony of repeated misfortune, which is at least as boring as the monotony of pleasure. But the joy that one gives to the poor and the sick is worth all this. And do not tell me that only the poor and the sick are benefited. My recompense upon thinking of their joy was great; it showed me the lofty and noble aspects of my nature.

158. Two Old Friends:

By the end of three or four years I was tired of this activity and abandoned it, not before making a large gift, which gave me the right to have my portrait in the sacristy. I shall not end the chapter, however, without relating that I saw an old friend die in the Order's hospital. Can you guess who it was? None other than the gorgeous Marcella. And I saw her die on the same day on which, visiting an overcrowded tenement to distribute gifts of charity, I found . . . this time you cannot possibly guess . . . I found the flower of the thicket, Eugenia, the daughter of Dona Eusebia and Villaça, as lame as when I had left her and much sadder.

When she recognized me she turned pale and lowered her eyes; but only for an instant. She quickly raised her head and met my gaze with great dignity. I understood that she would accept no charity from me, and I extended my hand as respectfully as if she had been the wife of a successful businessman. She accepted my hand, nodded politely, and shut herself in her cubicle. I never saw her again; I did not learn whether her mother was dead, nor what misfortune had brought her to this misery, nor anything else about her life. I know only that she was still lame and still sad.

It was with Eugenia deeply impressed on my mind that I arrived at the hospital, which Marcella had entered the day before, and where I saw her expire a half hour later, ugly, thin, decrepit . . .

159. Insane:

I knew then that I was an old man and that I needed strength from a source outside me; but Quincas Borba had left, six months earlier, for Minas Geraes and had taken with him the best of all philosophies. He returned four months later and, on a certain morning, came into my house in a state almost as bad as that in which I had found him in the Passeio Publico. The striking difference was in his eyes. He was now clearly insane. He told me that, in order to perfect Humanitism, he had burned the whole manuscript and was going to begin all over again. He had finished the theological part although he had not written it down; it would become the true religion of the future.

"Do you swear loyalty to Humanity?" he asked me.

"You know I do."

My voice caught in my throat, and yet I had not discovered the entire truth in all its cruelty. Quincas Borba not only was mad but knew he was mad; and this remaining shred of self-understanding, like a flickering in the midst of lurking shadows, added to the horror of the situation. He knew he was mad, and he did not try to fight his madness; on the contrary, he told me that it was still another manifestation of Humanity, which was trying to amuse itself. He recited by memory long chapters from his book and followed these with antiphonies and litanies. He even demonstrated a sacred dance that he had devised for the ritual of Humanitism. The lugubrious grace with which he lifted his legs and kicked was singularly fantastic. At times he would sulk in a corner, staring into space with eyes in which, at long intervals, there would shine a persistent gleam of sanity, as sad as a tear . . .

He died in my house a few days later, swearing repeatedly that pain and grief were illusions and that Pangloss, the calumniated Pangloss, was not so great a fool as Voltaire thought.

160. Negatives: Between Quincas Borba's death and my own, there occurred the events narrated at the beginning of the book. Chief among them was the invention of the Braz Cubas Plaster, which died with me. Divine plaster, you would have given me first place among men, above the learned and the wealthy, because you were a genuine inspiration direct from heaven. Chance determined the contrary; and so, my friends, you will remain eternally melancholy.

This last chapter consists wholly of negatives. I did not achieve celebrity, I did not become a minister of state, I did not really become a caliph, I did not marry. At the same time, however, I had the good fortune of not having to earn my bread by the sweat of my brow. Moreover, I did not suffer a death like Dona Placida's nor did I lose my mind like Quincas Borba. Adding up and balancing all these items, a person will conclude that my accounts showed neither a surplus nor a deficit and consequently that I died quits with life. And he will conclude falsely; for, upon arriving on this other side of the mystery, I found that I had a small surplus, which provides the final negative of this chapter of negatives: I had no progeny, I transmitted to no one the legacy of our misery.